Space Is Just a Starry Night

Space Is Just a Starry Night

short fiction by

Tanith Lee

Aqueduct Press

Seattle

Aqueduct Press, PO Box 95787
Seattle, WA 98145-2787
www.aqueductpress.com

ISBN: 978-1-61976-031-8
First printing, July 2013

Library of Congress Control Number: 2013932286

10 9 8 7 6 5 4 3 2 1

Cover Design by Lynne Jenson Lampe
Cover illustration credits:
Fornax Galaxy Cluster: NASA/JPL-Caltech/UCLA
CabeusCrater: NASA/GSFC/Arizona State University

Book Design by Kathryn Wilham

Printed in the USA by Thomson-Shore, Inc.

Publication Acknowledgments

"The Beautiful Biting Machine," Cheap Street, 1984; Arrows of Eros. London, New English Library, 1989. Alex Stewart, editor.

"Moon Wolf," *Asimov's Magazine*, August 2004.

"Felixity," *Sisters in Fantasy*, editors Susan Shwartz and Margin Greenberg, New York: Penguin/Roc, 1995.

"The Thaw," *Asimov's Magazine*, Vol 3 No 6, June 1979.

"You Are My Sunshine," *Chrysalis 8*, edited by Roy Torgeson, New York: Doubleday & Company, Inc., 1980.

"Black Fire," *Light Speed*, edited by John Joseph Adams, Issue 8, January 2011; *Lightspeed Year One*. San Francisco: Prime Books, 2011. Reprint anthology.

"Written in Water," *Perpetual Light*, edited by Alan Ryan, New York: Warner Books, 1980.

"Tonight I Can Sleep Quietly," *Emblemes* (Editions de l'Oxymore), ed. Lea Silhol, 2005.

"Stalking the Leopard," *Realms of Fantasy Magazines*, edited by Shawna McCarthy, Vol 10 No 5, June 2004.

"Dead Yellow," *Nature*, edited by Henry Gee, Vol 453 No 7199, June 2008.

"By Crystal Light Beneath One Star," *Tales from the Forbidden Planet*, edited by Roz Kavney, New York: Titan Books, 1987.

"A Day in the Skin (Or...)," *Habitats*, edited by Susan Shwartz, New York: DAW Books, 1984.

"With a Flaming Sword" and "Within the Ghost" are original stories for this book.

To my Husband and Angel, John Kaiine."
From whom great inspiration I gaiine;
And whose name is such fun,
Since almost no one
Can pronounce it—until we explaiine.

Contents

I left my world to wander in
This endless midnight sky,
For space is just a starry night
Where no suns ever rise.

"Dana's Song" by Tanith Lee
from Sarcophagus, her first episode for the BBC
TV Series Blake's 7

The Beautiful Biting Machine

When the two suns go down and it starts to get dark, the Nightfair wakes up, a beast with a thousand bright eyes.

Five miles long, four miles wide, the valley is full of lights, noises, musics, between the tall and echoing hills.

This world's a pleasure planet. It has many and various attractions. The Nightfair is only one. Here there are spinning wheels of yellow sparks against the dusk, and glimmering neon ghost towers ringing with screams, and carousels that maybe come alive. Not everyone cares for these, or the candy awnings, the peppermint arenas, the cries of fortune-tellers in glass cages, the crashing of pre-arranged safe vehicular accidents, the soaring space-flights that never leave the ground. Those that don't care for them don't come. But for those that do, there are the cuisine and superstition and popular art, the sex and syntax and the sin of twenty worlds, to be sampled for a night, or a week of nights. (Who could tolerate more?)

So visit the Valley of Lights. Hurry, hurry, don't be slow or sly or shy.

Welcome to the Nightfair.

"This gentlevyrainian's gotta slight complaint."

"Tell him to see a doctor."

"Don't cheek me, Beldek."

"No, Mr Qire. What seems to be the trouble, sir?"

Beldek and Qire looked through the one-way window at the gentleman from Vyraini. Like all Vyrainians, he was humanoid, greenish, fretful. Vyraini did not esteem the human race, but was patronizingly intrigued by it and its culture.

Anything human, where possible, should be experienced, explored. Now this Vyrainian had come to Qire's pavilion at the Nightfair and was not quite satisfied, had a slight complaint.

"Go and talk to it—him," said Qire.

"Me, sir?"

"You. You speak their lingo. You speak half the damn gurglings of half the damn galaxy, don't you, Beldek? You lazy son-of-a-ghex."

"If you say so, Mr Qire."

Beldek opened the long window and stepped through. The other side of the window looked like a door, glamorous with enamel paint and stained glass. Beldek bowed to the gentlevyrainian with his hands to his face, which was the correct form of greeting from an outworlder. The Vyrainian stood impassive, ears folded.

"*Fo ogch m'mr bnn?*" Beldek inquired courteously.

The Vyrainian seemed gratified; it lifted its ears and broke into staccato Vyrainese.

The glottal conversation continued for two and a half minutes. After which, feeling Qire's beady little eyes on him through the one-way door-window, Beldek leisurely set the computer for a twenty percent refund.

The Vyrainian took its cash and offered Beldek the salute used when bidding farewell to an inferior but valuable alien. Not all Earthmen knew exactly what the salute implied (a rough translation was: I will let you lick my feet another time, O wise one). Beldek, who did, smiled pleasantly.

The whaal-ivory screens of the outer doors closed on the Vyrainian's exit.

Beldek turned as Qire came storming from the inner office. Qire was a bulging, broad-faced type, the little eyes somewhat slanting, the mane of golden hair an implant. His clothes, though gaudy, were the best—real silk shirt, whaal-leather sandals. A ruby in his neck-chain.

"Why d'yah do that?"

"What, Mr Qire, sir?"

"Refund the bastard his money."

"Twenty percent. The amount he agreed would compensate for the slight complaint."

"What was wrong with her?"

Beldek said, ultra-apologetically, fawningly, "A little something I told you about, that clicks—"

"Why the Garbundian Hell didn't you, for Christ's sake, get it fixed?"

"I have tried, Mr Qire," said Beldek humbly. "I truly have."

Qire glowered.

"I should put you out on your butt. Why don't I?"

"I'm useful?" Beldek said, attempting humbly to be helpful now.

"Like urx-faron you are. All right. Give me the receipts. I'm going over to Next Valley. I'll be here again five-day week. Chakki'll be by in three days."

Beldek keyed the computer for the cash receipts, tore them off when they came, and presented them to Qire. Qire riffled through them, glancing for mistakes. "Okay, Beldek. I want to hear from Chakki that she's back in good order, you savvy?"

"Oh yes, Mr Qire, sir."

Qire swore. At the whaal-ivory doors he turned for one last snarl.

"I've got other concerns on this planet, Beldek. If Malvanda packs up, it's no great loss to me. You're the one'll suffer. Back to hoofing the space-lanes with your card tricks and your dipscop seventh-rate jaar. You get me?"

"To the heart, sir," said Beldek. "And all the way up yours, Mr Qire."

Qire cursed him and slammed out.

The doors, ever serene, whispered shut in his wake.

Beldek leaned on the ornamental counter, keying the computer, which he had long ago rigged to count the amount he had creamed off Qire's takings for the last five-day period. Qire, of course, guessed he did this. It was an inevitable perk of the job. All told, Qire seemed to value disliking Beldek. Value the hypertensive rage that came to the boil whenever Beldek's cool clear eyes met his with such angelic sweetness above the long, smiling mouth that said: Yes, Mr Qire, *sir*. Most of the human portion of the Valley of Lights knew about Qire's hatred of his employee Beldek, the drifter from the space-lanes. Beldek who could speak half the languages of the galaxy and could charm rain from a desert sky, if he wanted. Usually he didn't want to. Beldek, whose un-implanted, long thick lank brass-colored hair hung on his shoulders and over his high wide forehead. Lean as a sculpture and tall, from birth on some unspecified lower-gravity world. Pale and pale-eyed. Something about him: more than the rumored past, card-shark, kept creature of male, female, humanoid...tales of a man murdered out among the stars.... More than the fact of working for Qire, in attendance on one of the weirdest novelties of the Nightfair. Be careful of Beldek.

The pavilion stood on a rise. A quarter of a mile below, a bowl of dizzy fires, the Arena of Arson, flashed and flared. Back a way, one of the great wheels whirled gold against the black sky. But the crimson pavilion was clouded round with Sirrian cedars. Far-off lamps winked on their branches; the apex of the pavilion, a diadem of rose-red glass lit subtly from within, just pierced, with a wicked symbolism of many carnal things, from the upper boughs. Once among the trees, the rest of the Fair seemed siphoned off. You came to the kiosk with the ivory doors. You went in, read something, signed something, paid something, and were let through another door, this one of black Sinoese lacquer. And then the Fair was very far-away indeed. For then you were in the Mansion of Malvanda. And she was there with you...

A faint bell chimed on the console. Beldek killed the read-out and looked urbanely at the door-screens. Another customer.

The doors opened.

A New-Worlder stepped through. He was alone. Most of them came alone, the same as most were men, or rather, most were male. A mixture of human and some genetically-adhesive other-race, the New-Worlder was fresh-skinned, grinning, handsome, and without whites to his eyes.

"Say," he said.

"Good-evening, gentlenewman. You wish to visit Malvanda's Mansion?"

"Su-ure," said the New-Worlder.

"Take a seat, please.

Grinning, the New-Worlder rippled onto a couch.

Double-jointed, too. That should offer Malvanda a challenge.

Beldek came around the counter and extended a small steel wafer.

"You understand, this entertainment being of the kind it is, you must first—"

"Sign a disclaimer? Yes, su-ure." The New-Worlder was already excited, a little drunk or otherwise stimulated. That had usually happened too, before they got themselves to these doors.

The Newman accepted the wafer, which hummed and spoke to him, telling him of possible dangers involved in what he was about to experience. As it droned on, the Newman grinned and nodded, nodded and grinned, and sometimes his all-blue eyes went to Beldek, and he grinned wider, as if they were in a conspiracy. When the machine finished, the New-Worlder was already up at the counter, his six fingers out for the disclaimer and stylus. He signed with a flourish. He paid the fee in one large bill and shiftily counted his change from habit, not really concentrating.

"What now?"

"Now you meet the lady."

"Say," said the Newman.

Beldek fed the disclaimer into the computer. The back of the kiosk murmured and rose, revealing the black lacquer door. The New-Worlder tensed. There was sudden sweat on his face, and he licked his lips. Then the door opened inward.

Standing well back by the counter, Beldek got a glimpse of somber plush, sulky, wine-smoked light, the vague shimmer

of draperies in a smooth wind scented with camellias and
sorrow-flowers, the floral things of drugged funerals. He had
seen the poisonously alluring aperture, that throbbing carnelian camellia vulva of doorway, many thousands of times.
The New-Worlder had not. Mindlessly, helplessly, he went
forward, as if mesmerized, and poured over the threshold. A
heavy curtain fell. The door swung shut. The ultimate orifice
had closed upon him.

Beldek moved around behind the counter and touched the
voyeur-button. He watched for less than a minute, his face
matt as fresh linen, ironed young and expressionless. Then he
cut off the circuit.

Such a device, mostly unknown to clients, was necessary
by law, which did not call it a voyeur-button. Persons who
underwent such events as Malvanda had to be monitored
and easy of access should an emergency occur. Twice, before
Beldek joined the show, a client had died in there. Because the
disclaimers were in order, and medical aid was rushed to the
spot, Qire was covered and no action resulted. The Newman,
however, had registered healthy on the wafer. Beldek had told
at a glance he was strong. There was no need to watch.

Qire sometimes came around just to do that. There was a
more private extension of the voyeur-button in the cubicle
off the inner office. Qire had not invented Malvanda's Mansion, only sponsored the design and then bought the product.
But he liked it. He liked to watch. Sometimes, Qire brought a
friend with him.

Beldek went into the inner office and dropped crystals in
his ears that would play him an hour of wild, thin music, a
concerto for Celestina and starsteel.

He did not need to watch Malvanda.

He knew what happened.

When the hour was up, Beldek tidied the office and reset the
computer. The panels dimmed one by one as the lamps soft-
ened in the kiosk, and the carnal peak on the roof went out.

The New-Worlder was the last customer of the night. In thirty minutes, dawn would start to seep across the eastern hills.

As Beldek was re-vamping the computer program for the next night, the black lacquer door shifted open behind him. He heard the Newman emerge, stumbling a little on his double joints.

The hiccupping footsteps got all the way to the whaal-ivory doors before the voice said, "Say." The voice had changed. It was husky, demoralized. "Say."

Reluctantly, abrasively polite, Beldek turned. He leveled a wordless query at the sagging male by the kiosk doors. The Newman's eyes were muddy, looking sightless. He seemed to go on trying to communicate.

"Yes, sir?"

"Nothing," said the New-Worlder. "Just—nothing." The doors opened, and like a husk he almost blew into the diluting darkness and away through the dregs and embers of the Fair.

Whatever else, the click in the mechanism obviously hadn't spoiled it for him at all.

By day, the Nightfair goes to ground. Some of the big architectures and marts sink down literally into the bedrock. Others close up like clams. Coming over the hills too early, you get a view of acres of bare earth, burned-looking, as if after some disaster. Here and there the robot cleaning-machines wander, in a snowstorm of rinds, wrappers, drugstick butts, lost tinsels. Places that stand naked to the two eyes of heaven, the pair of dog-suns, have a look of peeled potatoes, indecent and vulnerable.

Awnings of durable wait like rags, dipped flags, for the glow and glitter of neon night.

The peoples of the Nightfair are wolves, foxes, coomors; they sleep by day in their burrows or their nests up in the scaffolded phantom towers, among the peaceful wrecks of sky buses, their wry lemon dreams filling the air with acids.

In the last of the afternoon there begins to be some movement, furtive, rats on a golden hill of rubbish littered with tin-can calliopes.

"Beldek, is that you, you ghexy guy?"

Qire's runner, Chakki, having used his key to the whaal-ivory doors, peered about the office.

"Who else did you hope to find?"

Beldek was tinkering with a small box of wires and three or four laser-battery tools. He did not turn round. Chakki now and then dropped by, never when expected, checking up for Mr Qire, or just nosing. Scrawny and pretty, Chakki was a being of instinct rather than thought or compunction, an alley cat that runs in, steals a chicken dinner, pees in a corner, and, soulless physical ghost, is gone.

"What ya doing, lovely Beldek?"

"Trying to repair a click."

"My…Malvanda clicketh. Yeah, I heard about it. Better now?"

"We shall see."

"You going in to give it her?"

Beldek walked past him toward the back wall of the kiosk, which was going up to reveal the door of Sinoese lacquer.

"You lucky buck. Bet she bends ya."

"So long, Chakki."

The lacquer door started to open. Chakki stared tiptoe over Beldek's shoulder into camellia, carnelian, lilies-go-roses, funereal virgo unintacta.

"Let's have a piece, Bel?"

"If you can afford it. Come back tonight with the other clientele."

"Go swiff yourself, Bellrung."

The curtain fell. The door had dosed.

Beyond the door, no matter the time of day or season, it was always midnight in Indian Summer.

Around the great oval room long windows seemed to give on to a hot perfumed night, mobile only with the choruses of crickets. There were lush gardens out there, under the multiplicity of stars, the best constellations of ten planets, and beyond the garden, hills, the backs of black lions lying down. Now and then a moth or two fluttered like bright flakes of tissue past the open glass. They never came in. It might distract the customer.

The roof apparently was also of glass, ribbed into vanes, like the ceiling of a conservatory. You saw the stars through it, and soon a huge white moon would come over, too big to be true.

There were carpets on the walls. Draperies hung down, plum velvets, transparencies with embroidery and sequins, dividing the room like segments of a dream. Everything bathed in the aromatic smoke of a church of incense candles. The other scent was flowers. They bloomed out of the bodies of marble animals grouped around little oases of water thick with sinuous snakefish. Redblack flowers, albino flowers, flowers stained between red and white and black, gray flowers, fever and blush flowers, bushes of pale, sighing faints.

The marble stair went up to shadows, reflected in the polished floor. If you looked in the floor at the reflection, presently something moved, upside down, a figure in fluid. Then you looked up again at the stair. And saw Malvanda, out of the shadows, coming down.

Malvanda was tall and twenty-two years old, slim but not slender, her shoulders wide for elegance, her hips wide as if to balance panniers, her waist to be spanned by a man's hands, her breasts high and firm and full to fill them, spill them. Malvanda's skin was as white as the sorrow-flowers, with just that vague, almost-colorless flush at the temples, ear-lobes, hollow of the throat, insteps, wrists...that the sorrow-flowers had at the edges of their petals. She was platinum blonde. Flaxen hair without a trace of gold or yellow, hair white, like moonlight blanching metal. Her eyebrows were just two shades darker, but her lashes were like tarnished brass, and her eyes like untarnished brass. Wolf-color eyes, large; glowing now, fixed on him.

A small movement of her head shifted the coils of platinum hair away, over her shoulder. The column of her throat went down and down into the crimson dress. The V of the neckline ended just under her breasts. She smiled a little, just a very little. Her lips were a softer crimson than the gown. Rose mouth. She began to come toward him, and her hand stole from her side, moving out to him ahead of her, as if it couldn't wait to make contact.

Beldek walked up to her, and, as the smooth hand floated to his arm, guided her fingers away. He ran his own hand in under the heavy silk hair to the base of her skull and touched.

Switched off, Malvanda stood quite still, her lips slightly parted, her eyes dreaming, brazen, swimming with late afternoon veldt.

Beldek ran his thumb around her throat and jabbed into the hollow. He pressed the second disc under her right ear and the third under her left index fingernail, deactivating the safety. There had to be a suitably obtuse series of pressures, to avoid random deactivation by a client when caressing her. Beldek knelt at Malvanda's feet. He raised the hem of her gown and drew one flawless foot onto his knee. He gripped under the instep and drew out the power-booster from the panel.

Then he got up and went around, undoing the cling-zip on the back of her gown. The keyboard opened where her lower spine should be. He compared it to the box of wires he had brought in, then selecting one of the fine plumbing needles, he began to work on her.

After four and a half minutes he found the fault that might be responsible for the unfortunate click that had offended the aesthetic values of the Vyrainian. Two levers, the size of whiskers, had unaligned and were rubbing together. Looking through the magnifier, he eased them away and put in a drop of stabilizer. That area of the board could be overheating, causing the levers' unwanted expansion together. He would need to check it again in a couple of days.

Having closed the panel and sealed her dress, he replaced the power-booster in her foot. The gauge in her board had showed nearly full, so it was time to empty the sac before reactivating.

Very gently, Beldek parted her beautiful carmine lips and reached in, past the beautiful teeth, to the narrow tube of throat.

The sac was not too easy to come at, of course. When Qire took him on, the first two things he had wanted to see were Beldek's hands. Articulate and long-fingered, they had passed the test.

Beldek was halfway through disposing of the sac's contents when he heard a noise behind him.

The moon was coming up over the glass ceiling, augmenting the candle-and-lamplight. Not that he really needed it to see Chakki, transfixed there, against the curtain with his mouth open and his eyes bulging.

Before coming in, Beldek always cut off the voyeur-button, both on the console and in the office cubicle. At such times as this, the computer would only release the black lacquer door to Beldek. Somehow, Chakki had found a way either to fool the computer or to force the door.

"What the Garbundian Hop-Hell are you doing, Beldek?" said Chakki, all agog.

"Emptying the sac," said Beldek. "As you saw."

"Yeah but—" Chakki burst into a wild laugh. "Holla, man. You're kinkier than I ever thought."

Chakki, unable to spy in the usual way, had obviously badly wanted to see Beldek in operation with Malvanda. Chakki had always, blatantly, imagined Beldek liked to get free what the patrons paid for. If he'd managed an entry one minute earlier, or one minute later, it need not have mattered.

"Kinkier than you thought? Of course I am, Chakki."
Beldek resettled the sac in Malvanda's mouth and let it go
down the throat. Always an easier maneuver this, than retrac-
tion. He keyed on the relays. Malvanda did not move just yet.
She took a moment to warm up after de-activation. "I suppose
I'll have to bribe you, now, Chakki. Won't I?"

Chakki giggled. He looked nervous. In a second he would
start to back away.

"How about," said Beldek, "a free ride with Malvanda?"
Then he sprinted, faster than any alley cat, straight through
the candlelamp moonlight. He caught Chakki like a lover.
"How about that?" he asked, and Chakki shivered against him,
scared now, but not quite able to make up his mind to run.

Beldek led him firmly, kindly stroking him a little, to the
center of the floor where Malvanda had been left standing.

As they got near, her eyelids flickered.

"She's something," said Chakki. "Maybe I could come
round tonight."

"Busy tonight. Do it now. You always wanted to. Have fun."

Chakki's shiver grew up into a shudder; he glanced toward
the curtained door. Then Malvanda woke up.

Beldek moved aside. Malvanda's hand went to Chakki's
face, sensuous and sure.

She was taller than Qire's runner, Beldek's height. Her
mouth parted naturally now, the wonderful strange smile in-
viting, certain. Just showing the tips of the teeth.

This time, Beldek would watch.

Chakki wriggled, still afraid. But the drugs in the candles
were affecting him by now, and the water-lily touches, on
the neck, the chest, slipping, lingering. He put out one hand,
careful, into her neckline, and found a breast. Half-fright-
ened, aroused, wanting approval, he looked at Beldek. "She
feels real."

"She's meant to, Chakki."

"Hey, I never really saw what you—"

"That's okay, Chakki. Enjoy."

Malvanda's strawberry tongue ran over Chakki's lips. Her left arm held him like a loved child; her right hand moved like a small trusting animal seeking shelter, and discovered it, there in Chakki's groin, and played and tickled, and burrowed and coiled.

They were on the couch now. Chakki with his clothes off, handfuls of Malvanda's gown clenched in his fists, his nose between her breasts, was writhing and squeaking. Malvanda bent her head to do the thing they paid for, the thing Chakki had not paid for—the true thrill, the perverse unique titillation that Malvanda offered. Her platinum hair fell over them, obscuring. But Beldek knew what went on under the wave of hair. Chakki was coming, noisily and completely, the way most of them did.

Beldek walked quickly across to the couch. He tapped Malvanda on the right shoulder, just once.

He had had the maintenance of her a long while. He had been able to innovate a little, a very little. Enough. Provision for a Chakki day.

Chakki was subsiding. Then struggling.

"Beldek," he said, "she's still—ah—Christ—Beldek!" His arms flailed and his legs as, naked and puny, Chakki tried to push Malvanda away. But Malvanda was strong as only a machine could be. She held him down, pinned beneath her, her marmoreal body oblivious of the kicks and scratches that did not even mar its surface as she went on doing what Beldek had just told her to go on doing.

Ignoring the screams that gradually became more frenzied and hopeless, Beldek walked out of Malvanda's Mansion.

The marks where the door had been forced were not bad but quite plain. A paint job would see to it. Chakki would have planned to do that before Qire got back. Now Qire would have to see them.

Beldek shut the door, and Chakki's last wailing thinning shrieks were gone.

Just before suns' set, Beldek called Qire on the interphone. He broke the news mildly: Qire's runner had got through the Mansion door when Beldek was in the bathroom. Entering the Mansion to check Malvanda, Beldek found Chakki. He had died of hemorrhage and shock, the way the two others had. There was, obviously, no disclaimer. What did Quire want him to do?"

He could hear the boss-man sweating all along the cable from Next Valley.

"You called anyone else, Beldek?"

"No."

"The pol?"

"Not yet."

He listened to Qire bubbling over, over there. The two prior deaths in Qire's pavilion made things awkward, despite all the cover on the world. This third death, minus cover, could look like shoddy goods. And Chakki was a private matter. Beldek had known what Qire would do.

"All right. Don't call 'em. You listening, Beldek?"

"Oh yes, Mr Qire. Most attentively."

"Don't scad me, Beldek. I'm gonna give you a number. You call *that*. Someone'll come see to things. Okay?"

"Anything you say, Mr Qire."

"And keep your mouth shut."

"Yes, *sir*."

Qire gave him the number, and he used it. The voice at the other end was mechanized. He said to it the brace of phrases Qire had briefed him with; then there were noises and the line went blind.

The suns were stubbed out, and the wild flame wheels began to turn on the sky of Indian ink, and the colored arsons shot across the arena bowl below, and the carousels practiced their siren-songs and got them perfect.

Someone came and tried to breach the darkened pavilion.

Beldek went out and stood on the lawn.

Two Pheshines stared from their steamy eyes, lashing their tails in the grass.

"*Dena mi ess, condlu ess, sollu ess. Dibbit?*"

Beldek told them, in Phesh, the show was closed. The gentlephesh did *dibbit* and went off spitting to each other.

The nondescript carry-van drew up an hour later. Men walked into the kiosk and presently into the Mansion. They walked out with a big plastic bag and took it away.

Beldek had already cleaned up, before they came. Not much later, Beldek lit the pavilion and opened for business, but no one else stopped by that night.

Beldek sat up in the tall echoing hills, watching the dawn borning and the Nightfair slink to ground.

Malvanda, had she been real, would not have been able to do this. Sunlight was anathema to Malvanda's kind. Sunlight and mirrors and garlic-flowers, and thorns and crucifixes and holy wafers, and running water. It just went to show.

Beldek leaned back on the still-cool slate, looking down the four-by-five miles of the valley.

Gorgeous Malvanda, Terran turn-on, Phesh *tashsa-mi*, Venusian wet dream; Angel of Orgasm, kiss of death. Malvanda, the Beautiful Biting Machine. Malvanda the robot vampire.

He didn't know her whole history, how some sick-minded talent had thought her up and put her together. Her place of origin was a mystery. But what she did; he knew that. A connoisseur's sexual desideratum. The actual bite was controlled to a hair's breadth by her keyboard. The teeth went in, naturally. She sucked out blood. That's what they paid for, was it not? Money's worth. Blood money. Only a little, of course. More would be dangerous. And the teeth left built-in coagulant behind them, zippering up the flesh all nice. Unimpaired, the client staggers forth, only a bit whoozy. A bite whoozy.

Some of them even came back, days, months, years later, for another turn.

It was harmless, unless you were sick, had some weakness...

Or unless Beldek tapped Malvanda's right shoulder that particular way he had when she was with Chakki. Then another key snapped down its command through her wires and circuits. And Malvanda kept on biting, biting and sucking like a bloody vacuum cleaner. Till all the blood was in Malvanda's throat sac and spilling over and on the floor and everywhere. But Beldek had cleaned that away and bathed her and changed her gown before Qire's goon friends arrived with their big plastic bag.

It had been fairly uncomplex to tidy his mistake, this time. But he must beware of mistakes from now on. Tomorrow, today, Beldek would work something out to make the Mansion door impregnable.

Even so, Beldek didn't really mind too much. It had been a bonus, all that blood. Better than just the contents of the sac, which Chakki had, unfortunately for Chakki, seen Beldek drinking earlier.

Beldek sunned himself on the hills for several hours. He never browned in sunshine, but he liked it, it was good for him. His hair, the tone of Malvanda's eyes, gleamed and began playfully to curl.

When he strolled back through the valley, the Fair was in its somnolent jackal-and-bone midday phase. Qire's buggy was at the entry to the pavilion. Qire was inside, in the Mansion, pawing Malvanda over, and the furnishings, making sure everything had been left as the customers would wish to find it.

Beldek followed him in.

"I should throw you out on your butt," said Qire.

"Throw me out," said Beldek. "I'll have some interesting stories to tell."

Qire glared.

"Don't think you can make anything outa what happened. It was your, for Christ's sake, negligence."

They both knew Qire would never fire him. Beldek was too handy at the job. And knew too much. And would be too difficult to dispose of.

Presently they went into the office, and Qire handed Beldek a sheaf of large notes. "Any noise," said Qire, "something might happen you might not be happy about. And fix that damn door. *She* seems okay. She damaged at all?"

"No. Still what your pamphlets say. The Night-Blooming Bella Donna of Eternal Gothic Fantasy."

When Qire had gone, Beldek listened to symphonies on music crystals in the office.

It had always rather fascinated him, the way in which vampires, a myth no one any longer believed, had become inextricably and dependently connected with sex. Actually, vampirism had nothing to do with sex. Beldek could have told them that. Just as it had nothing to do with sunlight or mirrors or crosses. It was simply and solely (though not soully) about basic nourishment.

Later, he set the program for the night. He had a premonition there would be a lot of custom. Somehow, without anyone knowing about it in any logical way, some enticing whiff of velvet morbidity would be blowing around the pavilion, luring them in like flies. The sac would have to be emptied many times tonight, in Beldek's own special way, which was not the way in which the instruction manual advocated.

Just before it got dark and he lit up the lights to match the exploding ignition of the Fair, Beldek looked in on Malvanda. She had been returned to her shadowy alcove above the marble stair and was waiting there for the first client to come in and gaspingly watch her descend. Beldek climbed the steps, and brushed her platinum hair and refilled the perfumery glands behind her ears.

He cared nothing for the sentient races that were his prey. But for the beautiful biting machine, he felt a certain malign affection. Why not? After a century or so of insecure, monotonous, and frequently inadequate hit-and-miss hunting, which left little space for other pursuits, the Nightfair had provided Beldek the softest option on twenty worlds. Now Malvanda saw to everything. She paid his bills. She kept him fed.

Moon Wolf

The carrier rose into the clear sky of dusk. Below, the shadowy trees whispered on the darkening hills. Above, the white moon waited.

"You for Crisium Base?" said Edwards. "Me too. Guess we'll ride out together."

Bayley nodded. She looked away from the see-through, where the earth had already shrunk aside and the night of space begun, littered with its incendiaries.

"Been some funny stories," said Edwards.

"Ha, ha."

"No, I mean weird-funny."

"So I heard."

"What do you think?"

She shrugged. "I think people on the bases get bored sometimes. Or primally scared. All that white naked desert. The black sky with the Earth hanging in it."

"Come on. After all this time?"

"Why else do we go?" she said.

Edwards, sitting now across from her, narrowed his eyes along the length of the otherwise empty carrier.

"You always were fanciful, Chrissie."

Bayley smiled.

He said, "OK, but you are."

Bayley said, "Never go to a horror movie, Al?"

"So what?"

"We sometimes like to get frightened. Don't you remember when you were a kid, staying behind in the park after the gates shut, in the wild bits where the lights don't shine—"

"Lots of times. But I had several *good* reasons. They were usually blonde."

"Fine. But what I mean is the *darkness*, what might be in the dark. That electric, almost drunken terror—either you know what I mean or you don't."

Edwards now shrugged. This was what their conversation was always likely to become, now.

Shrugs, shrugging things off.

For a while they did not speak at all. Beyond the see-through, liquid black, a shark's carapace, space rushed like a sea.

"Three hours. Guess I'll sleep awhile," said Edwards.

"Yes," she said softly. You were always good for that.

In childhood, she thought, that was where she first heard stories of werewolves, as of vampires, ghosts, ghouls, and dragons. That plethora of fearsome exotic things that plagued the lives (fictionally?) of mankind. To her, they had that element of old pagan supernaturals. They were like the dark wood, the coming of night—events, beings, over which man had no control—or very little—but which nipped endlessly at his heels, no matter how clever he was or how high he built his walls. Like the Greek god Dionysos, in the *Bacchae*, they broke through reason, demanding tribute in a dark leopard-speckled by moonlight.

Crisium Base 15 was long and low and ugly. Appearing through the faint shimmering mist of the nighttime moon, it caught the transport's headlights gracelessly.

It was built for its purpose, nothing more.

Bayley (Chrissie at Crisium—an old tired joke) looked at it with familiar but no longer interested disapproval. How unlike the mooted fairy-tales of crystal domes and delicate glacial structures, pure as if carved from moon-frost, on the covers of old magazines. The moon had been romantic, then possible. Then it had been living Science Fiction, *then* the money ran out, and it became nowhere you could go. Finally, things changed. And there it was again, like something someone had just invented, all the way up in the air—and accessible, for a few.

Bayley parted from Al Edwards in the lock foyer. She checked in, then took the moving walk straight to her quarters. There were only five other persons on the base this month. She had not even looked at the names and meeting Edwards, her once-lover, had felt only mild irritation. Like the base, he was old news. He didn't matter now.

In her cabin, she took another shower, to get rid of the static from the journey.

Beyond the see-through, here set in long, curved windows, she watched the blue-chalked earth lambent in the blackness. It gave more light than the full moon ever gave on earth, edging the long strands of the boulder-strewn plain with rifts and darts of thin pale silver. Indigo shadows stretched backward from every object, shadows that shone, as earth shadows did not.

Nothing was out there, only men, men and women, from the various bases. And yet, now and then, you saw them, nearly everyone did, those sudden, half-glimpsed forms that came and went at the corners of the eyes…like "seeing cats"—but nothing like that really.

The first time, though she had been warned, Bayley had been scared—entranced. What had it been, that luminously slender apparition—almost like a floating stone, yet light and weightless—borne transparently along by legs of finest glass—and with embers-of-opal eyes? Turning—only a swirl or flick of vapor. You knew it was an optical delusion, a moon delusion. Uls, they were playfully called: unreal lunar sightings. But also, you *knew* it had been there. A phantom of something lost long ago, or else a ghost that had traveled with you.

It was noisy at dinner.

Pal Al was in good form, as were the other three men on the maintenance team. Bayley, the hygiene operative, sat modestly, listening to their grouses and sallies and then, when they had broken out some beers, to their jokes and full-scale complaints. She volunteered little, beyond accepting a can. Fevriere and Sporch she knew from previous stints of duty; Edwards she knew from long ago. The fourth man, Case, was red-haired and loud. The geologist, Reza, a haughty woman from Central Industries, had taken her food in her cabin. All this, predictable.

By 23 on the GMT clock, Bayley felt more than ready to leave the main saloon. She had shown willing, as you had to, but now Case and Sporch were well into a beery, angry diatribe. She'd heard it all before.

As she started to get up, Fevriere spoke to her very low, under the blare of hearty whinging.

"Bayley—can I ask you—"

"What, Fevriere?" Silence. She said, "I'm ready to turn in. Tomorrow is a long day, and it's getting on for midnight."

"Sure. Just a word." The silence again. Then: "You've seen uls, haven't you?"

"Yes, now and then."

"You log them?"

"At first. But well, everyone sees them. Almost everyone. Now and then."

"Yes. I have too, sometimes. But Bayley—have you ever *heard* things?"

"Of course. Whisperings, sighs—it's to do with the air-pressure in the suits and—"

"No, I don't mean—look, Bayley. You were here on the last shift. Did you come across that story going round?"

She said, cautiously, putting down the half-full can, "Which story?"

"About something that came down here on one of the survey ships. Something that had got in the hold somehow, lay up by the energy vent—got out when the ship touched down over by C. Serenum?"

"Fevriere, I've heard lots of stories about things stowing away on ships—carriers, survey vessels—I've heard of alien things flying in on meteorites too, and landing smack in the impact crater, and then just getting up, shaking themselves, and sprinting off over the rocks."

"That wasn't the story," he said. His narrow dark face was serious, uneasy.

"What did you see, Fevriere, and what did you hear?"

Edwards, Case, and Sporch had ambled away back towards the bar dispenser. They were going to need detox tablets tomorrow when the machine checked their levels. Fevriere leaned toward her even so, lowering his voice almost to a whisper, and she heard Case laugh leeringly, pointing them out, as if they were two kids caught in a clinch in the back of a car. She ignored that and listened.

Fevriere said, "It was from the side of my eye, like always—but I turned, as you always do. I turned, and for a second—it was still there. It was white, like the desert-sea. Like ice-glass. It stood up like a man, but it wasn't in a suit—nothing. It didn't need one. Eyes. I saw eyes. Then it gave a sound—a cry. A kind of—I heard it."

"You couldn't, Fevriere. Sound doesn't—"

"I'd swear, *not* in my head. That's what frightens me most."

⑤ ⑤ ⑤

How did the story of the wolf, the werewolf, start? Some drunk scenario maybe, like the one tonight, but with a spooky storyteller theme rather than a grievance recital.

She hadn't been there that time. She hadn't heard it. Only that other occasion, last month—no, six months ago, going down one of the ramps, riding the roller-mop, and Box and Ryan, talking at the edge of the hydroponics area.

What had they said? She could not recall the words, only the substance. About a wolf, about a wolf that ran across the surface of the moon. They were saying it had been spotted by several outside teams, and from two or three bases. But the whole thing could have been a spoof. Ryan thought he was court-jester. And bases sometimes liked to play tricks on each other—out of boredom, or rivalry.

Why a wolf, though? Or, why a *were*wolf?

In all the stories, the werewolf—part man, part beast—was roused to shapechange at full moon. The three nights, approaching full, total full, and diminishing full. The moon would drive a werewolf crazy. And that was when it was deep inside the forests and mountain places of the earth.

So what if a werewolf were on the moon, no longer subject to that reverse-telescopic far-off view, but here, in the *middle* of the view, on the face of the snow-white satellite, running between the boulders and leaping in and out of the craters, the sourceless spanglings—the tidal pull all around, the lunar tide coming and going over its body and over its savage brain—

But nothing could live on the surface, not without a suit, not without air or life-support.

Even in the peculiar and unsubstantiated tales of foxes, gophers, and rabbits that had stowed away and got here in the baggage holds or electric vents…these little critters were found and rescued before they could escape into the airless icy death outside.

C. Serenum, the tiny "ocean-bed," only mapped west of Crisium in the first years of man's return, was void. Nothing landed there. There was nothing to land for, even for the survey teams.

We go a little mad, perhaps, she thought, lying on her bunk in the dim light and the gleam of the flaming stars beyond the window, in the night of space. Of *course* we go mad. We're *lunatics*, aren't we.

Bayley rode the roller-mop along the lit-up corridors. She had traveled maybe two miles, through the spider-web of the base complex, meeting no one, for this month the base was scarcely manned at all.

A mechanical apparatus moved continually about, it and the mop nimbly avoiding each other, with no attention needed from her. In most sections other robotic life went on, the deciphering, weighing and measuring, the assessment and notation of things. Lamps twinkled, tinselly wires strummed like harps.

Once, ghostly, at an intersection of the corridors, Bayley heard the distant cursing of the mile-off, but already unmistakable Case.

Outside it was lunar day. Darkly bright, the sky the color of chocolate tin-foil.

Reza's lab was shut tight, and the neon *keepout* posted on the doors. All the other laboratories were locked up and unoccupied.

"Ill met by moonlight, proud Titania," murmured Bayley as the mop veered by Reza's lab and round to the central maintenance station. Presently, she glimpsed Al Edwards climbing like an overalled monkey across one of the rigs. He did not notice her. Frankly, in the carrier, she had been surprised he even remembered her. They had been together only a few months. He hadn't seemed to bear a grudge, but then, neither had she. What had she seen in him?

Where the corridor ended in a ramp, passing down beside the see-through, an uls shivered across the corner of her eye. It was like a statue of milky ice, moving, rushing, among daggers of aquamarine. Bayley did not turn. Over the steady noise of the roller-mop, she did not expect to hear any other fainter sound. And so, the slender piping siren notes, rising, falling in her ear, were imagination—an ula—unreal lunar audition.

Not even a wolf-howl. You would think your brain, in its inventively deranged moments, would still get that right. If it could supply the uls of a white wolf-thing, upright, with long hair of milk-ice and beryl, it could surely also lay on the throaty music of such a child of night.

But it was no longer a child of night, this wolf, naturally. It was now a child of space and moon.

Would it be wonderful to be a werewolf, then, brought here, by accident or design, forced through the magnetic ecstasy of lunar transformation, and *kept* always thereafter transformed, by proximity to, contact *with*, the fully engorged lunar disc:

Or would it be an agony—a horror?

At the bottom of the ramp, the roller-mop swam through into hydroponics, and Bayley looked up between the pagodas of green and bronze mutated leaves.

I'm being rational about it now. Trying to figure it out. True madness.

A light water-spray flew across the high ceiling, a dragonfly of peppermint rain, and the leaves tinkled, also turning their faces upwards.

Everything changed here, and having changed, *stayed* changed.

That too, was why you came to this place?

"Hi, Chrissie. Look, I have some whisky."

"Good for you."

"Wait, wait—I thought we might share?"

"Share what, Al?"

"The bottle. Perhaps…a little warmth?"

This was predictable too. Bayley shook her head. "No thanks, Al. No sore feelings, but I'm tired." How often this or similar scenes? But this man had a partial obligation to misunderstand, so gently does it.

"Or you'd rather be with Fev," Edwards snapped, sure enough.

"Fevriere? You're kidding. Fevriere, as you and Case are obviously the last to know, is—er—sharing with Sporch."

"Really? Right. So—"

"Good night, Al. Take care."

She remembered how she had once thought it would be, off-earth. Only the best chosen for the moon, the most fit, the most intelligent and able. And with that would go courtesy and finesse, maybe even artistry and charisma.

But it was like the built bases and stations. The buildings were functional and squat, and the people who came down there were ordinary in every particular, except for some relevant routine skill or talent. And so you got the creeps like Edwards, and the geegs like Case and Sporch, the nervous ones like Fev, and the beautiful clever rotten ones like Marisha Reza. And the failures, like Christina Bayley.

"You know your trouble," said Edwards, in the morning.

"Yes, I know my trouble."

"Don't get funny. It's why we split up."

"Did we split up?" Careful, she thought. We are here on this shift for eleven more days, and if we row, four square miles of Base 15 may not be big enough for both of us. "Sorry, Al. What's the matter?"

"You." He slouched there glumly. He had a magnificent body (had *that* been what she saw in him? Probably. That and the rich brown hair and the smile.) But even so, despite his work-outs in the gym and his active physical job in maintenance, he was starting to alter somehow. Thickening a little; bending, burly, and aggressive. His eyes were way too small. Had they always been like that?

Yes, Al, actually we split up because you slapped my face twice one night, when you were high, and I knocked you out stone cold and left. *That* was why, Al. But we won't go into that.

"You see, Chrissie, your problem—" Yes, always *my* problem, of course— "you can't relate to anyone. I mean, can you?"

"I'm sorry." She sounded quite contrite. Too contrite? Apparently not.

"Damn it, Chrissie. You might just as well be one of your fucking machines. The roller-mop, the wall-skinner—you just do what you think we'll expect. Think that makes us happy? Think you got us fooled, huh? Well think again."

She *thought*, I didn't make you happy when I clocked you, Al, and you woke up with a bruised jaw. Nor did I reckon I would.

She said, calmly, "Look, Al, this isn't the place. Why don't we—well, discuss it, next break? Somewhere more private, over a drink. Back on Earth."

He grinned.

So I've done what you expect, given in, because you are so irresistible. And you are fooled. She thought, I'll deal with all this then, back on Earth. But a sour surge of rage went through her, because, unless she could get the rostas changed, she might have to quit her job if this kept up. There were other bases, of course. But each one had its established hygiene unit. It had taken her four years to get here. Four years after the other four, training for lab work and work on the surface—failing to make the grade.

"Oh ho, here's the Witch Queen," said Edwards.

Naturally he hated the Rezas of any world even more than the Chrissies. The Rezas would *never* say Yes.

"Hi, Rez. Seen the wolf yet?"

Reza looked at him, her china-pale face immaculate, ink-black brows lifted over ebony eyes.

"Wolf?"

This, Bayley thought, is almost ritualistic now...

"Haven't you heard the stories, Rez? We're haunted by a werewolf. Came up on a carrier and stayed out on the surface. Been seen by teams from Crisium Bases 13 and 9. And out at C. Serenum, by several passing craft—"

"Bayley," said Reza, turning her back on Edwards and addressing her apparent quarry. "You've finished corridor-and-general-cleanse yet?"

"Yes."

"OK. Then I want you to carry out a task for me, outside. The other cleaning work can wait. You are the only one on-base this month that I can trust with this."

Queen Reza.

Bayley heard Edwards swear softly.

"All right," said Bayley.

"I want a match for some rock samples. The Machine has it. Only guidance is required. Snake Ridge. Further is no use."

"Why can't you do it, Rez?" said Edwards.

Reza again ignored him. She handed Bayley the sandwich-sized match-coder, turned, and walked beautifully away.

"She sure has a lovely glide," said Edwards. "Pity she's a bitch."

Bayley and he were apparently comrades again, providing she held out the promise of more.

Reza was working on the Point Ridge, Bayley thought, that was what the match was for, mineral deposits, the trace of ancient humors and oils.

It would be good to get outside. Away from all of them. Surface work was the thing she had wanted to do in the beginning, but not been good enough for; at least her training meant that sometimes she got sent on these errands, by others of greater ability.

A machine. Am I really what he said? Come on, don't fall for that. They always tell you you're to blame. But perhaps I am.

When she was suited up and had the sleigh ready by the lock, Bayley turned once, looking back into the web of the base.

Yes, I am a robot, with them. I always was. Acting. Giving them what I think they want and will put up with. Attacking as a last resort. Running away.

She walked into the lock.

The sleigh followed her, and the doors closed without a sound.

Sometimes there had been dust, and long ago earthly arguments about how this dust (noted in relayed visuals) could exist, since the idea of Moon Dust was long ago relegated to fantasy. Generally it was put down to some camera fault. Yet too, there seemed to be "dusty seasons," not logical, like winter or fall, simply, now and then, *there*. Satin, pearly, with unseen, unheard winds to stir it, rustling, like autumn leaves.

Out there, there were sounds. On the plains, in the mountains, you heard them, everyone did. Voices made of thinnest platinum, the calls and flutings of invisible birds, nacre-spun nightingales and hawks of hollow electrum. And the roar—like an ancient train, some said, like a tidal wave; and someone else, like an avalanche or forest fire. And sometimes voices spoke inside your head. They…whoever they were, if ever they had been, or were to be anyone, vocal ghosts of time. Usually only one or two words. As with the light-colored male voice Bayley heard once speaking, clear in her left ear, as she waited with others to load chippings on the slopes of Mount Tranquility. "Deft Amereen," he said. She did not know what it meant. Some other language?

It was always easy, you were warned, to believe things were here that were *not*, and never *could* have been, things for which there was never, and never would be, any proof or evidence.

Faces were seen in formations of the terrain, in the sides of mountains; they shaped themselves in the rock and blew away on the silent, non-existent winds. Gigantic statues were sighted near the Mare Nectaris, sighted by ten sober people, and vanished by earthrise. There had been a solar eclipse, the Earth standing, a black hole, between the moon and the sun. The landscape altered to amber and honeycomb, sweet enough to break off pieces and devour. There were purple shadows that seemed to contain fireflies, sparks— And at that time, many sightings, solar eclipse uls. A pillared cathedral balconied from a cliff, a fleet of fin-sailed dhows went drifting by on a river of molten copper.

Bayley had not seen that, not any of that.

She had only seen flat, perspectiveless pictures of a new-penny-colored moon, sent back to earth. The eclipse was before her time down here.

And she had been told, *No, the moon had not actually become like amber. Only dun, like a sienna wash on paper.*

The sleigh shot, weightless, south and west. Toward the Snake Ridge, fancifully named. Beyond the Snake Ridge lay the miniature dry sea, C. Serenum.

Sea C. Serenum
See sea is so
Solar
Solace so
Silver sea...

What...? Oh, phonetic alliteration exercise, yes, all those years back, that's where the little chant came from. Bayley had written it in her student notebook. But even then — *where* had it come from? She didn't write, ever, anything like that. Only that one time.

Sea C. Serenum
See sea is —

The dust sprayed up in great radiant wings on either side the sleigh. Looking ahead out of the see-through, in the polarized solar glare, she expected, every instant, something to pierce, needle-white, in the dust-foam, emerging like a star. But nothing did. Even the dust was an illusion.

And then, there ahead, was the ridge.

Eight years she had been coming down to the moon. Before that, eight years waiting. And she had begun training when she was just sixteen. Everything seemed in blocks of eight. Did that mean anything? She was thirty-two.

Bayley stood on First Spine, under the head of the ridge, watching the match-coder trundle lightly to and fro, now and then pausing to scoop up relevant debris. When she thought it had enough from one area, she pointed it another way.

Who am I kidding? Anyone could do this.

She need not have come so far out, either, so far from base.

On some days, it was sometimes possible to glimpse the lights of Base 9 from the top of the Snake Ridge, but not always. The non-atmosphere, the strange shortened horizon, played tricks not only with vision, but with distance and illumination.

Bayley climbed the ridge. She looked out. Base 9 was invisible, and might not exist.

Instead, the vast sweep of the dry sea that was not a sea, folded open like a dead marble flower. Beyond, lay mountains, low and pinnacled as some city of stone.

And the wind that was no wind came and stirred the unreal powders of the sea floor, so for a moment they rippled like long waves, and she heard the crisp fall-leaf sound that was also like the swarming of a tidal ocean.

I can hear it.

I'd swear, *not* in my head—Fevriere, that first night, whispering—*That's what frightens me most.*

Bayley had seen Fevriere next day, drinking with Sporch, laughing and hearty, like the others, like Edwards and the loud red Case. Fevriere had said nothing else to her. His worries seemed entirely forgotten. He was embarrassed, maybe?

Something—

From the corner of her eye—

Bayley turned so suddenly, the whole white world seemed to snap over. But it would only seem like that. The anchoring boots, the heavy suit, must make her slow, even in gravity-zero.

And yet. She had been quick enough.

I am *seeing* this. What am I seeing?

The wind blew, and the white hair flattened to the body, rippled, like the sand-waves of the sea C. Serenum.

His eyes were the blue of irises, all iris blue, and the dark pupils glowed in them like eclipsing planets dropped from the sky.

He was a wolf that was a man. He had, as wolves did, human eyes. Naked, but for the white-platinum petals of the hair, which covered him yet let him be seen, and the mane of head-hair, a white chrysanthemum, a moonburst, flaring behind his face that had a wolf's features and a man's eyes, and a silence that belonged only in this place of silver seas.

The sea is moving. Waves are coming in. A sea of silver coins, flooding softly to the shore.

Bayley stared through her face-plate, and gradually the man-wolf, the wolf-man, darkened. She thought, *Breathe*— take a *breath*—

She breathed.

The blood thundered in her ears, sea-sound, solace so, rush, push, washing away and away.

She could see.

Nothing was there. Only the bleak carved spines of the Snake Ridge, knife-cut-edged with sharp solar glare. The machine, trundling up and down between the pebbles that were like the shells of albino tortoises.

"That's enough," she said to the machine, over the link.

It heard her and stopped abruptly, a guilty child who had shoveled up too much sand from the beach as the adult slept.

⑤ ⑤ ⑤

Werewolf: it wasn't just the thing of night, the haunt, the horror. It represented—was—the inner creature, the animal spirit, resident in all men, all women, triggered into life by a malediction or a wry blessing; by magic or only at the madness of full moon. Not every culture or people feared the werewolf. Shamans conjured and became such a beast, not to terrify or kill, but only to release their own pent energies and so find the knowledge that mortal life hides from itself under the veils of flesh, under the lenses of sight.

Bayley lay on her bunk. She dreamed of a pack of moon wolves, like the moon wolf she had seen. They chased a phantom thing, a glimmering energy that might have been a deer, but was nothing like that. One wolf, two, leapt. They killed swiftly.

She watched them in the dream, as they ate the fresh-slaughtered energy that had not been a deer. She saw, across their couth and quiet feeding, a shambles of rocks, a sea that moved, slow quick-silver, on the shore. A city of low, calm buildings, with here and there slender skeins of translucent steeples.

When the pack rose and sped away, she was taken with them. She ran with them up and over the slopes by the sea and came into the city.

Clouds drifted through wide-open avenues, clouds of breath or thought. Flowers, pale-pink and like velvet to the touch (she touched them) grew out of the stones, their narrow, serpentine leaves twisting, sighing. The streets were broad. There was a kind of music.

She saw no women among the wolves. She realized they were there nevertheless. It was only that they were, everyone, all alike. What she had seen on the ridge was then not necessarily a man. It was simply—a wolf.

Bayley opened her eyes, and the dream ebbed away and away.

She thought, But that was what I saw. *That* was what I truly saw. I saw it in one split second, just before the face-plate darkened or seemed to, because I hadn't breathed. *Why* didn't I breathe? Where—where had I gone out of my body so it stopped breathing, and so that I saw all this, and only now I remember it?

She watched them at dinner, Case, Edwards, Sporch, Fevriere. How they were. Just as she had watched Reza earlier, in the lab, having found some excuse to intrude, checking up on the gathered samples.

They were all so predictable. They did, each of them, only what you expected they would. Reza cold and a bitch, rude and intolerant, interested solely in her work. Edwards lustful—worse than she ever recalled—rolling his eyes at Bayley, and Sporch and Case also acting up together, and Fevriere gladly joining in, over the growing array of beer cans.

They're the robots, not me. They're like automata. Were they always like that? I don't remember.

Only three days to go now, before the carrier would come to take her off, up to earth, that jewel hanging there, unbelievable, the same color blue as the moon wolf's eyes.

"Communication from Base 13," said Sporch, as Bayley came in to breakfast. "They lost a sleigh, over near the Snake Ridge. See anything, Bay, when you were up there?"

"No. Do you mean they lost personnel?"

"Seems not. Some guy called Stanlevy. He got back OK, but says he lost the sleigh."

"How d'ya lose a sleigh for Chrissake?" said Case.

They all laughed. Was it funny?

None of them was serious.

Things got lost.

Bayley thought of the moon wolf suddenly there on the ridge. She thought of the man called Stanlevy going back on his boots to Base 13, way over south, and *leaving something behind*. She thought how things vanished in the moon dark, and even when the dark went away, how you never found them, only other things that seemed to have been mislaid or jettisoned by other persons, other bases, other survey teams or machines.

Reza walked into the saloon. The men quietly sniggered, all of them, in unison, like an entity, then cleaned their faces off.

"Bayley, these samples are useless. What were you playing at?"

Bayley stared at Reza.

"I thought—"

"Don't think, then. I expect you to go out again and make good. I can't work with this rubbish."

One of the men cheered sotto voce—probably Case.

Reza took no notice, nor did Bayley.

"You want me to go back—"

"*I* haven't the time. I have to get on with the other samples."

She wants me to go back, go out. It's nuts. The samples aren't useless; I checked them anyway. They're what she asked for, and of course the match-coder does all the work, and there's nothing wrong with it, and why has she waited—

She sounds like a school ma'am. I'd like to slap her. Can't, damn her; she's senior status. But Bayley knew she was pretending to be annoyed, was *not* aggravated at all, didn't care. She might as well admit to that.

"OK, Reza."

In the hydroponics area, Bayley stood looking at the green earth leaves, lifting their heads towards the rain dragonfly. She sniffed the minty herbal scent, the aroma of peppermint and thyme.

She touched a leaf, and it turned out of her hand, as if alive.

No plant had any flowers. All were healthy, even productive, but without blooms. As if—as if the flowers had gone elsewhere.

I have a choice. You always have a choice.

I'll make some excuse to Reza, and stay in until the last days of my stint are done and I can ride the carrier up to earth. And then I'll have to change my job, won't I? Because even if Reza doesn't get me thrown out, every time I come back—

Why has this taken eight years?

Blocks of eight, everything.

Eight years old when she first saw the moon and *knew* the moon, from a roof, on Earth. Looking into that face that was like no other thing, not a lamp, not a sun, not *even*—a face.

And then the eight years of training, failing, waiting, and then the eight years coming down and going back. Back—you never said now, going home. As you never said, on Earth, going *up* to the moon. *Earth* was *up*. Up in the black lunar sky, an iris-blue gem among its shifting cloud-breaths.

Anyway, she thought, even if I don't go out today, sometime I will. I mean—I don't even have to *go* out, do I? For it to happen.

She felt strange, Chrissie Bayley. She knew the near-drunk terror of the dark wood, where Dionysos called his maenads. It wasn't being scared at all. It was the madness of the moon. The lunacy. (The lunar sea...) Joy.

I suppose I've never got close to anyone. Not ever.

Not even the ones like Al, who tried to get close to *me*. He did try. He slapped me once, twice, because he wanted something from me, more than sex, more than friendship or even love, and I didn't or couldn't give it. That doesn't excuse him, but it explains. He wasn't always like he is now. But was I? A robot. Chrissie of Crisium.

Can a robot be enamored of a moon?

Bayley watched herself go through the base on the moving walkways, suit up, take the sleigh and open the lock.

Bayley watched the sleigh, with Bayley in it, shooting out over the moon surface. Bayley ran beside the sleigh with Bayley riding in it. Bayley in the sleigh still breathed this time. The running Bayley was not breathing, not needing to breathe. Not needing to smile or lie any more, warm in her fur. Piping her siren song to the dark and the light.

Later, much later, she ran back, all the way to the base, and standing on the milky drifts of the dark outside, she looked in at the see-through, and saw herself plod in from the lock, and take off her suit, and shower and go to dinner.

Chrissie saw herself, window after window, laughing and drinking beer. She saw herself in Edwards' cabin, and having sexual relations with Edwards, and then, that established, she went away again. She left herself to it.

She knew where the others would be, and she found them. This was in the marble city that had seemed to be mountains, among the fragile spires and gracious low buildings, all the architecture that had never happened here, except in wishful thinking. She could smell the scent of the pink flowers and the ice-cool smell of the vanilla clouds.

The ocean came in, sigh on sigh, quintessential sea, to solace the onyx shore, under the solar light that did not glare any more but was smooth as the taste of cream.

It was what she had always looked for, when she looked—thought—of the moon, what she had anticipated, failed to see, and now discovered.

Everyone was there who had ever come here, or returned here. They were all alike, and all one. There was no need for conversation or remorse, for laughter, alcohol, or oxygen, or love. Moon wolves.

They hunted and ate the silver deer that felt no pain, they swam in the seas and leaped across the mountains. They drank moonlight.

Sometimes with her iris eyes she would see, as did they all, the alien mechanisms at work on the moon, the soulless ships coming and going, the shells of people, the autometons, carrying on their abandoned lives.

Sometimes, sleeping in the indigo sleeve of night, she dreamed distinctly of the base, real as if she lived there too, or of earth. Of things she did in those places, or that her robot self did there, mechanically.

Silly dull dreams, which meant nothing at all.

Felixity

Felixity's parents were so beautiful that everywhere they went they were attended by a low murmuring, like that of a beehive. Even when pregnant with her child, Felixity's mother was lovely, an ormolu madonna. But when Felixity was born, her mother died.

Among the riches of her father, then, in a succession of elaborate houses, surrounded by gardens that sometimes led to a cobalt sea, Felixity grew up, motherless. Her father watched her grow, he must have done, although nannies tended her, servants waited on her, and tutors gave her lessons. Sometimes in the evening, when the heat of the day had settled and the stars come out, Felixity's father would interview his daughter on the lamplit terrace above the philodendrons.

"Now tell me what you learned today."

But Felixity, confronted by her beautiful and elegant father burnished on the dark with pale electricity, was tongue-tied. She twisted her single plait around her finger and hunched her knees. She was an ugly child, ungraceful and gauche, with muddy skin and thin, unshining hair. She had no energy, and even when put out to play, wandered slowly about the garden walks, or tried tiredly to skip, giving up after five or six heavy jumps. She was slow at her studies, worried over them and suffered headaches. She was meek. Her teeth were always needing fillings, and she bore this unpleasantness with resignation.

"Surely there must have been something of note in your day?"

"I went to the dentist, Papa."

"Your mother," said Felixity's father, "had only one tiny filling in her entire head. It was the size of a pin's point. It was gold." He said this without cruelty, more in wonder. "You must have some more dresses," he added presently.

Felixity hated it when clothes were bought for her. She looked so awful in anything attractive or pretty, but they had never given up. Glamorously dressed she resembled a chrysalis dressed in the butterfly. When she could, she put on her drabbest, most nondescript clothes.

After half an hour or so of his daughter's unstimulating company, Felixity's father would send her away. He was always tactful but Felixity was under no illusions. Beneath the dentist's numbing cocaine she was aware her teeth were being drilled to the nerve and that shortly, when the anesthetic wore off, they would hurt her.

Inevitably, as time passed, Felixity grew up and became a woman. Her body changed, but it did not improve. If anyone had been hoping for some magical transformation, they were disappointed. When she was sixteen, Felixity was, nevertheless, launched into society. Not a ripple attended the event, although she wore a red dress and a most lifelike wig fashioned by a famous coiffeur. Following this beginning, Felixity was often on the edges of social activities, where she was never noticed, gave neither offense nor inspiration, and before some of which she was physically sick several times from neurasthenia. As the years went by, however, her terror gradually left her. She no longer expected anything momentous with which she would not be able to cope.

Felixity's father aged marvelously. He remained slim and limber, was scarcely lined, and that only in a way to make him more interesting. His hair and teeth were like a boy's.

"How that color suited your mother," he remarked to Felixity, as she crossed the room in a gown of translucent lemon silk, which made her look like an uncooked tuber. "I remember three such dresses, and a long, fringed scarf. She was so partial to it." Again, he was not being cruel. Perhaps he was entitled to be perplexed. They had anticipated an exquisite child, the best of both of them. But then, they had also expected to live out their lives together.

When she was thirty-three, Felixity stopped moving in society and attended only those functions she could not, from politeness, avoid. Her father did not remonstrate with her, indeed he only saw her now once a week, at a rite he referred to as "Dining with my Daughter." Although his first vision of her was always a slight shock, he did not disenjoy these dinners, which lasted two hours exactly, and at which he was able to reminisce at great length about his beautiful wife. If anyone had asked him, he would have said he did this for Felixity's sake. Otherwise, he assumed she was quite happy. She read books and occasionally painted rather poor watercolors. Her teeth, which had of necessity been over-filled, had begun to break at regular intervals, but aside from this her life was tranquil and passed in luxury. There was nothing more that could be done for her.

❡ ❡ ❡

One evening, as Felixity was being driven home to one of her father's city houses, a young man ran from a side street out across the boulevard, in front of the car. The chauffeur put on his brakes at once. But the large silver vehicle lightly touched the young man's side, and he fell in front of it. A crowd gathered instantly, at the periphery of which three dark-clad men might be seen looking on. But these soon after went away.

The chauffeur came to Felixity's door to tell her that the young man was apparently unhurt, but shaken. The crowd began to adopt factions, some saying that the young man was to blame for the accident, others that the car had been driven too fast. In the midst of this, the young man himself appeared at Felixity's door. In years he was about twenty-six, smartly if showily dressed in an ice-cream white suit now somewhat dusty from the road. His blue-black hair curled thickly on his neck; he was extremely handsome. He stared at the woman in the car with amontillado eyes. He said, "No, no, it was not your fault." And then he collapsed on the ground.

The crowd ascended into uproar. The young man must be taken immediately to the hospital.

Felixity was flustered, and it may have been this that caused her to open her door and to instruct the chauffeur and a bystander to assist the young man into the car. As it was done, the young man revived a little.

"Put him here, beside me," said Felixity, although her voice trembled with alarm.

The car door was closed again and the chauffeur told to proceed to a hospital. The crowd made loud sounds as they drove off.

To Felixity's relief and faint fright, the young man now completely revived. He assured her that it was not essential to go to the hospital, but that if she were kind enough to allow him to rest a moment in her house, and maybe swallow a glass of water, he would be well enough to continue on his way. He had been hurrying, he explained, because he had arranged to see his aunt, and was late. Felixity was afraid that the drive to her house would prolong this lateness, but the young man, who said his name was Roland, admitted that he was often tardy on visits to his aunt, and she would forgive him.

Felixity, knowing no better, therefore permitted Roland to be driven with her to the house. Its electric gates and ectomorphic pillars did not seem to antagonize him, and ten minutes later, he was seated in the blond, eighteenth-century drawing room, drinking bottled carbonated water with slices of lime. Felixity asked him whether she should call her father's doctor, who was in residence. But Roland said again that he had no need of medical attention. Felixity believed him. He had all the hallmarks of strength, elasticity, and vitality she had noted in others. She was both glad and strangely sorry when he rose springingly up again, thanked her, and said that now he would be leaving.

When he left, she shook all over, sweat beaded her fore-head, and she felt quite sick. That night she could not sleep, and the next morning, at breakfast, she broke another tooth on a roll.

Two days after, a bouquet of pink roses, from a fashionable florist, arrived for Felixity. That very afternoon Roland came to the gates and inquired if he might see her. The servants, the guards at the gate, were so unused to anyone seeking Felix-ity—indeed, it was unique—that they conveyed the message to her without question. And of course Felixity, wan with nau-seous amazement and a hammering heart, invited Roland in.

"I've been unable to stop thinking about you," said Roland. "I've never before met with a woman so gracious and so kind."

Roland said many things, more or less in this vein, as they walked about the garden among the imported catalpas and the orchids. He confessed to Felixity that his aunt was dead; it was her grave he had been going to visit. He had no one in the world.

Felixity did not know what she felt, but never before had she felt anything like it. In the dim past of her childhood, when some vague attempts had been made to prepare or alter her, she had been given to understand that she might, when she gained them, entertain her friends in her father's houses, and that her suitors would be formally welcomed. Neither friend nor suitor had ever crossed the thresholds of the houses, but now Felixity fell into a kind of delayed response, and in a while she had offered Roland wine on the terrace.

As they sat sipping it, her sick elation faded, and a mute sweetness possessed her.

It was not that she thought herself lovable; she thought herself nothing. It was that one had come to her who had made her the center of the day. The monumental trees and exotic flowers had become a backdrop, the heat, the house, the servants who brought them things. She had met before people like Roland, the gorgeous magicians who never saw her. But Roland did see her. He had fixed on her. He spoke to her of his sad beleaguered life, how his father had gambled away a fortune, how he himself had been sadistically misled on his chances of film stardom. He wanted her to know him. He gazed into her eyes and saw in her, it was plain, vast continents of possibility.

He stayed with her until the dinner hour and begged that he might be able to return. He had not told her she was beautiful or any lie of that nature. He had said she was good, and luminously kind, and that never before had he met these qualities in a young woman, and that she must not shut him out, as he could not bear it.

On his second visit, under a palm tree, Felixity was taken by compunction. "Six of my teeth are crowned," she said. "And this—is a wig!" And she snatched it off to reveal her thin cropped hair.

Roland gave a gentle smile. "How you honor me," he said. "I'm so happy that you trust me. But what does any of this matter? Throw the silly wig away. You are yourself. There has never been anyone like you. Not in the whole world."

When Felixity and Roland had been meeting for a month, Felixity received a summons from her incredible father.

Felixity went to see him with a new type of courage. Some of her awe had lessened, although she would not have put this into words. She had been with a creature of fires. It seemed she knew her father a little better.

"I'm afraid," said Felixity's father, "that it is my grim task to disillusion you. The young man you've made your companion is a deceiver."

"Oh," said Felixity. She looked blank.

"Yes, my child. I don't know what he has told you, but I've had him investigated. He is the bastard son of a prostitute and has lived so far by dealings with thieves and shady organizations. He was in flight from one of these when he ran in front of your car. Obviously now he is in pursuit of your money, both your own finances and those that you'll inherit on my death."

Felixity did not say she would not hear ill of Roland. She thought about what her father had told her, and slowly she nodded. Then, from the patois of her curtailed emotions she translated her heart into normal human emotional terms. "But I love him."

Felixity's father looked down at her with crucial pity. It was a fact, he did not truly think of her as his daughter, for his daughter would have been lovely. He accepted her as a pathetic dependent, until now always needing him, a jest of God upon a flawless delight that had been rent away.

"If you love him, Felixity," he said, "you must send him to me."

Felixity nodded again. Beings of fire communicated with each other. She had no fears.

The next day she waited on the terrace, and eventually Roland came out of the house into the sunlight. He seemed a little pale, but he spoke to her brightly. "What a man he is. We are to marry, my beloved. That is, if you'll have me. I'm to care for you. What a golden future lies before us!" Roland did not detail his conversation with Felixity's father. He did not relate, for example, that Felixity's father had courteously touched on Roland's career as crook and gigolo. Or that Felixity's father had informed Roland that he grasped perfectly his aims, but that those aims were to be gratified, for Felixity's sake. "She has had little enough," said Felixity's father. "Providing you are kind to her, a model husband, and don't enlighten her in the matter of your real feelings, I am prepared to let you live at her expense." Roland had protested feebly that he adored Felixity, her tenderness had won his heart. Roland did not recount to Felixity either that her father had greeted this effusion with the words: "You will not, please, try your formula on me."

In the days that succeeded Roland's dialogue with Felixity's father, the now betrothed couple were blissful, each for their own reasons.

Then Felixity's father flew to another city on a business venture, the engine of his plane malfunctioned, and it crashed into the forests. Before the month was up, his remarkable but dead body had been recovered, woven with lianas and chewed by jaguars. Felixity became the heiress to his fortune.

During this time of tragedy, Roland supported Felixity with unswerving attention. Felixity was bewildered at her loss, for she could not properly persuade herself she had lost anything.

The funeral took place with extreme pomp, and soon after the lovers sought a quiet civil wedding. Felixity had chosen her own dress, which was a swampy brown. The groom wore vanilla and scarlet. When the legalities were complete, Roland drove Felixity away in his new white car, toward a sixty-roomed villa on the coast.

As she was driven, a little too fast, along the dusty road, Felixity was saturated by an incoherent but intense nervousness.

She had never had any female friends, but she had read a number of books, and she guessed that her unease sprang from sexual apprehension. Never, in all their courtship, had Roland done more than press her hands or her lips lightly with his own. She had valued this decorum in him, even though disappointment sometimes chilled her. At the impress of his flesh, however light, her pulses raced. She was actually very passionate, and had never before had the chance of realizing it. Nevertheless, Roland had told her that, along with her kindness, he worshipped her purity. She knew she must wait for their wedding night to learn of the demons of love.

Now it seemed she was afraid. But what was there to dread? Her reading, which if not salacious, had at least been comprehensive, had given her the gist of the nuptial act. She was prepared to suffer the natural pain of deflowerment in order to offer joy to her partner. She imagined that Roland would be as grave and gentle in lovemaking as he had always been in all their dealings. Therefore, why her unease?

Along the road the copper-green pyramids of coffee trees spun past, and on the horizon's edge, the forests kept pace with the car.

By midnight, Felixity thought, I shall be different.

They arrived before sunset at the villa, where Felixity had spent some of her childhood. Felixity was surprised to find that no servants came out to greet them. Her bafflement grew when, on entering the house, she found the rooms polished and vacant.

"Don't concern yourself with that," said Roland. "Come with me. I want to show you something."

Felixity went obediently. Roland had somehow given her to understand that, along with kindness and purity, he liked docility. They moved up the grand stairway, along corridors, and so into the upper regions of the house, which were reached by narrow twining flights of steps.

Up there, somewhere, Roland unlocked and opened a door.

They went into a bare whitewashed room.

A few utilitarian pieces of furniture were in it, a chair or two, a slender bed, a round mirror. In one wall a door gave on a bathroom closet. There was a window, but it was caged in a complex if ornamental grill.

"Here we are," said Roland. Felixity looked at him, confused. "Where?" she asked.

"Your apartment."

Felixity considered this must be a joke and laughed falsely, as she had sometimes done in her society days.

"I have you at a disadvantage," said Roland. "Let me explain."

He did so. This room was where Felixity was to live. If there was anything else she wanted—he knew she was fond of books—it could be supplied. Food would be put in through that flap, there, near the bottom of the door. She should return her empty trays via the same aperture. She would find the bathroom stocked with clean towels, soap, and toothpaste. These would be replaced at proper intervals. Whatever else she required she should list—see the notepad and pencil on the table—and these things too would be delivered. She should have a radio, if she liked. And perhaps a gramophone.

"But—" said Felixity, "but—"

"Oh surely you didn't think I would ever cohabit with you?" asked Roland reasonably. "I admit, I might have had to awhile, if your father had survived, but maybe not even then. He was so glad to be rid of you, a letter from you every six months, dictated by me, would have sufficed. No, you will live up here. I shall live in the house and do as I want. Now and then I'll ask you to sign the odd document in order to assist my access to your money. But otherwise I won't trouble you at all. And so, dear Felixity, thank you, and au revoir. I wish you a pleasant evening."

And having said this, Roland went out, before Felixity could shift hand or limb, and she heard the key turning in the lock. And then a raucous silence.

At first she did not credit what had happened. She ran about like a trapped insect, to the door, to the window. But both were closed fast, and the window looked out on a desolate plain that stretched away beyond the house to the mountains. The sun was going down, and the sky was indelibly hot and merciless.

Roland would come back, of course. This was some game, to tease her.

But darkness came, and Roland did not. And much later a tray of bread and chicken and coffee was put through the door. Felixity ran to the door again, shrieking for help. But whoever had brought the tray took no notice.

Felixity sat through her wedding night on a hard chair, shivering with terror and incipient madness, by the light of the one electric lamp she had found on the table.

In the villa, far off, she thought she heard music, but it might only have been the rhythm of the sea.

Near dawn she came to accept what had occurred. It was only what she should have expected. She wept for half an hour and then lay down on the mean bed to sleep.

For weeks, and probably months, Felixity existed in the white-washed room with the grilled window.

Every few days books were put through her door, along with the trays of meals. The food was generally simple or meager, and always cold; still it punctually arrived. A radio appeared too, a few days after Felixity's internment. It seemed able to receive only one station, which put out endless light music and melodramatic serials, but even so Felixity came to have it on more and more. At midnight the station closed down. Then it was replaced by a claustrophobic loud silence.

Other supplies were promptly presented through the door on her written request. Clean towels, new soap, shampoo, toothpaste, and toothbrushes, Felixity's analgesics for her headaches and her preferred form of sanitary protection.

There was no clock or calendar in the room, but the radio station repeatedly gave the day and hour. At first Felixity noticed the progress of time, until eventually she recognized that she was counting it up like a prisoner, as if, when she had served her sentence, she would be released. But of course her freedom would never come. Felixity ceased to attend to the progress of time.

In the beginning, too, she went on with her normal routines of cleanliness and order. In her father's houses her bathrooms had been spectacular, and she had liked using them, experimenting there with soaps and foams, and with preparations that claimed they might make her hair thicker, although they did not. With only the functional white bathroom at her disposal Felixity lost interest in hygiene, and several days would sometimes elapse before she bathed. She had also to clean the bathroom herself, which initially proved challenging, but soon it became a chore she did not bother with. Besides, she found the less she used the bathroom the less cleaning it needed.

Felixity would sit most of the day, listening with unfixed open eyes to the radio. Now and then she would read part of a book. Occasionally she would wander to the window and look out. But the view never changed, and the glare of the distant mountains tired her eyes. Often she found it very hard to focus on the printed word and would read the same phrase in a novel over and over trying to make sense of it.

After perhaps three months had gone by, an afternoon came when she heard the key turn in the lock of her door.

She was now too apathetic to be startled. Yet when Roland, gleaming in his ice-cream clothes, came into the room, she knew a moment of shame. But then she acknowledged it did not matter if he saw her unwashed in her robe, her thin hair and unpowdered face greasy, for he had never cared what she looked like, she was nothing to him.

And Roland approached with his usual charm, smiling at her and holding out some papers.

"Here I am," he said, "I won't keep you a minute. If you'd just be kind enough to sign these."

Felixity did not get up at once only because she was lethargic. But she said softly, "What if I refuse?"

Roland continued to smile. "I should be forced to take away your radio and books, and to starve you."

Felixity believed him. After all, if he starved her to death, he would inherit everything. It was really quite good of him to allow her to live.

She went to the table and signed the papers.

"Thank you so much," said Roland.

"Won't you let me out?" said Felixity.

"Obviously I can't." He added logically, "It's much better if you stay here. Or you might be tempted to run away and divorce me. Or if you didn't do that, you'd be horribly in my way."

Roland had, prior to their drive to the villa, sacked the original servants and installed a second set, all of whom were bribed to his will, served him unquestioningly, and held their tongues. Roland now lived the life that ideally suited him, answerable to no one. He lay in bed until noon, breakfasted extravagantly, spent the day lazily, and in the evening drove to the nearest city to gamble and to drink. Frequently he would return to the villa in the small hours with beautiful women, to whom, in a great scrolled bed, he made ferocious love, casting them out again at dawn, in their spangled dresses, like the rinds of eaten fruits.

"But," said Felixity," "you see I'm afraid—if I have to stay here—I may lose my mind."

"Oh don't worry about that," said Roland. "The servants already think I locked you up because you were insane."

Then he left her, and Felixity went to gaze from her window. The mountains looked like the demarcation line at the end of the world. Felixity turned on her radio.

That night, as she ate a piece of hard sausage, she broke a tooth.

She felt curiously humiliated by this, yet she had no choice but to set the fact down on a page of her notepad, and append a request for a dentist. This she slipped out through the flap in the door with a pallid misgiving. She did not suppose for an instant Roland would permit her to leave the house, and what kind of mechanic would he send in to her?

For nine days, during which the broken tooth tore at her mouth and finally made it bleed, Felixity awaited Roland's response. On the tenth day she came to see he would not trouble to respond at all. He had spared her what suffering he could, under the circumstances, but to put himself out over her teeth was too much to ask of him.

This, then, was where she had sunk to.

Four hours passed, and Felixity sat in her chair listening to a serial about a sensational girl who could not choose between her lovers. Behind her the window became feverish then cool, and darkness slid into the room.

Suddenly something strange happened. Felixity sprang to her feet as if she had been electrically shocked. She rushed towards the cheap mirror on the wall and stared at herself in the fading crepuscule. She did not need light, for she knew it all. She reached up and rent at her thin hair and a scream burst out of her, lacerating her mouth freshly on the sharp edge of broken enamel.

"Nonononono!" screamed Felixity.

She was denying only herself.

She jumped up and down before the mirror, shrieking, galvanized by a scalding white thread inside her.

Only when this huge energy had left her, which took several minutes, did she crawl back to the chair and collapse in it, weeping. She cried for hours out of the well of pain. Her sobs were strong and violent and the room seemed to shake at them.

At midnight, the radio station closed down and the shattering silence bounded into the room. Felixity looked up. Everything was in blackness, the lamp unlit, and yet it seemed there had been a flash of brilliance. Perhaps there was a storm above the mountains. Or, incredibly, perhaps some human life went over the plain, a car driving on the dirt tracks of it with headlights blazing.

Felixity moved to the window. Night covered the plain and the mountains were like dead coals. Above, the stars winked artificially, as they had done in the planetarium where once she had been taken as a child.

The whip of light cracked again. It was not out on the plain but inside the room.

Felixity was still too stunned for ordinary fear.

She walked back slowly to her chair, and as she did so, she saw her reflection in the round mirror on the wall.

Felixity stopped, and her reflection stopped, inevitably. Felixity raised her right arm, let it fall. Her left arm, let it fall. The reflection did the same. Felixity began to walk forward again, towards the mirror. She walked directly up to it, and halted close enough to touch.

Earlier, in the twilight, the mirror had reflected Felixity only too faithfully. It had shown the apex of her ungainly figure, her drab, oily complexion, her ugly features and wispy hair. Now the mirror contained something else. It was illuminated as if a lamp shone on it out of the dark room. In the mirror, Felixity's reflection was no longer Felixity.

Instead a woman stood in the mirror, copying exactly every gesture that Felixity made.

This woman, to judge from her upper torso, was slender, with deeply indented breasts. Her skin, which was visible in the low-cut bodice and at the throat and the lower part of the face, was the mildest gold, like dilute honey. Her tightly fitting gown was a flame. On her upper face, across her forehead and eyes, she wore a mask like yellow jade, from which long sprays of sparkling feathers curved away. And above the mask and beneath ran thickly coiling gilded hair, like golden snakes poured from a jar.

Felixity put both her hands up over her mouth. And the woman in the mirror did as Felixity did. She wore long gloves the color of topaz, streaked with scintillants.

The flash of brilliance snapped again. It was up in the black air above the woman. A lyre of sparks came all unstrung: a firework. As it faded, an entire scene was there at the woman's back.

It was a city of steps and arches, plazas and tall buildings, through which a brimstone river curled its way. But over the river slim bridges ran that were fruited with lamps of orange amber, and on the facades all about roared torches of lava red. All these lights burned in the river too, wreathing it with fires.

Figures went across the levels of the city, in scarlet, brass, and embers. Some led oxblood dogs or carried incandescent parrots on their wrists. A bronze alligator surfaced from the river, glittered like jewelry, and was gone.

Felixity saw a large red star hung in the sky.

Within the woman's mask, two eyes glimmered. She lowered her hands from her mouth and Felixity found that she had lowered her hands. But then the woman turned from the mirror and walked away.

Felixity watched the woman walk to the end of a torchlit pier, and there she waited in her gown of flame until a flaming boat came by and she stepped into it and was borne off under the bridges of lamps.

After this the scene melted, all its fires and colors spilling together downward and out by some non-existent gutter at the mirror's base.

Felixity took two or three paces back. In sheer darkness now she went and lay on her bed. But the afterimages of the lights stayed on her retinas for some while, in flickering floating patches. The mirror remained black, and in it she could dimly see the room reflecting. Felixity closed her eyes and beheld the alligator surfacing in a gold garland of ripples, and as it slipped under again, she slept.

In the morning, when she woke, Felixity did not think she had been dreaming. It did occur to her that perhaps Roland had played some kind of trick on her, but she quickly dismissed this idea, for Roland had no interest in her, why should he waste effort on such a thing? Had she then suffered an hallucination? Was this the onset of madness? Felixity discovered that she did not thrill with horror. She felt curiously calm, almost complacent. She took a bath and shampooed her hair, ate the meals that were shunted through the door, ignoring as best she could the difficulty with the broken tooth, and listened to the radio. She was waiting for the darkness to come back. And when it did so, she switched off the radio and sat in her chair, watching the mirror.

Hours passed and the mirror kept up its blackness, faintly reflecting the room. Once Felixity thought there was a spark of light, but it was only some spasm in her eyes.

Eventually Felixity put on the radio again. It was midnight and the station was closing down. Felixity became alert, for it was at this moment on the previous night that the mirror had come alive. However, the station went off the air, and that was all. Felixity watched the mirror from her bed until sleep overcame her.

Somewhere in the markerless black of early morning, she awakened, and over the mirror was flowing a ribbon of fire.

Felixity leapt from the bed and dashed to the mirror, but already the fire had vanished, leaving no trace.

Felixity set herself to sleep by day and watch by night. This was quite easy for her, for rather like a caged animal she had become able to slumber almost at will. In the darkness she would sit, without the lamp, sometimes not looking directly at the mirror. She let the radio play softly in the background, and when the close-down came she would tense. But nothing happened.

Seven nights went by.

Felixity continued her bat-like existence.

Only one magical thing had ever taken place in her life before, her betrothal to Roland, and that had been proved to be a sham. The magic of the mirror she recognized, as sometimes a piece of music, never heard before, may seem familiar. This music was for her.

On the eighth night, just after the radio had announced it was eleven o'clock, the mirror turned to a coin of gold.

Without a sound, Felixity got up, went to the mirror, and stared in.

It was a golden ballroom lit by bizarre chandeliers like the rosy clustered hearts of pomegranates. There on the floor of obsidian a man and woman danced in an austere yet sensual fashion. His were sophisticated carnival clothes of black and blood, and he was masked in jet. She was Felixity's reflection, and now she wore a dress of sulfur beaded by magma rain. There was a tango playing on the radio, and it seemed they moved in time to it.

Felixity felt herself dancing, although she did not stir, and the man's arm around her.

In a tall window was a sort of day, a sky that was coral pink and a huge red sun or planet lying low.

The tango quivered to its end.

The man and woman separated, and all the colors pooled together and sluiced down the mirror. Felixity made a wild motion, as if to catch them as they flushed through the bottom of the glass. But of course nothing ran out.

In the blackness of her room then, Felixity solemnly danced a tango alone. She was stiff and unwieldy and sometimes bumped into the flimsy furniture. She knew now a raw craving and yearning, a nostalgia as if for an idyllic childhood. She had come to understand who the woman was. She was Felixity, in another world. Felixity's brain had made the intellectual and spiritual jump swiftly and completely. Here she was a lump, unloved, unliked even, so insignificant she could be made a prisoner forever. But there, she was a being of fire.

Oh to go through the mirror. Oh to be one with her true self.

And at last she touched the mirror, which was very warm against her hand, as if the sun had just shone on it. But otherwise it gave no clue to its remarkable properties. And certainly no hint of a way in.

After the vision at eleven o'clock on the eighth night, a month elapsed, and the mirror never altered by night or day.

Felixity grew very sad. Although she had been thrown into an abyss, idly tossed there, her reaction had been mostly passivity rather than despair, for she was used to ill-treatment in one form or another. But the images in the mirror had raised her up to a savage height, to a plateau of lights she had never before achieved. That she grasped almost at once their implication demonstrated how profoundly she had been affected. And now she was left with the nothing which had always encompassed her and which Roland had driven in beside her, into her cage.

She ceased to eat the scanty meals and only sipped the coffee or water. In order to hide what she did—she was incoherently afraid of force-feeding—she dropped the portions of food into the lavatory. Felixity became extremely feeble, dizzy, and sick. Her head ached constantly, and she could not keep down the pain-killers. She lay on the bed all day, sinking in and out of sleep. She could hardly hear the radio for the singing in her ears. At night she tried to stay conscious, but the mirror was like a black void that sucked her in. Her head whirled, and spots of light burst over her eyes, deceiving her, for there was nothing there. She cried softly without passion. She hoped she would die soon. Then she could sleep indefinitely.

On the first morning of the new month, before sunrise, Felixity raised her gluey lids and saw the woman who was herself standing up against the inside of the mirror in her mask of yellow jade, a dress like naphtha, and the glinting vipers of her golden hair.

Felixity's heart palpitated. She tried to get up, but she was too weak.

Behind the woman who was the real Felixity, there was, as at the start, only blackness. But now the mirror-Felixity lifted her ruby glove, and she held in her fingers a single long, coppery feather, the plume of some extraordinary bird.

If she would only take off her mask, Felixity thought, I'd see that she is me. It would be my face, and it would be beautiful.

But the woman did not remove the mask of yellow jade. Instead she turned her head toward the feather, and she blew gently on it.

The breath that came out of her mouth was bloomed with a soft lightning. It enveloped the tip of the feather, which at once caught fire.

Felixity watched, dazzled, until the flame went out and the woman dissolved abruptly into glowing snow, and the mirror was only a mirror again. Then Felixity turned on her side and fell asleep.

When it was light, she woke refreshed and, going into the bathroom, bathed and washed her hair. Presently when the tray of food came, she ate. Her stomach hurt for some while after but she did not pay any attention. She put on the radio and hummed along with the melodies, most of which she now knew by heart.

In the afternoon, after the lunch tray, from which she ate everything, the door was unlocked and Roland entered the room.

Felixity stood up. She had not realized he would arrive so quickly.

"Here I am," he said, "I won't detain you a moment. Just some more of these dull papers to sign."

Felixity smiled, and Roland was surprised. He expected acquiescence, but not happiness.

"Naturally I'll sign them," said Felixity. "But first, you must kiss me."

Roland now looked concerned.

"It seems inappropriate."

"Not at all," said Felixity. "I'm your wife."

And at this, the gigolo must have triumphed over the thief, for Roland approached Felixity and gravely bowed his head. Indeed, at the press of her flesh on his, after the libidinous life he had been leading, his lips parted from force of habit, and Felixity blew into his mouth.

Roland sprang away. His face appeared congested and astonished. He went on, stumbling backwards, until he reached the door, and then he turned as if to rush out of it.

So Felixity saw from the back of him, the tailored suit and blue-black hair, and two jets of white flame that spouted suddenly from his ears.

Roland spun on the spot, and now she saw his face, with yellow flames gouting from his nose and purple gases from his mouth. And then he went up in a noiseless scream of fire, like petrol, or a torch.

The doorway was burning, and she could not get out of it. Flames were darting round the room, consuming the sticks of furniture as they went. The bed erupted like an opening rose. The mirror was gold again, and red.

How cold the flames were. Felixity felt them eating her and gave herself eagerly, glad to be rid of it, the vileness of her treacherous body. The last thing she saw was half the burning floor give way and crash down into the lower regions of the house, and the mirror flying after it like a bubble of the sun.

⑤ ⑤ ⑤

The servants escaped the blazing villa and stood in the gardens of the house above the sea, wailing and exclaiming. It was generally concluded that their employer, Roland, and his mad invalid wife, had perished in the inferno. With amazing rapidity the house collapsed, sending up a pillar of red smoke that could be seen for miles.

Unseen by anyone, however, Felixity emerged out of the rubble.

She had not a mark or a smut upon her. She had instead the body of a goddess and the face of an angel. Her skin was like honey and her hair like a cascade of golden serpents, and in her mouth were the white and flawless teeth of a healthy predator.

Somehow she had had burned on to her, also, a lemon dress and amber shoes.

She went among the philodendrons, Felixity, out of sight. And so down toward the road, without a backward glance.

The Thaw

Ladies first, they said.

That was OK. Then they put a histotrace on the lady in question and called me.

"No thanks," I said.

"Listen," they said, "you're a generative bloodline descendant of Carla Brice. Aren't you interested, for God's sake? This is a unique moment, a unique experience. She's going to need support, understanding. A contact. Come on. Don't be frigid about it."

"I guess Carla is more frigid than I'm ever likely to be."

They laughed, to keep up the informalities. Then they mentioned the Institute grant I'd receive, just for hanging around and being supportive. To a quasi-unemployed artist, that was temptation and a half. They also reminded me that on this initial bout there wouldn't be much publicity, so later, if I wanted to capitalize as an eyewitness, and providing good old Carla was willing—I had a sudden vision of getting very rich, very quick, and with the minimum of effort, and I succumbed ungracefully.

Which accurately demonstrates my three strongest qualities: laziness, optimism, and blind stupidity. Which in turn sums up the whole story, more or less. And that's probably why I was told to write it down for the archives of the human race. I can't think of a better way to depress and wreck the hopes of frenzied, shackled, bleating humanity.

But to return to Carla. She was, I believe, my great-great-great-great-great grandmother. Give or take a great. Absolute accuracy isn't one of my talents, either. The relevant part is, however, that at thirty-three, Carla had developed the rare heart complaint valu—val—well, she'd developed it. She had a few months, or less, and so she opted, along with seventy other people that year, to undergo Cryogenic Suspension till a cure could be found. Cry Sus had been getting progressively more popular, ever since the 1980s. Remember? It's the freezing method of holding a body in refrigerated stasis, indefinitely preserving, thereby, flesh, bones, organs, and the rest, perfect and pristine, in a frosty crystal box. (Just stick a tray of water in the freezer and see for yourself.) It may not strike you as cozy anymore, but that's hardly surprising. In 1993, seventy-one persons, of whom four-or-five-or-six-great granny Carla was one, saw it as the only feasible alternative to death. In the following two hundred years, four thousand others copied their example. They froze their malignancies, their unreliable hearts, and their corroding tissues, and as the light faded from their snowed-over eyes, they must have dreamed of waking up in the fabulous future.

Funny thing about the future. Each next second is the future. And now it's the present. And now it's the past.

Those all-together four thousand and ninety-one who deposited their physiognomies in the cold-storage compartments of the world were looking forward to the future. And here it was. And we were it.

And smack in the middle of this future, which I naively called Now, was I, Tacey Brice, a rotten little unskilled artist, painting gimcrack flying saucers for the spacines. There was a big flying saucer sighting boom that year of 2193. Either you recollect that, or you don't. Nearly as big as the historic boom between the 1930s and '90s. Psychologists had told us it was our human inadequacy, searching all over for a father-mother figure to replace God. Besides, we were getting desperate. We'd penetrated our solar system to a limited extent, but without meeting anybody on the way.

That's another weird thing. When you read the speculativia of the 1900s, you can see just how much they expected of us. It was going to be all or nothing. Either the world would become a miracle of rare device with plastisteel igloos balanced on the stratosphere and metal giblets, or we'd have gone out in a blast of radiation. Neither of which had happened. We'd had problems, of course. Over two hundred years, problems occur. There had been the Fission Tragedy, and the World Flood of '14. There'd been the huge pollution clean-ups complete with the rationing that entailed, and one pretty nasty pandemic. They had set us back, that's obvious. But not halted us. So we reached 2193 mostly unscathed, with a whizz-bang technology not quite as whizz, or bang, as prophesied. A place where doors opened when they saw who you were, and with a colony on Mars, but where they hadn't solved the unemployment problem or the geriatric problem. Up in the ether there were about six hundred buzz-whuzzes headed out into nowhere, bleeping information about earth. But we hadn't landed on Alpha Centauri yet. And if the waste-disposal jammed, brother, it jammed. What I'm trying to say (superfluously, because you're ahead of me) is that their future, those four thousand and ninety-one, their future, which was our present, wasn't as spectacular as they'd trusted or feared. Excepting the Salenic Vena-derivative drugs, which had rendered most of the diseases of the 1900s and the 2000s obsolete.

And suddenly, one day, someone had a notion.

"Hey, guys," this someone suggested, "you recall all those sealed frosty boxes the medic centers have? You know, with the on-ice carcinomas and valu-diddums in 'em? Well, don't you think it'd be grand to defrost the lot of them and pump 'em full of health?"

"Crazy," said everybody else, and wet themselves with enthusiasm.

After that, they got the thing organized on a global scale. And first off, not wanting to chance any public mishaps, they intended to unfreeze a single frost box, in relative privacy. Perhaps they put all the names in a hat. Whatever, they picked Carla Brice, or Brr-Ice, if you liked that Newsies' tablotape pun.

And since Carla Brr-Ice might feel a touch extra chilly, coming back to life two hundred years after she'd cryonised out of it, they dredged up a bloodline descendant to hold her cold old thirty-three-year hand. And that was Tacey Brr-Ice. Me.

The room below was pink, but the cold pink of strawberry ice cream. There were forty doctors of every gender prowling about in it and round the crystal slab. It put me in mind of a pack of wolves with a carcass they couldn't quite decide when to eat. But then, I was having a nervous attack, up on the spectator gallery where they'd sat me. The countdown had begun two days before, and I'd been ushered in at noon. For an hour now, the crystal had been clear. I could see a sort of blob in it, which gradually resolved into a naked woman. Straight off, even with her lying there stiff as a board and utterly defenseless, I could tell she was the sort of lady who scared me dizzy. She was large and well-shaped, with a mane of dark red hair. She was the type that goes outdoor swimming at all seasons, skis, shoots rapids in a canoe, becomes the coordinator of a moon colony. The type that bites. Valu-diddums had got her, but nothing else could have done. Not child, beast, nor man. Certainly not another woman. Oh my. And this was my multiple-great granny that I was about to offer the hand of reassurance.

Another hour, and some dial and click mechanisms down in the strawberry ice room started to dicker. The wolves flew in for the kill. A dead lioness, that was Carla. Then the box rattled and there was a yell. I couldn't see for scrabbling medics.

"What happened?"

The young medic detailed to sit on the spec gallery with me sighed.

"I'd say she's opened her eyes."

The young medic was black as space and beautiful as the stars therein. But he didn't give a damn about me. You could see he was in love with Carla the lioness. I was simply a pain he had to put up with for two or three hours, while he stared at the goddess beneath.

But now the medics had drawn off. I thought of the Sleeping Beauty story, and Snow White. Her eyes were open indeed. Coppery brown to tone with the mane. She didn't appear dazed. She appeared contemptuous. Precisely as I'd anticipated. Then the crystal box lid began to rise.

"Jesus," I said.

"Strange you should say that," said the medic. His own wonderful eyes fixed on Carla, he'd waxed profound and enigmatic. "The manner in which we all still use these outdated religious expletives: *God, Christ, Hell,* long after we've ceased to credit their religious basis as such. The successful completion of this experiment in life-suspense and restoration has a bearing on the same matter," he murmured, his inch-long lashes brushing the plastase pane. "You've read of the controversy regarding this process? It was seen at one era as an infringement of religious faith."

"Oh, yes?"

I kept on staring at him. Infinitely preferable to Carla, with her open eyes, and the solitary bending medic with the supadermic.

"The idea of the soul," said the medic on the gallery. "The immortal part that survives death. But what befalls a soul trapped for years, centuries, in a living yet statically frozen body? In a physical limbo, a living death. You see the problem this would pose for the religious?"

"I—uh—"

"But, of course, today..." He spread his hands. "There is no such barrier to lucid thought. The life force, we now know, resides purely in the brain, and thereafter in the motor nerves, the spinal cord, and attendant reflexive centers. There is no *soul.*"

Then he shut up and nearly swooned away, and I realized Carla had met his eye.

I looked, and she was sitting, part reclined against some medic's arm. The medic was telling her where she was and what year it was and how, by this evening, the valu-diddums would be no more than a bad dream, and then she could go out into the amazing new world with her loving descendant, whom she could observe up there on the gallery.

She did spare a glance for me. It lasted about .09 of a mini-instant. I tried to unglue my mouth and flash her a warming welcoming grin, but before I could manage it, she was back to studying the black medic.

At that moment somebody came and whipped me away for celebratory alcohol, and two hours later, when I'd celebrated rather too much, they took me up a plushy corridor to meet Carla, skin to skin.

Actually, she was dressed on this occasion. She'd had a shower and a couple of post-defrosting tests and some shots and the anti-valu-diddums stuff. Her hair was smoldering like a fire in a forest. She wore the shiny smock medical centers insisted that you wore, but on her it was like a design original. She'd even had a tan frozen in with her, or maybe it was my dazzled eyes that made her seem all bronzed and glowing. Nobody could look that good, that *healthy*, after two hundred years on ice. And if they did, they shouldn't. Her room was crammed with flowers and bottles of scent and exotic light paintings, courtesy of the Institute. And then they trundled me in.

Not astoundingly, she gazed at me with bored amusement. Like she'd come to the dregs at the bottom of the wine.

"This is Tacey," somebody said, making free with my fore-name. Carla spoke, in a voice of maroon velvet.

"Hallo, er, Tacey." Patently, my cognomen was a big mistake. Never mind, she'd overlook it for now. "I gather we are related."

I was drunk, but it wasn't helping.

"I'm your gr—yes, we are, but—" I intelligently blurted. The "but" was going to be a prologue to some nauseating, placatory, crawler's drivel about her gorgeousness and youth. It wasn't necessary, not even to let her know how scared I was.

She could tell that easily, plus how I'd shrunk to a shadow in her high-voltage glare. Before I could complete my hiccupping sycophancy, anyway, the medic in charge said: "Tacey is your link, Mz Brice, with civilization as it currently is."

Carla couldn't resist it. She raised one manicured eyebrow, frozen exquisite for two centuries. If Tacey was the link, civilization could take a walk.

"My apartment," I went on blurting, "it's medium, but—"

What was I going to say now? About how all my grant from the Institute I would willingly spend on gowns and perfumes and skis and automatic rifles, or whatever Carla wanted. How I'd move out and she could have the apartment to herself. (She wouldn't like the spacine murals on the walls.)

"It's just a bri—a bridge," I managed. "Till you get acclimatozed—atized."

She watched me as I made a fool of myself, or rather, displayed my true foolishness. Finally I comprehended the message in her copper eyes: Don't bother. That was all: Don't bother. You're a failure, Carla's copper irises informed me, as if I didn't know. Don't make excuses. You can alter nothing. I expect nothing from you. I will stay while I must in your ineffectual vicinity, and you may fly round me and scorch your wings if you like. When I am ready, I shall leave immediately, soaring over your sky like a meteor. You can offer no aid, no interest, no gain I cannot garner for myself.

"How kind of Tacey," Carla's voice said. "Come, darling, and let me kiss you."

Somehow, I'd imagined her still as very cold from the frosty box, but she was blood heat. Ashamed, I let her brush my cheek with her meteoric lips. Perhaps I'd burn.

"I'd say this calls for a toast," said the medic in charge. "But just rose-juice for Mz Brice, I'm afraid, at present."

Carla smiled at him, and I hallucinated a rosebush, thorns too, eviscerated by her teeth. Lions drink blood, not roses.

I got home paralyzed and floundered about trying to change things. In the middle of attempting to re-spray-paint a wall, I sank onto a pillow and slept. Next day I was angry, the way you can only be angry over something against which you are powerless. So damn it. Let her arrive and see space shuttles, mother ships, and whirly bug-eyed monsters all across the plastase. And don't pull the ready-cook out of the alcove to clean the feed-pipes behind it that I hadn't seen for three years. Or dig the plant out of the cooled-water dispenser. Or buy any new garments, blinds, rugs, sheets. And don't conceal the Wage-Increment checks when they skitter down the chute. Or prop up the better spacines I'd illustrated on the table where she won't miss them.

I visited her one more time during the month she stayed at the Institute. I didn't have the courage not to take her anything, although I knew that whatever I offered would be wrong. Actually, I had an impulse to blow my first grant check and my W-I together and buy her a little antique stiletto of Toledo steel. It was blatantly meant to commit murder with, and as I handed it to her I'd bow and say, "For you, Carla. I just know you can find a use for it." But naturally I didn't have the bravura. I bought her a flagon of expensive scent she didn't need and was rewarded by seeing her put it on a shelf with three other identically packaged flagons, each twice the size of mine. She was wearing a reclinerobe of amber silk, and I almost reached for sunglasses. We didn't say much. I tottered from her room, sunburned and peeling. And that night I painted another flying saucer on the wall.

The day she left the Institute, they sent a mobile for me. I was supposed to collect and ride to the apartment with Carla, to make her feel homey. I felt sick.

Before I met her, though, the medic in charge wafted me into his office.

"We're lucky," he said. "Mz Brice is a most independent lady. Her readjustment has been, in fact, remarkable. None of the traumas or rebuttals we've been anxious about. I doubt if most of the other subjects to be revived from Cryogenesis will demonstrate the equivalent rate of success."

"They're really reviving them, then?" I inquired lamely. I was glad to be in here, putting off my fourth congress with inadequacy.

"A month from today. Dependent on the ultimately positive results of our post-resuscitation analysis of Mz Brice. But, as I intimated, I hardly predict any hitch there."

"And how long—" I swallowed— "how long do you think Carla will want to stay with me?"

"Well, she seems to have formed quite an attachment to you, Tacey. It's a great compliment, you know, from a woman like that. A proud, volatile spirit. But she needs an anchor for a while. We all need our anchors. Probably, her proximity will benefit you, in return. Don't you agree?"

I didn't answer, and he concluded I was overwhelmed. He started to describe to me that glorious scheduled event, the global link-up, when every single cryogone was to be revived, as simultaneously with each other as they could arrange it. The process would be going out on five channels of the Spatials, visible to us all. Technology triumphant yet again, bringing us a minute or two of transcendental catharsis. I thought about the beautiful black medic and his words on religion. And this is how we replaced it, presumably (when we weren't saucer-sighting), shedding tears sentimentally over four thousand and ninety idiots fumbling out of the deep-freeze.

"One last, small warning," the medic in charge added. "You may notice—or you may not, I can't be positive—the occasional lapse in the behavioral patterns of Mz Brice."

There was a fantasy for me. Carla, *lapsed.*

"In what way?" I asked, miserably enjoying the unlikelihood.

"Mere items. A mood, an aberration—a brief disorientation even. These are to be expected in a woman reclaimed by life after two hundred years, and in a world she is no longer familiar with. As I explained, I looked for much worse and far greater quantity. The odd personality slip is inevitable. You mustn't be alarmed. At such moments the most steadying influence on Mz Brice will be a non-Institutional normalcy of surroundings. And the presence of yourself."

I nearly laughed.

I would have, if the door hadn't opened, and if Carla, in mock red-lynx fur, hadn't stalked into the room.

I didn't even try to create chatter. Alone in the mobile, with the auto driving us along the cool concrete highways, there wasn't any requirement to pretend for the benefit of others. Carla reckoned I was a schmoil, and I duly schmoiled. Mind you, now and again, she put out a silken paw and gave me a playful tap. Like when she asked me where I got my hair *done*. But I just told her about the ready-set parlors, and she quit. Then again, she asked a couple of less abstract questions. Did libraries still exist, that was one. The second one was if I slept well.

I went along with everything in a dank stupor. I think I was half kidding myself it was going to be over soon. Then the mobile drove into the auto-lift of my apartment block, the gates gaped, and we got out. As my door recognized me and split wide, it abruptly hit me that Carla and I were going to be hand in glove for some while. A month at least, while the Institute computed its final tests. Maybe more, if Carla had my lazy streak somewhere in her bronze and permasteel frame.

She strode into my apartment and stood flaming among the flying saucers and the wine-ringed furniture. The fake-fur looked as if she'd shot it herself. She was a head taller than I was ever going to be. And then she startled me, about the only way she could right then.

"I'm tired, Tacey," said Carla.

No wisecracks, no vitriol, no stare from Olympus.

She glided to the bedroom. OK. I'd allocated the bed as hers, the couch as mine. She paused, gold digit on the panel that I'd preset to respond to her finger.

"Will you forgive me?" she wondered aloud.

Her voice was soporific. I yawned.

"Sure, Carla."

She stayed behind the closed panels for hours. The day reddened over the city, colors as usual heightened by the weather control that operates a quarter of a mile up. I slumped here and there, unable to eat or rest or read or doodle. I was finding out what it was going to be like, having an apartment and knowing it wasn't mine anymore. Even through a door, Carla dominated.

Around nineteen, I knocked. No reply.

Intimidated, I slunk off. I wouldn't play the septophones, even with the ear-pieces only, even with the volume way down. Might wake Granny. You see, if you could wake her from two hundred years in the freezer, you could certainly wake her after eight hours on a dormadais.

At twenty-four midnight, she still hadn't come out.

Coward, I knocked again and feebly called: "Night, Carla. See you tomorrow."

On the couch I had nightmares, or nightcarlas, to be explicit. Some were very realistic, like the one where the trust bonds Carla's estate had left for her hadn't accumulated after all and she was destitute and going to remain with me forever and ever. Or there were the comic-strip ones where the fake red-lynx got under the cover and bit me. Or the surreal ones where Carla came floating toward me, clad only in her smoldering hair, and everything caught fire from it, and I kept saying, "Please, Carla, don't set the rug alight. Please, Carla, don't set the couch alight." In the end there was merely a dream where Carla bent over me, hissing something like an anaconda—if they do hiss. She wanted me to stay asleep, apparently, and for some reason I was fighting her, though I was almost comatose. The strange thing in this dream was that Carla's eyes had altered from copper to a brilliant topaz yellow, like the lynx's.

It must have been about four in the morning that I woke up. I think it was the washer unit that woke me. Or it could have been the septophones. Or the waste-disposal. Or the drier. Or any of the several gadgets a modern apartment was equipped with. Because they were all on. It sounded like a madhouse. Looked like one. All the lights were on, too. In the middle of chaos: Carla. She was quite naked, the way I'd seen her at first, but she had the sort of nakedness that seems like clothes, clean-cut, firm, and flawless. The sort that makes me want to hide inside a stone. She was reminiscent of a sorceress in the midst of her sorcery, the erupting mechanisms sprawling around her in the fierce light. I had a silly thought: *Carla's going nova.* Then she turned and saw me. My mouth felt as if it had been security-sealed, but I got out, "You OK, Carla?"

"I am, darling. Go back to sleep now."

That's the last thing I remember till ten A.M. the next day.

I wondered initially if Carla and the gadgets had been an additional dream. But when I checked the energy-meter I discovered they hadn't.

I was plodding to the ready-cook when Carla emerged from the bedroom in her amber reclinerobe.

She didn't say a word. She just relaxed at the counter and let me be her slave. I got ready to prepare her the large breakfast she outlined. Then I ran her bath. When the water-meter shut off half through, Carla suggested I put in the extra tags to ensure the tub was filled right up.

As she bathed, I sat at the counter and had another nervous attack.

Of course, Carla was predictably curious. Back in 1993, many of our gadgets hadn't been invented, or at least not developed to their present standard. Why not get up in the night and turn everything on? Why did it have to seem sinister? Maybe my sleeping through it practically nonstop was the thing that troubled me. All right. So Carla was a hypnotist. Come to consider, should I run a histotrace myself, in an attempt to learn what Carla was—had been?

But let's face it, what really upset me was the low on the energy-meter, the water-meter taking a third of my week's water tags in one morning. And Carla luxuriously wallowing, leaving me to foot the bill.

Could I say anything? No. I knew she'd immobilize me before I'd begun.

When she came from the bathroom, I asked her did she want to go out. She said no, but I could visit the library, if I would, and pick up this book and tape list she'd called through to them. I checked the call-meter. That was down, too.

"I intend to act the hermit for a while, Tacey," Carla murmured behind me as I guiltily flinched away from the meter. "I don't want to get involved in a furor of publicity. I gather the news of my successful revival will have been leaked today. The tablotapes will be sporting it. But I understand, by the news publishing codes of the '80s, that unless I approach the Newsies voluntarily, they are not permitted to approach me."

"Yes, that's right." I gazed pleadingly into the air. "I guess you wouldn't ever reconsider that, Carla? It could mean a lot of money. That is, not for you to contact the Newsies. But if you'd all—allow me to on your beh—half."

She chuckled like a lioness with her throat full of gazelle. The hair rose on my neck as she slunk closer. When her big, warm, elegant hand curved over my skull, I shuddered.

"No, Tacey. I don't think I'd care for that. I don't need the cash. My estate investments, I hear, are flourishing."

"I was thinking of m—I was thinking of me, Carla. I cou—could use the tags."

The hand slid from my head and batted me lightly. Somehow, I was glad I hadn't given her the Toledo knife after all.

"No, I don't think so. I think it will do you much more good to continue as you are. Now, run along to the library, darling."

I went mainly because I was glad to get away from her. To utter the spineless whining I had, had drained entirely my thin reserves of courage. I was shaking when I reached the auto-lift. I had a wild plan of leaving town and leaving my apartment with Carla in it, and going to ground. It was more than just inadequacy now. Hunter and hunted. And as I crept through the long grass, her fiery breath was on my heels.

I collected the twenty books and the fifty tapes and paid for the loan. I took them back to the apartment and laid them before my astonishing amber granny. I was too scared even to hide. Much too scared to disobey.

I sat on the sun-patio, though it was the weather control day for rain. Through the plastase panels I heard the tapes educating Carla on every aspect of contemporary life: social, political, economic, geographical, and carnal.

When she summoned me, I fixed lunch. Later, drinks and supper.

Then I was too nervous to go to sleep. I passed out in the bathroom, sitting in the shower cubicle. Had nightcarlas of Carla eating salad. Didn't wake up till ten A.M. Checked. All meters down again.

When I trod on smashed plastase, I thought it was sugar. Then I saw the cooled-water dispenser was in ninety-five bits. Where the plant had been, there was only soil and condensation and trailing roots.

I looked, and everywhere beheld torn-off leaves and tiny clots of earth. There was a leaf by Carla's bedroom. I knocked, and my heart knocked to keep my hand company.

But Carla wasn't interested in breakfast, wasn't hungry.

I knew why not. She'd eaten my plant.

You can take a bet I meant to call up the Institute right away. Somehow, I didn't. For one thing, I didn't want to call from the apartment and risk Carla catching me at it. For another, I didn't want to go out and leave her, in case she did something worse. Then again, I was terrified to linger in her vicinity. A *lapse,* the medic in charge had postulated. It was certainly that. Had she done anything like it at the Institute? Somehow I had the idea she hadn't. She'd saved it for me. Out of playful malice.

I dithered for an hour, till I panicked, pressed the call button, and spoke the digits. I never heard the door open. She seemed to know exactly when to—*strike;* yes, that *is* the word

I want. I sensed her there. She didn't even touch me. I let go the call button.

"Who were you calling?" Carla asked.

"Just a guy I used to pair with," I said, but it came out husky and gulped and quivering.

"Well, go ahead. Don't mind me."

Her maroon voice, bored and amused and indifferent to anything I might do, held me like a steel claw. And I discovered I had to turn around and face her. I had to stare into her eyes.

The scorn in them was killing. I wanted to shrivel and roll under the rug, but I couldn't look away.

"But if you're not going to call anyone, run my bath, darling," Carla said.

I ran her bath.

It was that easy. Of course.

She was magnetic. Irresistible.

I couldn't—

I could *not*—

Partly, it had all become incredible. I couldn't picture myself accusing Carla of houseplant-eating to the medics at the Institute. Who'd believe it? It was nuts. I mean, too nuts even for them. And presently, I left off quite believing it myself.

Nevertheless, somewhere in my brain I kept on replaying those sentences of the medic in charge: *the occasional lapse in the behavioral patterns…a mood, an aberration….* And against that, point counterpoint, there kept on playing that phrase the beautiful black medic had reeled off enigmatically as a cultural jest: *But what befalls a soul trapped for years, centuries, in a living yet statically frozen body?*

Meanwhile, by sheer will, by the force of her persona, she'd stopped me calling. And that same thing stopped me talking about her to anybody on the street, sent me tongue-tied to fetch groceries, sent me groveling to conjure meals. It was almost as if it also shoved me asleep when she wanted and brought me awake ditto.

Doesn't time fly when you're having fun?

Twenty days, each more or less resembling each, hurried by. Carla didn't do anything else particularly weird, at least not that I saw or detected. But then, I never woke up nights anymore. And I had an insane theory that the meters had been fiddled, because they weren't low, but they felt as if they should be. I hadn't got any more plants. I missed some packaged paper lingerie, but it turned up under Carla's bed, where I'd kicked it when the bed was mine. Twenty days, twenty-five. The month of Carla's post-resuscitation tests was nearly through. One morning, I was stumbling about like a zombie, cleaning the apartment because the dustease had jammed and Carla had spent five minutes in silent comment on the dust. I was moving in that combined sludge of terror, mindlessness, and masochistic cringing she'd taught me, when the door signal went.

When I opened the door, there stood the black medic with a slim case of file-tapes. I felt transparent, and that was how he treated me. He gazed straight through me to the empty room where he had hoped my granny would be.

"I'm afraid your call doesn't seem to be working," he said. (Why had I the notion Carla had done something to the call?) "I'd be grateful to see Mz Brice, if she can spare me a few minutes. Just something we'd like to check for the files."

That instant, splendid on her cue, Carla manifested from the bathroom. The medic had seen her naked in the frosty box, but not a naked that was vaguely and fluently sheathed in a damp towel. It had the predictable effect. As he paused transfixed, Carla bestowed her most gracious smile.

"Sit down," she said. "What check is this? Tacey, darling, why not arrange some fresh coffee?"

Tacey darling went to the coffee cone. Over its bubbling, I heard him say to her, "It's simply that Doctor Something was a little worried by a possible amnesia. Certainly, none of the memory areas seem physically impaired. But you see, here and there on the tape—"

"Give me an example, please," drawled Carla.

The medic lowered his lashes as if to sweep the tablotape.

"Some confusion over places and names. Your second husband, Francis, for instance, who you named as Frederick. And there, the red mark—Doctor Something-Else mentioned the satellite disaster of '91, and it seems you did not recall—"

"You're referring to the malfunction of the Ixion II, which broke up and crashed in the Midwest, taking three hundred lives," said Carla. She sounded like a purring textbook. She leaned forward, and I could watch him tremble all the way across from the coffee cone. "Doctor Something and Doctor Something-Else," said Carla, "will have to make allowances for my excitement at rebirth. Now, I can't have you driving out this way for nothing. How about you come to dinner, the night before the great day. Tacey doesn't see nearly enough people her own age. As for me, let's say you'll make a two-hundred-year-old lady very happy."

The air between them was electric enough to form sparks. By the "great day" she meant, patently, the five-channel Spatial event when her four thousand and ninety confreres got liberated from the subzero. But he plainly didn't care so much about defrosting anymore.

The coffee cone boiled over. I noticed with a shock I was crying. Nobody else did.

What I wanted to do was program the ready-cook for the meal, get in some wine, and get the hell out of the apartment and leave the two of them alone. I'd pass the night at one of the all-night Populars, and creep in around ten A.M. the next morning. That's the state I frankly acknowledged she had reduced me to. I'd have been honestly grateful to have done that. But Carla wouldn't let me.

"Out?" she inquired. "But this whole party is for you, darling."

There was nobody about. She didn't have to pretend. She and I knew I was the slave. She and I knew her long-refrigerated soul, returning in fire, had scalded me into a melty on the ground. So it could only be cruelty, this. She seemed to be experimenting, as she had with the gadgets. The psychological dissection of an inferior inhabitant of the future.

What I had to do, therefore, was to visit the ready-set hair parlor, and buy a dress with my bimonthly second W-I check. Carla, though naturally she didn't go with me, somehow instigated and oversaw these ventures. Choosing the dress, she was oddly at my elbow. *That* one, her detached and omnipresent aura instructed me. It was expensive, and it was scarlet and gold. It would have looked wonderful on somebody else. But not me. That dress just sucked the little life I've got right out of me.

Come the big night (before the big day, for which the countdown must already have, in fact, begun), there I was, done up like a New Year parcel, and with my own problematical soul wizened within me. The door signal went, and the slave accordingly opened the door, and the dark angel entered, politely thanking me as he nearly walked straight through me.

He looked so marvelous, I practically bolted. But still the aura of Carla, and Carla's wishes, which were beginning to seem to be communicating themselves telepathically, held me put.

Then Carla appeared. I hadn't seen her before, that evening. The dress was lionskin, and it looked real, despite the anti-game-hunting laws. Her hair was a smooth auburn waterfall that left bare an ear with a gold star dependent from it. I just went into the cooking area and uncorked a bottle and drank most of it straight off.

They both had good appetites, though hers was better than his. She'd eaten a vast amount since she'd been with me, presumably ravenous after that long fast. I was the waitress, so I waited on them. When I reached my plate, the food had congealed because the warmer in the table on my side was faulty. Anyway, I wasn't hungry. There were two types of wine. I drank the cheap type. I was on the second bottle now and sufficiently sad I could have howled, but I'd also grown uninvolved, viewing my sadness from a great height.

They danced together to the septophones. I drank some more wine. I was going to be very, very ill tomorrow. But that was tomorrow. Verily. When I looked up, they'd danced themselves into the bedroom, and the panels were shut. Carla's cruelty had had its run, and I wasn't prepared for any additions, such as ecstatic moans from the interior, to augment my frustration. Accordingly, garbed in my New Year parcel frock, hair in curlicues, and another bottle in my hand, I staggered forth into the night.

I might have met a thug, a rapist, a murderer, or even one of the numerous polipatrols that roam the city to prevent the activities of such. But I didn't meet anyone who took note of me. Nobody cared. Nobody was interested. Nobody wanted to be my friend, rob me, abuse me, give me a job or a goal, or make me happy, or make love to me. So if you thought I was a Judas, just you remember that. If one of you slobs had taken any notice of me that night—

I didn't have to wait for morning to be ill. There was a handsome washroom on Avenue East. I'll never forget it. I was there quite a while.

When the glamorous weather-control dawn irradiated the city, I was past the worst. And by ten A.M. I was trudging home, queasy, embittered, hard-done-by, but sober. I was even able to register the tabloes everywhere and the holoid neons, telling us all that the great day was here. The day of the four thousand and ninety. Thawday. I wondered dimly if Carla and the Prince of Darkness were still celebrating it in my bed. She should have been cold. Joke. All right. It isn't.

The door to my apartment let me in. The place was as I'd abandoned it. The window blinds were down, the table strewn with plates and glasses. The bedroom door firmly shut.

I pressed the switch to raise the blinds, and nothing happened, which didn't surprise me. That in itself should have proved to me how far the influence had gone and how there was no retreat. But I only had this random desultory urge to see what the apartment door would do now. What it did was not react. Not even when I put my hand on the panel, which method was generally reserved for guests. It had admitted me, but wouldn't let me out again. Carla had done something to it. As she had to the call, the meters, and to me. But how—personal power? Ridiculous. I was a spineless dope; that was why she'd been able to negate me. Yet—forty-one medics, with a bevy of tests and questions, some of which, apparently, she hadn't got right, ate from her hand. And maybe her psychic ability had increased. Practice makes perfect.

...*What befalls a soul trapped for years, centuries, in a living yet statically frozen body?*

It was dark in the room, with the blinds irreversibly staying down and the lights irreversibly off.

Then the bedroom door slid wide, and Carla slid out. Naked again, and glowing in the dark. She smiled at me, pityingly.

"Tacey, darling, now you've gotten over your sulks, there's something in here I'd like you to clear up for me."

Dichotomy once more. I wanted to take root where I was, but she had me walking to the bedroom. She truly was glowing. As if she'd lightly sprayed herself over with something mildly luminous. I guessed what would be in the bedroom, and I'd begun retching, but, already despoiled of filling, that didn't matter. Soon I was in the doorway, and she said, "Stop that, Tacey." And I stopped retching and stood and looked at what remained of the beautiful black medic, wrapped up in the bloodstained lionskin.

Lions drink blood, not roses.

Something loosened inside me then. It was probably the final submission, the final surrender of the fight. Presumably I'd been fighting her subconsciously from the start, or I wouldn't have gained the ragged half-freedoms I had. But now I was limp and sodden, so I could ask humbly: "The plant was salad. But a man—what was he?"

"You don't quite get it, darling, do you?" Carla said. She stroked my hair friendlily. I didn't shudder anymore. Cowed dog, I was relaxed under the contemptuous affection of my mistress. "One was green and vegetable. One was black, male, and meat. Different forms. Local dishes. I had no inclination to sample you, you comprehend, since you were approximate to my own appearance. But of course, others who find themselves to be black and male may wish to sample pale-skinned females. Don't worry, Tacey. You'll be safe. You entertain me. You're mine. Protected species."

"Still don't understand, Carla," I whispered meekly.

"Well, just clear up for me, and I'll explain."

I don't have to apologize to you for what I did then, because, of course, you know all about it, the will-less indifference of the absolute slave. I bundled up the relics of Carla's lover-breakfast and dumped them in the waste-disposal, which dealt with them pretty efficiently.

Then I cleaned the bedroom and had a shower and fixed Carla some coffee and biscuits. It was almost noon, the hour when the four thousand and ninety were going to be roused and to step from their frost boxes in front of seven-eighths of the world's Spatial-viewers. Carla wanted to see it too, so I switched on my set, minus the sound. Next Carla told me I might sit, and I sat on a pillow, and she explained.

For some reason, I don't remember her actual words. Perhaps she put it in a technical way, and I got the gist but not the sentences. I'll put it in my own words here, despite the fact that a lot of you know now anyway. After all, under supervision, we still have babies sometimes. When they grow up they'll need to know. Know why they haven't got a chance, and why we hadn't. And, to level with you, know why I'm not a Judas, and that I didn't betray us, because I didn't have a chance either.

Laziness, optimism, and blind stupidity.

I suppose optimism more than anything.

Four thousand and ninety-one persons lying down in frozen stasis, aware they didn't have souls and couldn't otherwise survive, dreaming of a future of cures, and of a reawakening in that future. And the earth dreaming of benevolent visitors from other worlds, father-mother figures to guide and help us. Sending them buzz-whuzzes to bleep, over and over, *Here* we are. *Here. Here.*

I guess we do have souls. Or we have something that has nothing to do with the brain, or the nerve centers, or the spinal cord. Perhaps that dies too, when we die. Or perhaps it escapes. Whatever happens, that's the one thing you can't retain in Cryogenic Suspension. The body, all its valves and ducts and organs, lies pristine in limbo, and when you wake it up with the correct drugs, impulses, stimuli, it's live again, can be cured of its diseases, becoming a flawless vessel of—nothing. It's like an empty room, a vacant lot. The tenant's skipped.

Somewhere out in the starry night of space, one of the bleeping buzz-whuzzes was intercepted. Not by pater-mater figures, but by a predatory, bellicose alien race. It was simple to get to us—hadn't we given comprehensive directions? But on arrival they perceived a world totally unsuited to their fiery, gaseous, incorporeal forms. That was a blow, that was. But they didn't give up hope. Along with their superior technology they developed a process whereby they reckoned they could transfer inside of human bodies and thereafter live off the fat of the Terrain. However, said process wouldn't work. Why not? The human consciousness (soul?) was too strong to overcome, it wouldn't let them through. Even asleep, they couldn't oust us. Dormant, the consciousness (soul?) is still present, or at least linked. As for dead bodies, no go. A man who had expired of old age, or with a mobile on top of him, was no use. The body had to be a whole one, or there was no point. Up in their saucers, which were periodically spotted, they spat and swore. They gazed at the earth and drooled, pondering mastery of a globe and entire races of slaves at their disposal. But there was no way they could achieve their aims until—until they learned of all those Cryogenic Suspensions in their frost boxes, all those soulless lumps of ice, waiting on the day when science would release and cure them and bring them forth healthy and *void.*

If you haven't got a tenant, advertise for a new tenant. We had. And they'd come.

Carla was the first. As her eyes opened under the crystal, something looked out of them. Not Carla Brice. Not anymore. But something.

Curious, cruel, powerful, indomitable, alien, deadly.

Alone, she could handle hundreds of us humans, for her influence ascended virtually minute by minute. Soon there were going to be four thousand and ninety of her kind, opening their eyes, smiling their scornful thank-yous through the Spatials at the world they had come to conquer. The world they did conquer.

We gave them beautiful, healthy, movable houses to live in, and billions to serve them and be toyed with by them, and provide them with extra bodies to be frozen and made fit to house any leftover colleagues of theirs. And our green depolluted meadows wherein to rejoice.

As for Carla, she'd kept quiet and careful as long as she had to. Long enough for the tests to go through and for her to communicate back, telepathically, to her people, all the data they might require on earth, prior to their arrival.

And now she sat and considered me, meteoric fiery Carla-who-wasn't-Carla, her eyes, in the dark, gleaming topaz yellow through their copper irises, revealing her basic inflammable nature within the veil of a dead woman's living flesh.

They can make me do whatever they want, and they made me write this. Nothing utterly bad has been done to me, and maybe it never will. So I've been lucky there.

To them, I'm historically interesting, as Carla had been historically interesting to us, as a first. I'm the first Slave. Possibly, I can stay alive on the strength of that and not be killed for a whim.

Which, in a way, I suppose, means I'm a sort of a success, after all.

You Are My Sunshine

(Tape running.)

—For the record: Day two, Session two, Code-tape three. Earth Central Investigation into the disaster of the *S.S.G. Pilgrim*. Executive Interrogator Hofman presiding. Witness attending, Leon Canna, Fifth Officer, P. L. Capacity. Officer Canna being the only surviving crew member of the *Pilgrim*. Officer Canna?

—Yes, sir.

—Officer Canna, how long have you been in the Service?

—Ten years, sir.

—That would be three years' service in exploration vessels and seven in the transport and passenger class. How many of those seven years with Solarine Galleons?

—Six years, sir.

—And so, you would know this type of ship pretty well?

—Yes, sir. Pretty well. .

—And was the *Pilgrim* in any way an unusual ship of its kind?

—No, sir.

—Officer Canna, I'm aware you've been through a lot, and I'm aware your previous record is not only clear, but indeed meritorious. Naturally, I've read your written account of what, according to you, transpired aboard the Solarine Space Galleon *Pilgrim*. You and I, Officer Canna, both know that with any ship, of any class or type, occasionally something can go wrong. Even so wrong as to precipitate a tragedy of the magnitude of the *Pilgrim* disaster. Now I want you to consider carefully before you answer me. Of all the explanations you could have chosen for the death of this ship and the loss of the two thousand and twenty lives that went with her, why this one?

—It's the truth, sir.

—Wait a moment, Officer Canna, please. You seem to miss my point. Of all the explanations at your disposal, and with ten years intimate knowledge of space, the explanation you offer us is, nevertheless, frankly ludicrous.

—Sir.

—It throws suspicion on you, Officer Canna. It blots your record.

—I can't help it, sir. Oh sure, I could lie to you.

—Yes, Officer Canna, you could.

—But I'm not lying. Suppose I never told you this because I was afraid of how it would reflect on me. And then suppose the same situation comes up, somewhere out there, and then the same thing happens again.

—That seems quite unlikely, Officer Canna.

(A murmur of laughter.)

—Excuse me, but I don't think this thing should be played for laughs.

—Nor do I, Officer Canna. Nor do I. Very well. In your own words, please, and at your own pace. Tell this investigation what you say you believe occurred.

The girl came aboard from the subport at Bel. There were thirty-eight passengers coming on at that stop, but Canna noticed the girl almost at once. The reason he noticed her was that she was so damned unnoticeable. Her clothes were the color of putty, and so was her hair. She had that odd, slack, round-shouldered stance that looked as though it came from .a lifetime of sitting on her poor little ass, leaning forward over a computer console or a dispensary plate. Nobody had ever told her there were machines to straighten you out and fine you down, and vitamins to brighten your skin, and tints to color your hair, and optic inducers to stop your having to peer through two godawful lenses wedged in a red groove at the top of your nose. Nobody had ever presumably told her she was human either, with a brain, a soul, and a gender.

Watch it, Canna. A lost cause is lost. Leave it alone.

Trouble was, it was part of his job to get involved.

P.L.—Passenger Link—required acting as unofficial father, son, and brother to the whole shipload; sometimes you got to be priest-confessor and sometimes lover too. It took just the right blend of gregariousness coupled to the right blend of constraint. Long ago, the ships of the line had reasoned that passengers, the breadwinning live cargo that took up half the room aboard a Solarine Galleon, were liable to run amok without an intermediary between themselves and the crewing personnel topside. The role of P.L. was therefore created. Spokesman and arbiter, the P.L. officer knew the technical bias up top, but he represented the voice of the nontechnical flock lower side. He related to his flock what went on behind the firmly closed doors of the Bridge and Engine Bay. If he sometimes edited, he took care not to admit it. He belonged, ostensibly, to the civilians, and that way he stopped them rocking the boat.

To do this job at all, you had to be able to communicate with your fellow mortals, and they had to be able to communicate with you. In that department, Canna did excellently. Sometimes better than excellently. Dark, deeply suntanned, as were all Solarines, and with a buoyant, lightly sardonic good humor, he had found early on that women liked him very well, sometimes too well. This had been one of the score of reasons that had driven him off the exploration vessels, where for one or two years at a stretch, you rubbed shoulders with all the same stale passions and allergies. The EVs took on no passengers to provide diversion, stimulus and, in the most harmless of ways, fair game. Conversely, the Solarines had a low percentage of female crew: since women had realized their intellectual potency, they tended to go after the big-scale jobs, which pleasure cruisers didn't offer. However, the passengers provided plenty of female scenery, women who came and went, the nicest kind. For the rest, the grouses of transient passengers Canna could easily stand because next stop the grousers got off. Canna's trick was that he found it easy to be patient, appreciative, and kind with all birds of passage.

So there was that little gray dab of a girl no one had ever been kind to, creeping into the great golden spaceship. Canna reminded himself of the story of the man who would go up to drab women on the street and hiss suddenly to them: "You're beautiful!" For the strange ego trip of seeing the dull face abruptly flare into a kindling of brief surprised loveliness: the magic a woman would find in herself with the aid of a man. Watch it, Canna. There were two day-periods and a sun-park of twenty before they turned for Lyra and this live cargo got off.

S.S.G.s operated, as implied, on stored solar power. Their original function was transport, and with a meton reactor geared into the solar drive, they had been the hot rods of the galaxy. The big suns, any of a variety of rainbow dwarfs, provided gas stations for these trucks. Parked in Orbit around the furnace, shields up and Solarine mechanisms gulping, the truck became a holiday camp. The beneficial side effects of S.S.G.s were swiftly noted. Golden-skinned crews, whose resistance to disease was 99 to a 100 percent, gave rise to new ideas of the purpose of the galleons. Something about the Solarine filter of raw sunlight acted like a miracle drug on the tired cells of human geography. Something did you a world of good, and you might be expected to pay through the nose to get it. From transport trucks, S.S.G.s became the luxury liners of the firmament, health cures, journeys of a lifetime, the only way to travel. The Solarina sun decks were built on, the huge golden bubbles that girdled the ship, wonderlands of glowing pools, root-ballasted palms and giant sunflowers, lizardia blooms and lillaceous cacti, through which poured the screened radiance of whichever sun the ship was roosting over, endless summer on a leash.

The sun between Bel and Lyra was a Beta-class topaz effulgence, a carrousel of fire.

The third period after lift-off, the "day" they settled around the sun, the little gray-putty girl was sitting in the sun lounge that opened off the entry-outs of the Solarina. Not sitting precisely, more crouching. Canna had checked her name on the passenger list. Her name was Hartley. Apollonia Hartley. He had guessed it all in a flash of intuition; though if he was right, he never found out. The guess was someone had died and left her some cash, enough to make a trip some place. And someone else had said to her: Gee, Apollonia honey, with your name you have to have a Solarine cruise. Apollo's daughter, child of a sun-god (they must have maliciously predicted she'd turn out this plain to crucify her with a name like that), could bask in the sun under the ballasted ballsy palms and fry her grayness golden. Except that she wasn't doing that at all. She was sitting-crouching here in the lead-off lounge, with a tiny glass of champazira she wasn't even sipping. A few people were going in and out, not many. Most of them were placed to grill like tacos within the outer-side bubble.

"Hi, Miss Hartley," said Canna, strolling up to her. "Everything OK?"

Apollonia jumped about ten centimeters off her couch and almost knocked her champazira over.

"All right, thank you," she muttered, staring at her knees.

It was a formula. It meant: Please go away; I'm afraid to talk to you. That was a professional slight, if nothing else. People had to *want* to talk to Leon Canna. It was what he was there for.

"Had enough of the Solarina for today?" he asked.

"Oh yes. That is—yes," said Apollonia. She must be seeing something about her knees which no one but she ever would.

He sat on the arm of the couch beside her.

"You haven't been out there at all, have you?" Silence, which meant go away, go away. "Why's that?" Silence, which had become an abstract agony. "Maybe you've got sun fright. Is that it? It's quite common. Fears of strong radiation. But

I can assure you, Miss Hartley, it's absolutely safe. Do I look sick, Miss Hartley?"

Inadvertently, she glanced at him. Her eyes got stuck somewhere on the white uniform casuals, the sun blaze over the pocket. Black hair and eyes and cleft golden jaw and the golden hands with their fine smoke of black hirsuteness, these she avoided.

"I'm not," she said, "that is, there are so many-people out there." She might have said lions, tigers.

"Sure. I know," he said. He didn't know. People to him were a big fun game. "But I'll tell you what, you know when it gets really quiet in the Solarina?"

"When?" Whispered.

He liked that. He understood what was happening. Fascinated by him, she was beginning to forget herself.

"Twenty-four midnight by the earth clock below. Come back then, you'll get a good three or four hours, maybe alone." She didn't speak. "Or I might come up," he said. Christ, Canna, what did I say to you? He could see her breathing, just like a heroine in an old romance, bosom, as they said, heaving. "Why don't you drink your champazira?" he said.

"I don't—I only—"

"Ordered it for something to play with while you sat here," he said. "I didn't see you at dinner the last two night-periods."

"I ate in my cabin."

"Oh, Miss Hartley—Apollonia, may I?—Apollonia, you'll get the *Pilgrim* a bad name. You're supposed to get something out of your voyage. Come on, now. Promise me. The Solarina at midnight. I have to make certain our passengers enjoy themselves. You don't want me to lose my job, do you?"

Startled, her eyes flew up like birds and collided with his jet-black ones. Her whole face stained with color, even her spectacles seemed to glaze with pink. "I'll try."

"Good girl."

Good God.

He told himself not to go up to the Solarina after midnight. Of course, he'd met women out there before, who hadn't. But not women like Apollonia.

At twenty-four thirty by the earth clock, he walked through the sun lounge. The passenger section of the ship was fairly still at this hour, as he had assured her. The Solarina was empty except for its flora and its light. In the sun lounge, Apollonia was huddled on her couch, without even the champazira to keep her company.

"I didn't think—you would come. I was," she said, "afraid to go through on my own. Is it—all right?"

"Sure it is."

"Will the doors open?"

"I have a tab if they don't."

"It looks so—bright. So fierce."

"It's like a hot shower or the sea at Key Mariano. You ever been there'?" He knew she had not. "Just above blood heat. The fish cook as they swim. Come on." She didn't move, so he moved in ahead of her, into the glowing summer, sloughing his robe as he went. He understood perfectly what he looked like in swim trunks. If he hadn't, enough women had told him, using the analogies of Greek heroes, Roman gladiators. "The harmful rays are filtered out by the Solarine mechanism," he said. Encouraged, mesmerized, she slipped through, and the wine water closed over her head.

She wore a long shapeless tunic. Probably just as well. She would be nearly as shapeless underneath.

"Will this do?" she said. "I didn't know what—"

"That's fine. The filtered sun soaks through any material. The tan is all over, whatever you wear. I just like to get directly under the spotlight when I can."

They folded themselves out among the palms, which threw down coffee-green papers of shade. The warmth was honey. You felt it osmose into you. You never grew bored with, it. The walls of the bubble, sun-amber hiding the actual roaring face of the sun, pulsed very faintly, rhythmically, sensually, with Solarine ingestation. The Galleon was a child, given suck by a fiery breast. All this to fuel a ship. Man oh man.

"It's beautiful," Apollonia said.

She lay on palm-frond shadows. Her eyes were wide behind the spectacles. Her putty-colored hair was ambiguously tinged, almost gilded. Her lips were parted. He hadn't noticed before, she had a nice mouth, the upper lip chiseled, the lower full and smooth, the teeth behind them even and white. He leaned over her and gently lifted the spectacles off the red groove in her nose. He was completely aware of the cliché—Oh, Miss Hartley, now I see you for the first without your glasses. . . .

She made a futile panicky little gesture after the spectacles.

"Relax," he said.

She relaxed, closing her eyes.

"I can see. But not so well But I can see without them."

"I know you can."

"I never felt the sun, any sun, like this before," she said presently. He saw it often, every journey in fact, how they grew drunken, wonderful solar drunks, with no morning after.

An hour later, one-thirty earth time, he looked at her again. There was something changed. Already, her skin was altered. Long lashes lay like satin streaks against her face. The red groove had faded, become a thin rose crescent. OK Canna, so you're Pygmalion. But the Solarina sun had got to him also, as it always did. He leaned over again, and this occasion he kissed her lightly on the lips.

"Oh," she said softly. "Oh."

"Baby," he said. "I have to go back to my quarters and put on tape for my captain what 976 people find wrong with *S.S.G. Pilgrim this* trip."

She didn't stir. He thought she'd gone to sleep, perhaps (fanciful) melodramatically passed out at the fragile kiss.

He left her to the Solarina, and when he closed the door of his cabin he found himself carefully locking it, and the sweat between his shoulder blades had nothing to do with the sun.

He didn't see Miss Hartley next day-period. This was partly deliberate and partly luck. There were plenty of things to do, reports to make, two hours' workout in the gym. Then some crazy dame lost a ruby pendant. He took a late dinner in the salon—as P.L., he had a place at the coordinators' table, alongside his flock. The golden wash was spreading over them all, just as usual. Then he saw the girl.

Something had happened to the girl.

She was tanned, of course, enough tan that she must have been back to the Solarina during the day, or else she'd stayed there all night. Or maybe both. But it wasn't only the tan. What the hell was it?

He couldn't stop staring, which was bad, because any moment she might look his way. But she didn't look. She wasn't even wearing her spectacles. She finished the tawny liqueur she was drinking, got to her feet, and walked unhurriedly out of the salon. She didn't move the same way, either.

"I don't remember that girl," said Fourth Officer Coordinator Jeans.

"Apollonia Hartley."

"Not the right mixture for you, Canna."

"Help yourself," said Canna.

After dinner there was the report to make on the rediscovery of the lost pendant. It looked like it was going to be one of those runs with a lot of desk work. Around midnight there was cold beer and nothing much left to do except wonder if little Miss Hartley was on the sun deck.

There were girls, and there were girls. Some girls you had to be wary of. Even birds of passage could turn around and fly straight back, and some had nest-building on their minds, and some had damn sharp claws. This girl now. She might be grateful. She might have taken it for what it was. Then again, she might not. And for godsakes anyway, what was there for him to be interested in?

At one o'clock earth time, Canna went up to the Solarina. No robe and trunks now, but the rumpled uniform casuals he'd had on all day. The sun lounge was empty. Canna went to the entry-out and glanced through the gold-leaf tunnels of shine under the lizardia. Miss Hartley was lying face down on a recliner, about thirty meters away. Her hair poured over onto the ground. He couldn't see her that well through the stripes of the palms, but enough to know that, aside from her hair, she was naked.

He stepped away from the entry-out noiselessly and walked soft all the way back to his cabin. Oh boy, Canna.

You're beautiful! he said to the plain woman. Her face kindled, she opened her mouth and swallowed him whole.

⑤ ⑤ ⑤

Ten o'clock next day-period, Jeans's jowly face appeared on the cab-com.

"Priority meeting, all officers non-Bridge personnel. Half an hour, Bridge annex."

"What's going on?" Canna asked.

"Search me."

"No thanks."

"OK, funny guy. Usual spiel to the mob, OK?"

"Sure thing."

"Usual spiel" was, as ever, necessary. Somehow, your passengers always knew when something was up, however mild, however closely guarded. Passing three groups on route topside, Canna was asked what emergency required a Bridge annex meeting. Usual spiel meant: "No emergency, Mr. Walters. *Pilgrim* always has an annex meeting third day of sun-parking." "But surely, if everything is going smoothly?" "Nothing ever goes quite smoothly on a vessel this size, Miss Boenek." "Then there *is* an emergency, Mr. Canna?" "Yes, Mr. Walters. We're all out of duck pâté."

"Sit down, gentlemen, if you will," said Andersen.

He had been captain of the *Pilgrim* since Canna had started with the ship, and Canna guessed he respected the man about as much as he'd ever respected any extreme authority. At least Andersen didn't think he was God, and at least he sometimes got off his tail.

"Gentlemen," said Andersen, "we have a slight problem. I'm afraid, Mr. Canna, yours, as ever, is going to be the delicate task."

"You mean it involves our passengers, sir?"

"As ever, Mr. Canna."

"May I know what the problem is?"

"We have some excess radiation, Mr. Canna."

There was the predictable explosion, followed by the predictable dumb show that greets the distant tolling of that bell, about which ask not for whom. Spake, Bridge Engineer Galleon Class, waited for the bell.

"With your permission, sir? OK, gentlemen, it's not big business. We have it under control. Every cubic centimeter of this tub is being checked."

"You mean," said Jeans, "you don't know the hell where it's coming from."

Andersen said: "We know where it isn't coming from. The meton is sound, and there's no bleed-off from the casings. That's our only source of internal radiation. Ergo, it can't be us. Therefore, it's coming in from outside. From the sun we're parked over. As yet, we don't know how or where, because every shield registers fully operational. According to topside computer there's no way we can have a rad-bleed at all. So naturally, we're double checking, triple checking until we pin the critter down. Even if we can't figure it, and there's no reason to suppose we eventually can't, all we have to do is weigh anchor and move out of sun range. Meantime (and here, Mr. Canna, is the rub), the most obvious danger zone is the Solarina."

Canna groaned.

"What you're saying, sir, is that we're going to put the Solarina off limits to the passengers, and I have to find some reason for it that won't cause an immediate panic."

"You know what passengers are like when radiation is involved," said Andersen.

"Mention the word and they're howling and clawing for the life launches," said Jeans.

"What's the rad level?" Canna asked,

Engineer Spake looked at the captain, got some invisible go-ahead, and answered: "At three o'clock this morning, point zero one zero. At nine o'clock, point zero two ten."

There was a second round of expletives.

"In other words, it's rising?"

"It appears to be. But we have a long way to go before it reaches anything like an inimical level."

"I guess that's topside's hang-up, not mine," said Canna. "My hang-up is what story I tell lower side."

"Just keep it simple, Mr. Canna, if you would."

"The simplicity isn't what's troubling me, sir."

"You'll think of something, Mr. Canna."

At noon by the earth clock, when nine hundred odd persons were shooed from the Solarina, Canna guided them into the major lower-side salon, and told them about the free drinks, courtesy of *Pilgrim*. Then, standing on the rostrum with the hand mike, gazing out at the pebbled-beach effect of cluster on cluster of grim, belligerent, nervous faces, Canna found himself reviewing the half a dozen times he had been required to make similar overtures; the time the number twenty Solarine Ingestor caught fire, the time they hit the meteor swarm coming up from Alpheus. A couple of those, and a point zero two ten radiation reading was a candy bar. And then he remembered the girl, and for five seconds his eyes ran over the crowd, and when he couldn't find her, he wondered why the mike was wet against his palm.

They were making a lot of noise, but they quieted down when he lifted his hand. He explained, apologetically, humorously, that *Pilgrim* needed to make up a fuel loss, caused by a minor failure, now compensated, in one of the secondary ingestors. Due to that, the ship would be channeling off extra power through the ship's main Solarine area, the sun deck. Hence the closure.

"For which inconvenience, folks, we are truly sorry."

Now came the questions.

A beefy male had commandeered one of the floor mikes.

"OK, mister, how long's this closure going to last?"

"A day-period, sir. Maybe a couple of days, at most."

"I paid good cash for this voyage, mister. The Solarina's the main attraction."

"The beneficial solar rays permeate every part of the ship, sir, not only the Solarina. The sun deck's function is mostly ornamental. But the company will be happy to refund any loss you feel you've suffered, when we reach Lyra."

"If the goddam Solarina's only ornamental, how can closing it affect the ship's power?"

"That's kind of a technical query. The Solarine pipe ingestors run out over the hull, you recall, and the Solarina's banks are the nearest to outer surface—"

"OK, OK."

A pretty young woman miked from the other side of the room: "Is there any danger?"

"Absolutely none, ma'am. We're just tanking up on gas."

"Well, then, let's tank up," someone yelled, and the free drinking began in earnest.

The *Pilgrim* had got off lightly, Canna thought.

He met Jeans near the bar, downing a large double paint-stripper. Grinning broadly for passenger benefit, Jeans muttered: "Guess what the number game was ten minutes ago?"

"Thrill me." Canna also grinning.

"Full point one."

"Great," said Canna.

"And you know what?" grinned Jeans. "Still climbing."

Far across the room there was a sort of eddy, a current of gold like a fish's wake in sunset water. He thought of a woman baking in the yellow-green cradle of the palms, her arms and her hair poured on the floor.

"The max is fifty, right?"

"Right, Canna, right."

The woman with the ruby was approaching. Miss Keen? Kane? Kone? "I think it's just lovely," she giggled to Canna. "These marvelous ships, and they still get caught with their pants down." She tried to buy him one of the free drinks.

The golden current had settled, become a pool of molten air. Where the girl was. Apollonia. She'd dyed her hair, the color of Benedictine. He couldn't be sure it was Apollonia, except there was nobody else who looked like her now, as none of them had looked like her before.

When he escaped from his flock and got back to his cabin, a slim sealed envelope had come in at the chute with the lower-side stamp over it. Canna opened the envelope.

I waited for you. That was all she had written, in rounded, over-disciplined letters. *I waited for you.*

Sure you did, baby.

He felt sorry for her, and disgusted. She'd improved herself. Perhaps he could palm her off on Jeans. No, he couldn't do that. He'd understood she was trouble the first moment. He should have left her alone. God knew why he hadn't been able to.

At four, Spake came through on the cab-com.

"Thought you'd like to hear it officially. The count is now point fifteen zero five."

"Jesus. Got a fix yet?"

"Nothing. It's everywhere lower side, from the Solarina to the milk bar."

"Not topside?"

"Sifting through."

"Then the source has to be down here."

"According to the computer, nothing leaks, nothing's bleeding off. Unless one of your sheep has a stash of plutonium tucked in his diapers.... It's got to be coming *in,* but the shields are solid as a rock."

"Maybe you're asking the computer the wrong questions."

"Could be. Know the right ones?"

"What does Andersen say?"

"He wants another meet, all available personnel, midnight plus three."

"Three in the *morning?*"

"That's it, Canna. Be there. And, Canna—"

"What?"

"Complete passenger drill tomorrow. Launches, suit-ups, the whole show."

"That'll certainly lend an atmosphere of calm. I'll get it organized."

Just then, the cabin lights faltered. The clear sheen of the Solarine lamps went white, then brown, steadied, and flashed clear again.

"What the hell did that?" Canna demanded, but Spake was gone. Somewhere there had been a massive drain-off of power. That could mean several things, none of them pleasing. Already he was spinning a story for the passengers, a switchover of batteries as the fabricated weak ingestor was shut down. You stood there with the smoke billowing and the walls red-hot and screaming people everywhere, and you told them: It happens every trip. It's nothing. And you made them believe it.

Canna went out of the cabin, strolling toward the lower-side salon, taking in the three TV theaters on the way. The flock came to him like filings to a magnet. He was amazed they'd noticed the lights faltering. It was only the spare ingestor shutting down. They believed him. Makes you feel good, huh, Canna?

But where was Canna when the lights went out? In the goddam dark.

He opened his eyes. It was half past one, the cabin on quarter lamp. Over by the tape cabinet, fastened to its stanchions, the grotesque survival suit stood, blackly gleaming, like a monster from a comic rag. He'd been checking the suit for the demonstration tomorrow and then lain on the bunk to snatch an hour's sleep before Andersen's meeting. What had awakened him?

The door buzzer sounded again. That was what had awakened him.

Two thirds of the way to the door, he knew who it was, and hesitated. Then he opened the door.

There in the corridor stood Apollonia Hartley. But it was not the Apollonia Hartley who had come aboard at Bel. The whole corridor seemed to shine, to throb and glow and shimmer. Maybe that was just the effect of full light after quarter lamp. Then she stepped by him into his cabin, and the throbbing, glowing, shimmering shine came in with her.

"I waited," she said quietly. "And then, when you didn't come, I realized you meant me to come here."

"Did I?"

She turned and looked at him. Without her glasses, there was a slight film across her eyes, making them large, enigmatic. Not seeing him quite so well seemed to make it easier for her actually to look at him. Her Benedictine golden hair hung around her, all around her, and all of her was pure gold, traced over by the briefest swimsuit imaginable. And she was beautiful. Shaped out of gold by a master craftsman, Venus on a gold medallion.

"You look fine," he said. "What have you done to yourself?"

"Nothing." she said. "You've done this for me, Leon,."

He thought, Christ, no woman could make herself look like this in two days, not starting on the raw material Apollonia had started with. Not even with the Solarina.

"You," she said, "and the strange wonderful sun. No man ever looked at me before, ever kissed me. I've never been this close to a sun."

As she breathed, regularly and lightly, planes of fire slid across her waist, her breasts, her throat. And the cabin gathered to the indrawn breath, spilled away, gathered, spilled—

"Can you let me into the Solarina, Leon?" she murmured. "I can do it this way, but it's better there."

He tried to smile at her.

"Sorry, the Solarina's out of bounds, Apollonia—Miss Hartley—until—"

"Leon," she said.

When she spoke, the room was full of amber dust and the scent of oranges, peaches, apricots; and volcanoes blazed somewhere. Then she put her hand against his chest, flat and still on the bare skin. Here he was, Leon Canna, with the best-looking lady he'd ever seen, and he was holding her at arm's length. He stopped holding her that way and held her a better way and she came to him like flame running up a beach.

Over by the cabinet, the black survival suit for tomorrow's drill rattled dully, as if sex vibrated the cabin.

When he opened his eyes the next time, it was with a sense of missing hours. He felt dizzy and the cab-com was bawling. The girl had gone.

"Canna!" For some reason no picture had come over to fit Spake's shouting.

"Yes. I'm sorry. I'm late for my very important date with the Bridge, right?"

"No, Canna. Canna, listen to me. The radiation count in your cabin is point forty-two, and rising."

Canna straightened himself, his eyes and brain focusing slowly. "Canna, are you there, for Christ's sake?"

"I'm here, Spake."

"We have a firework display over the panel here for the whole of lower side, centralized on your level, and through to the B entry-out to the Solarina."

Canna saw the *suit*, black as coal against the wall.

"I've got a demo suit with me, Spake."

"*Good*, Canna. Get it on in two seconds flat."

"Don't make any bets."

"*Canna*, it's forty-two point zero nine. *Forty-three, Canna.*"

"Why no alarms?" Canna inquired as he shambled over to the survival suit, cracked it open, and began to load its myriad pounds onto himself.

"The alarms are out, drained. This com. is working on emergency. Get suited-up, then get as many of the passengers suited as you can. You've got about ten minutes to do it before it goes above fifty in there. Oh, and, Canna, with the power shrinkage, half the auto-gears are jammed, including those of the Bridge exit and the seven lifts through from topside. That's why you're on your own. That's why we can't unpark this truck. Something's just eating up the Solarine, and we're glued over the bloody sun."

Now he was a black beetle. The casque clacked shut, and he hit the suit shields and they came on all around him. Did he fantasize the sudden coolness. His skin felt tender, blistered, but he forgot it.

Beyond his cabin everything was quiet. Innocently, the lower side of *Pilgrim* slumbered or fornicated, unaware that death lay thick as powder on every eye and nostril, every limb and joint and pore. Yet the lights were flickering again, and presently somewhere a dim far-off yelling arose, more anger than fear, the ship's insomniacs, God help them. He wasn't going to be in time. And then he ran at the door and it wouldn't shift.

"Spake," he said, "I'm suited-up, but I can't get the door open."

But the com. was beginning to crackle. Through the crackle, Spake said to him excitedly: "There's something happening in the Solarina— (yes, I have it on screen, sir)—"

"Spake, will you listen, the door—"

"My God," Spake said, in a hushed, low, reverent voice, "it's a woman, and she's on fire."

Canna stood in his cabin in the black coffin of the survival suit. He visualized Apollonia, her fingers in the pocket of his uniform casuals, the authorization tab, the entry-out of the sun deck softly opening.

He saw her, as the bridge was seeing her, lifting her amber arms, her golden body into the glare of the topaz sun. And the sun was shining through her, and like the bush on the holy mountain she was burning and yet not consumed.

A shock of sound passed through the ship. From the suit it seemed miles of cold space away. And then he felt the wild savage trembling like the spasm of an anguished heart, and the tapes and papers on his desk were smoking. The whole cabin was filling with steel-blue smoke he couldn't smell, like the heat he couldn't feel.

The screaming seemed to come all on one high frozen note, two thousand voices melted into one, as the ship bubbled like toffee in a pan. And then the screaming became in turn one with a long roar of light, a blinding rush of noise, and silence, and the dark.

The third time he opened his eyes, he was in a black box with white stars stitched over it. A few bits of unidentifiable wreckage went by, lazy as butterflies. Vast distances below, *Pilgrim's* charred embers fell into the pinpoint of a sun.

Automatically, Canna stabbed on the stabilizers in the suit that had saved his life, anchoring himself firmly to a point of nothing in space. The suit could withstand almost anything, and had just proved as much. It had liquid food and water sufficient for several day-periods, air for longer; it could probably even sing him songs. He had only to wait and keep sane. Every time a ship died, a red signal lit up on every scan board from Earth to Andromeda. Someone would come. He only had to wait.

If he could have got to any of his flock, he'd have had company. They had suits on the Bridge, of course, but they'd had the jammed doors too. And Bridge was right over the meton reactor. Even a suit couldn't take that on.

He drifted about the anchor point using up any foul words he could think of, like candles. He started to hurt. As all survivors did, he stared at the stars and wondered about God. He thought about the pretty girl in the salon who had asked if there was any danger, and he cried. He thought about Apollonia Hartley, and then the pain came, and he started to scream.

When the search ship found him two day-periods later, his voice was a hoarse wire splinter from screaming, and he spat blood from his torn throat.

(Tape running.)

—Thank you, Officer Canna. I think we are all in the picture. I should now like to analyze this vision. Or would you prefer a short recess?

—No, sir. I'd like to get this finished.

—Very well. Whatever you wish. Officer Canna, I hope you'll forgive me when I say, once again, that this story is preposterous. Having heard your account firsthand, I fear I must go further. You've somehow managed to turn a naval tragedy into an exercise in masculine ego. This tale of yours, the man who tells the woman she's beautiful, at which she magically makes herself beautiful for him. Can it really be that you credit—and expect us to credit—the notion that the sexual awareness you brought to this pathetic, rather unbalanced girl, triggered in her an unconscious response so enormous that she attempted to make herself beautiful by absorbing and eventually fusing with a solar body, becoming a fireball that consumed the S.S.G. *Pilgrim?*

—I don't know, sir. I only know what I saw and what I heard.

—But what *did* you see and hear, Officer Canna? You saw an ugly girl, who for some perverse reason attracted you, who then prettied herself for you, tanning quickly, as do all travelers on the Solarine Galleons, dyeing her hair, using a slimming machine. A girl who eventually offered herself to you. Coincidentally, there was a shield failure, which the computer of *Pilgrim* failed to localize. The computer may already have been affected by the loss of power from the Solarine system, hence its inability to identify the source of the trouble. A vicious circle ensues. The shield break degenerates the Solarine bank, the bank is unable to supply sufficient power to stem the break. On the other hand, assuming your bizarre hypothesis to be true, the computer should surely have traced the source. Do you agree, Officer Canna?

—A computer can't think on its own. You have to feed the right questions. Bridge was asking the computer to check for a specific *leakage,* in or out.

—Very well. I don't think we'll split any more hairs on that, Officer Canna. My comments on this phenomenon are amply recorded. The other phenomena you describe are due to the experience itself, but seen in the retrospect of your guilt.

—Excuse me, I don't like what happened, but I don't feel guilty. There was no way I could guess. When I did, there was nothing I could do.

—Perhaps not, but you were wasting precious hours with a female passenger when you might have been able to help your ship.

—I didn't know that at the time.

—Lastly, the woman on fire in the Solarina, by which garbled fragment you seem to set great store. With the radiation level where it was, and so near the outer surface of the ship as the sun deck, spontaneous combustion of tissue was not only possible but predictable. Er—Mr. Liles? Yes, please speak.

—As the witness's counsel, Mr. Hofman, I would respectfully draw your attention to the note appended to Leon Canna's written statement.

—This one? To do with the radiation burns Officer Canna received? But I would have thought such burns inevitable. After all, the exposure—

—The rad level in the cabin before Leon Canna suited-up was insufficient to cause burns of this magnitude.

—Well, I see. But what—

—Excuse me, Mr. Hofman. Leon, are you sure you want to go through with this?'

—I'm sure.

—Mr. Hofman, I'm setting up here a view screen, and on the screen I'm going to present to this investigation two shots of Officer Canna, taken before he underwent treatment and tissue regeneration. Lights, please. Thank you. Shot one.

(A faint growl of men unaccustomed to seeing raw human flesh.)

—Mr. Liles, is this strictly—

—Yes, Mr. Hofman, sir. And I'd ask you to look carefully, here and here.

—Yes, Mr. Liles, thank you.

—This is the frontal shot of Leon Canna's body. The second shot is of the hind torso and limbs.

(Silence. Loud exclamations. Silence.)

—I think you will take my point, gentlemen, that what might be a curious abstract in the first shot becomes a rather terrifying certainty when compounded by the second.

(Silence.)

—Mr. Liles—Officer Canna—gentlemen. I think—we must have a recess after all. Someone please stop that blasted tape.

(Tape stopped.)

Appendix: Two photographs.

1st Shot: A naked man about thirty-six years of age and of athletic, well-proportioned build, badly burned by a class-B radiation strike across the lower face, chest, arms, palms of the hands, pelvis, genitals, and upper legs.

2nd Shot: The same man, also nude; hind view. Burns of similar type, but small in area and fragmentally scattered across the shoulders and buttocks. Across the middle to upper region of the back, definitely marked as if with branding irons, the exact outline of two female arms and hands, tightly and compulsively pressed into the skin.

With a Flaming Sword

The Being had searched for a long while, through the star-shoals of space, before he found the planet. It was a young world, one of several clustered round the blazing youth of a new sun. Long before the instruments aboard his ship told him, he knew that this was the place.

For the Being had a Mission in the universe, a Mission that was both a happiness and a heartbreak to him. It had begun a very great time ago, in the galaxy of his own race, a race powerful and wonderful, but beginning then to die. There was no reason for this death. It had happened as if at the dictate of some irrefutable law, a relentless, dreadful dying. Nevertheless, there had been one remote last chance of propagation. Therefore, into the Being, and into several others chosen like himself, had been poured all the final spirit and might of their race. They had been given near immortality and the reserves of health and beauty that went with it. They had been given silver moons of ships to sail the vastnesses of space, searching. And they had been given the power to make again the life of their own galaxy on other planets resembling the worlds they had left behind.

And now, here, for the first time, lay an answer to the searching and the waiting, and the silent no-sound of space.

The ship slid downwards into the embrace of an alien gravity, not alien at all, and cruised high up, shining. The Being looked, and saw a world still in its infancy, not yet like a world of his lost galaxy, but reaching out toward that likeness. Above all else, it was a beautiful world, though still savage with its childhood. He saw the smoking greenness of jungle

105

forest, blue mirages of hills like clouds resting on the land. He saw vast sweeps of sea, twitching sunlight, rock-lands baking, mountains that snarled fire at the sky from the unhealed wounds of volcanic craters. The Being looked for a long while, resting on his gladness. And then the ship sank lower, and the second search began. And this time there was no reward. For he must find beings like himself through which his race could breed again. And he found none.

There were animals in abundance, animals that seemed familiar, the products of his own galaxy at their earliest evolution. Things moved on land, in sea, through air. But of his kind, the Being was alone amongst them. He left the ship and walked through the moist, throbbing forests, trod the smoldering mountain-flanks. He felt the angry weight of despair.

And then a morning came when he saw them.

Moving crazily and ungracefully, and much smaller, yet they seemed to him to be of his own species. They were trailing across an open tract of grassland, and he followed them in the ship, and came low enough to see their similarities—and all their differences, which were many. He came low enough for them in turn to see the silver thing hanging in the air, point and grunt and screech, and run away. He drew the ship back upwards into the sky, and thought about them. There was a war within him. He was uncertain and unconvinced. He did not know if he could make life out of these creatures, but then, there were no other creatures here so possible.

In the evening he found them again, and rushed low over them, scattering them. He picked out a female separated from the rest, and herded her toward the mountains. She was distressed and called at the others, presumably for help, but they were too afraid to come near the ship. When the rest of the tribe was far behind, he released a soporific gas, let down the nets, and gently lifted her into the ship with him.

He examined her minutely, shrinking a little from her alien stink and texture, but finding in her now many of the attributes he needed. Her organs were similar, both internally and externally, her features and structure also very like. She had neither the physical beauty nor the physical brain of the females of his own race, but he decided he must make her do, must see, must try, must hope. Perhaps this was the nearest chance he would ever have. And so he implanted in her the life-seed, stored for aeons in the womb-tube of the ship, seed that would make a male and a female from her body, providing her body could harbor it.

He took her to a valley he had found, high up, lovely. It was shielded by mountains that had ceased to spit fire; water-courses ran through it, and it was full of animals he had taken there earlier, experimenting gently with them to speed their evolution, hoping to see in them the animals of his own galaxy, before he went away. He set his captive free and watched her roaming the forests and grassland, solitary, blinking her small eyes. She plucked down fruit and ate it, but kept away from the other animals. She slept in tree-hollows at night. Soon he began to see that the life-seed lived in her womb, and he waited helpless, wondering if the magic would work, or if two monsters would break out of her, or if she would die and kill them at birth.

One day she hid herself. He searched in an agony; finally he found her with her two living infants. She had rolled away from them, and, as quickly as she was able, abandoned the place where they were. She felt no maternity for them because they were so alien to her. It did not matter. Her role was finished. Soon he took her out of the valley and left her where he had found her first, hoping she would make her way back to the tribe.

He lifted the infants into the ship and examined them. The miracle had happened. He found in them all the potential, both physical and mental, that had moved in his own lost race. They were shaped like the Being and his people, both beautiful, with the brain ready to grow in its case, with features delicate and strong, with limbs and eyes prepared to grasp skills, and see beyond seeing. He knew, of course, with sadness that the greatness of his own Galaxy would not come to them until their own race had advanced far into an unguessable future. He did not know what dangers and setbacks might slow their progress. He realized that he might never see their final fulfillment and the fruit of his task. But he believed that it would come, and that was enough.

When they had grown sufficiently, he put them out in the valley, and they bounded and played in the greenness as the lower animals did. They were still covered all over by the coarse, long hair their mother had had, a protection and a camouflage. The animals, gentle because of their environment, and the things the Being had adaptively done to them, came to the pair and would play and run about with them. Later, when the Being began their instruction, he tried to show his charges that they were superior to these other animals and must not identify with them totally. But as the process went on, and they grew from young to distinctive male and female, he knew he had little communion with them. They went in awe of him, speaking to each other, the animals, even the metallic robot tube he used to feed them from, rather than to him. Yet he loved to hear them speak, even though it was necessary for him to eavesdrop, for they spoke the old galactic tongue, clear and rounded. Despite their hairy bodies, nothing else of their mother remained in them. Even their occasional cries of anger or pain were sharp and formed; they seldom grunted as the tribe had done.

Eventually they spoke most often to the feeding tube. The Being imagined that in a way they identified it with him, as it brought them the special food he had prepared for them, so necessary for their development. The tube, long and shining, roamed around the valley freely. The Being realized that the male and female thought it was sentiently alive as they were and loved it because it could speak to them, as none of the animals could. It had a thin, metallic voice, which was mainly used in calling them to their meals.

As the time went by, and the Being had told them and taught them all they could grasp at this stage of their evolution, he began to be troubled by the growth of hair still clinging to their bodies. He had thought it might disappear naturally, or that the drugs he mixed with their food might disperse it. His own race had been entirely hairless, and the growth was anathema to him. He began to develop a new drug to use against it, gathering for energy, as he had always done, the power of the bright new sun that flamed overhead. The valley was full of the Being's experimental vats, where things metamorphosed under their sun-domes. Much of the food he had provided for the male and female had come from these. At first they had stood up, strange and sudden in the soft landscape, and the animals had kept away from them. But by now the vats had blended with the scenery of the valley, for the growth of the young world was so intense they had been covered by flowers and leaves and creepers, becoming at last almost indistinguishable from the large trees of the forest. Partly because of this, the Being put a force wall around the new vat to keep the animals out, and warned the male and female not to go near it either.It was very important to him. One day a deer brushed by the wall, and the current in the force field killed it. The male and female seemed afraid because of this. He had explained death to them, but as yet they could not understand it.

The Being began to see in them now the signs that they were discovering each other as of different sexes. Like children still, they giggled together in an intimate privacy, shutting out even the feeding tube. They would soon mate.

The need for the drug was thus urgent. If they mated now and produced offspring as hairy as themselves, he would have to start his teaching again, for the hair was a psychological deformity as much as a physical one. While they still had it, they thought of themselves as a species of lower animal, despite everything he had taught them.

As soon as the drug was prepared, he sent the feeding tube to take them to it. He watched them shaking their heads, saying: No, no, we were told not to go near that tree—they, like the animals, believed the vat was a tree—and anyway, the deer had died, they had seen it. To touch the tree meant death. But the tube persuaded them, somehow or other, and at last they went, and he saw them drinking through it out of the vat, laughing at how false all their fears had been. However, when the hair began to fall off them in patches, then in its entirety, they wept and screamed, and ran off into the forest.

At length the Being went after them. He called them, and his huge voice, so much larger than theirs, struck frightened birds out of the branches. When he found them they were crouched down, covering themselves with torn-off armfuls of leaves, shivering with fear. He accepted then, with a hurt in him, how afraid they really were of him, not just of his stature but of his powers, his knowledge, of everything about him.

He tried to calm their terror, but they seemed to think that he was angry with them for eating something he had previously told them not to eat. They blamed each other for doing it, and then they blamed the feeding tube, saying it had lured them to the vat, and now they were punished with this horrible, naked hairlessness. The male seemed to feel less guilty because there was still hair on his face and chest, as well as on his head and genitals (the drug had not been completely successful, unripe as it was). The female, more naked, was the more afraid.

The Being found that he could not evict the fear from their minds, so he left them alone, and later he took them to the ship and made them garments out of the deer's skin, showing them how it was done. This seemed to comfort them a little, but not much. When he told them that soon they must leave the valley and go into a world where animals would not play with them, and where snakes—they had thought the feeding tube was a snake—would be their enemies, they evidently believed they were truly being punished for what they had done. Later, when he explained to them the facts of their sex, how the female would carry the child and bring it forth not without discomfort, they clung together and would not look at him. They thought it was his curse on them for disobeying.

After that he gave them lessons on the world outside, fitted them for it, tried to console them. And he saw that his plan had been wrong, and that they were physically and mentally too young to understand what had happened to them.

When at last they climbed the path up out of the valley, he hung in his ship, watching them, resolving that next time he would be gentler, more subtle.

At the top of the path, the world stretched before them, unwelcoming and strange, the male and female halted. They heard the song of the ship's engines, and turning, saw between them and the valley, the long golden flame of the boost jet, lifting the ship like a silver halo, out into space. And because they were still bewildered and ashamed and afraid, they thought that the fire had been put there to stop them ever going back into the beautiful valley again.

They ran away before the flame vanished, and it stayed always in their minds, and in the minds of the tribe, and of the race, and of the people they founded. The fire that kept them out of the Garden, the fire which later, when they had learned how to make them, they would call a sword.

Black Fire

Witness A (One)

I first see it as I'm driving back that night up the road—you can bet I pulled over. I thought it was a fucking plane coming down. Like a plunge of flames right through the sky, as if the sky were tearing open from the top to the bottom. The car slams to a halt and I jump out—and I'm below the top of the hill, so I run the rest of the way and just as I get there, this—thing, whatever it was—it lands in the woods. Well, our house is around there, me and hers. Only a mouse-house—what she said—mid-terrace in the last street winds out the village.

I stand on the hill sort of frozen, sort of turned to stone, and I hold my breath, the way like you do, not knowing you're not breathing.

So while I watch, all this fire-thing just storms into and through the trees and down, and it hits the ground, and I think something's crazy then, because there should be a god-awful great bang, yeah? And great columns of fire and crap. But there ain't a sound. Not a bloody whisper.

And then I remember, and I take that missing breath. But it's so quiet. I think that's what struck me anyhow, even while I run up the hill. There's always some kind of noise out here, I mean we're not that far from town. And there's animals too, foxes and things snuffling and screeching. And cars. Only there isn't a single sound now.

I don't never drink when I drive. Not no more. I got pulled over a couple years ago, random check, and I was just over the limit—half a glass—well, a pint—of beer. But I won't take any chance now. So nobody can say I *imagined* what I seen. Go on, you can test me, if you like. No. I seen it. And I seen what come after too.

Witness E (One)

He was late. He's always late.

That's what they says about dead people, don't they? Well then, he must be dead.

Oh he's got some bint where he works. Says he hasn't.

He's got some—

Anyhow. I was washing my hair, and this blinding-like light sort of—I thought it was coming straight in the bleeding window—

I thought it was a bomb. You know. A *dirty* bomb like they always go on about. Terrorists. Why does everyone hate everyone?

So I runs out in the garden, and I look and this big light—it's like the sky's falling, and it's all on fire—only the fire is—it isn't red or nothing. It's—can't describe it really.

Right in the wood.

I started to cry. I was really scared. And *he* weren't there, the bugger.

But there's no crash. Nothing. Just—silence.

You know that thing someone said—hear a pin drop. Like that.

And my hair's so wet—but I shakes it back, and I thought, I can go next door—but the other three houses there, as we come like out of the village, no one lives in them now.

And then I sees him. This guy. He's walking out between the trees, i'nt he. Just walking.

Witness A (One)

Fucking car wouldn't start, would it, when I goes back to it. So I beats it up the fucking hill again and belts down the other side toward the house. I mean, I'm thinking of her, aren't I? Yeah?

I mean you do, don't you.

Witness E (One)

It wasn't just he was well fit. I mean he *was* fit. I can see that like. And like he's really—he's beautiful. And I'm standing there in my old jeans and an old bra and no slap on and my hair full of shampoo— But he's got a sort of like, he's sort of *shining*.

It's like—what's that stuff? Phosbros—is it?

He—gleams.

Only he's dark too. I don't mean he's a black guy. His skin is just kind of like summer tan, sort of like he's caught the sun but over *here*. Not a *real* tan. And his hair is black, but it's so long, all down his back, it's like silk.

And he has this face.

I don't think much of them movie celebs, do you? But *this* guy, he's like in films my mum used to watch before she went mad and ended up in Loonyville—I can't think who.

But he comes out the wood and up to the garden, where the dustbin is, and the broken gate, and he looks at me.

I say, "D'you see that flaming thing come down?"

And he smiles at me.

Witness A (Two)

Coming home on that train, it's always late and no trolley service. I dread the damn thing. But when I finally got to the station, what do you think? The shit Volvo won't start, will it.

So I walked.

Perfect ending to a perfect day, etc.

That's when I saw those fireworks all showering down on everything.

I admit I stopped and stared. I mean, I was recollecting that factory— God, where was it?—that place where all the fireworks blew up— the only difference was, and I eventually figured it out, *these* fireworks were all in a mass, just dropping in one area. They merely fell out of the sky. Glittering. The rather peculiar thing was, there were no colors. It was quite a naturally well-lit night—aside from the inevitable street lamp light-pollution—a half moon, and stars. And this fountain of fireworks looked somehow much darker. They were—the nearest I can get is something like black sequins, those kind of *gowns* sexy women wore in the forties of the last century.

Anyway, I started to walk again because even when the fountain hit the bloody houses on my street, which I could see from up there on the far side of the park, there wasn't any thudding noise, no detonations.

You get so anxious now. It's how they want to make you, isn't it. All these warnings. I'd been thinking, ever since the trouble years ago, I ought to relocate, just work from home.

But it's difficult. My partner. She likes the high life frankly, and her own job (she's a sort of PA) simply doesn't cover the rent.

It took me an hour to get back on foot. I steeled myself and didn't stop off at the King's Arms. I thought she might be worried. Sometimes I can be such a bloody fool.

By the time I reached the house the pyrotechnics were long gone. It was just this incredibly silent night. I noted that, you see. It struck me—how dead quiet it was.

When I unlocked the door, there seemed to be no one about. That was unusual. She's usually around. Even if she's asleep in front of the TV with an empty vodka bottle. I called out, I remember… I called her name— *Honey I'm home* sort of rubbish.

But no answer.

I felt fed up. I was tired and hungry. I admit, I felt *unloved.* Childish, stupid, but I'm trying to tell you the truth.

Then I thought I heard a noise upstairs. Had she gone up to bed early? (No care for me, get my own fucking meal even though she'd been home all day.) Or was she ill? She gets migraines sometimes—or she says she—she *said* she did.

I went upstairs.

This I can't really explain. I walked quietly. Maybe only because it really was so quiet. Not a sound. (Even when I'd passed the pub, now I come to think of it. Quiet as—well, is even a *grave* so quiet?)

Upstairs the dimmer was on, all the lights half doused.

Then I did hear something. Then I heard it again, through the bedroom door. *Our* bedroom. This cry.

You can't mistake a cry like that.

Unless, of course, you never ever heard it before.

Witness A (One)

I runs the last bit. I'm getting really scared, even though there'd been no bang nor nothing. I mean, the house lights were all out.

When I gets there I nearly has a heart attack because the front door is standing wide open.

No light—no, one on in the lounge—I say lounge, size of a kitchen table—nowhere else though.

Upstairs, in the tiny little mouse room we called our bedroom, I hear a long wild wailing noise.

And I fucking know that noise.

It's her, fetching off, like they say. It's sex.

I thought, hang on, maybe she's just fixed herself, me not being there.

Then I know.

Then I run upstairs fast as I could. Sounded like an elephant to myself, in all the quiet.

When I pushed the door open, there they are. Her and him. There they are.

Witness E (Two)

He rang the doorbell. I think that was it... He must have done.

So I opened the door. It wasn't that late. Anyway, I was bored.

The utter rubbish on TV. I'd been going to check the washing-machine because suddenly it seemed so silent that presumably it'd packed up, with all my gear in it, oh and his favorite three shirts—*unforgiveable!*

I thought I'd seen a kind of flash in the sky earlier. But I'm always seeing things in the sky. Altogether, in the past two years, I've seen six unidentified flying objects. Everyone laughs at me. But I did.

Anyway, standing outside the door is this entirely gorgeous man. There is no other way to describe him. He looks like—oh, God knows. Too good to be true. No, I don't remember what he was wearing.

Yes, I'd been drinking. I always mean to cut down, *never* do it when I'm at work. But sometimes, well. But not that much. I mean, I could see.

He was so beautiful.

And he said, "Here you are," and he smiled this wonderful smile. No, not *charismatic*, nothing so clichéd. You looked at him and—

I fell in love with him. On sight. I fell in love with him.

Can I stop now.

I need some water, please.

Witness E (Three)

We'd been going to go up to the ridge. There was supposed to be a meteor shower. He said so. We're both very interested in that sort of thing, space, you know. He has a wonderful collection of meteor bits—dark fusion crust—really special.

We'd only been together a year. It was awful when he lost his job, but luckily I still have mine. Very luckily, as it turns out. I mean it's just boring office work, but I'll still need a job, won't I. Or not for a bit, perhaps.

Anyway, we set off quite early, around sunset. It was lovely, the light sinking over the fields and the birds singing. I know the songs are only territorial, their way of saying *Keep Out!* to other birds. I never knew that till he explained it to me. I just thought they sang because they could do it so well.

The ridge is the highest open place for miles.

We sat down and looked at the dark coming, and then all the lights coming on all round, the two towns, and the city to the north, and the little villages. You can never go far here without seeing people, or signs of them.

It got dark then. The moon was already quite far over to the west, though still high enough to make the upper sky that deep night blue. Lots of stars.

We didn't see anything for a long time. Then this thing just *erupted* out of the zenith.

He jumped up. We both did.

"It's a fireball—" he shouted. "My God—it's colossal—"

It seemed to be falling straight on us, but somehow neither of us could move.

Then I remember being aware of turning, as if I were *being* turned, not doing it myself—and our shadows peeling out jet black behind us and then realizing the meteor was rushing down to the south, in front of us, not directly on to our heads.

He started to run. He was running after it. He didn't wait for me, or even call to me. I suppose he just thought I'd do exactly what he did, I'd be so desperate to *see*. But I was scared. You know. I mean, it was so big and blazing bright—and yet so *dark*. I didn't know you could have fire like that, *black* fire—it must be a phenomenon associated with certain types of extraterrestrial objects.

So he'd sprinted off, and the fireball went down on the land. And then—no shock wave, no sound—it just went out. Like a blown candle. Like that.

My legs had gone to jelly. I had to sit down. I thought he'd be all right, after all nothing had exploded or was burning. What a coward I was, and he was so brave. He'd really tell me off. Perhaps I could get up and follow him in a minute, pretend I'd fallen over something as I ran—

Then I noticed how completely quiet everything was. Nothing is ever that quiet. I've been out with him enough nights to know. Animals move about, there is the distant hum of traffic from the motorway, or a plane. Trees sort of *settle*. And even the quietest flick of breeze moves the leaves. And I could *see* the leaves on trees moving a little. So the silence was just for me, somehow I'd been closed in some sort of bubble of soundlessness—

Then I stood up.

And then he spoke to me. I mean *him*, the man. The—I mean *him*.

He said, "Are you here?"

I said, "Who are you? Where did you come from?"

And he smiled.

He was so wonderful to look at…long black hair. He wore—I can't remember. Just ordinary clothes, I expect. Because in fact he couldn't have been at all what he seemed. It was a sort of illusion he could create, just the way they do it in sf movies, CGI—in *Dr Who* for instance. Because he must be an alien, a species from beyond this world.

I was terrified. But then he touched me.

No, I'm all right. This isn't *my* blood.

Witness A (four)

I slung the door open and I ran straight at them. They were by the wall. No need to guess what he'd been doing with her—

She just looked sad. That was all. She didn't even protest.

And he—well, must have slipped out the side door while I was seeing to her, mustn't he. Bastard. *He never even tried to stop me.*

Is she going to be—?

OK. No. All right. Yes.

Witness E (Seven)

Of course I never want him near me again after what he did. Sure we've been married three years. So what? Yes, I'll press charges. Look at me.

I don't remember. Yes, there was another bloke. A stranger—so? So what. I don't remember. I must have done.

Dept. RUP/sub 3x6: ps

My profoundest apologies that the encl document did not accompany the (coded) transcript of this report.

Here then, belatedly, it is.

(I have to add at this point that whether it will shed any light of logic on the recorded eyewitness reports already transcribed and in your hands, remains to be seen. Those of us *here* are frankly baffled.

I will refer to that again at the end of the encl document.)

Docu 97/77/ Six. Six. Six.

On the night of July 20 __ (see transcript) a number of emergency calls began to be relayed to this department. They involved urgent requests for all emergency services: police, paramedics and, in some cases, fire fighters.

The peculiar feature of all these call-outs was the basic similarity of the claims of all the participants. Each seemed to involve an episode which, though variable, mentioned similar events and actions, and, significantly, one particular male person (as described in the transcripts), a youngish man, tall and slimly built, having very long dark hair and dark eyes. All the living victims—some were no longer alive—even those who did not regard themselves as victimized—were in a range of states representing shock, paranoid rage, or extreme exhilaration.

All reported a fundamentally similar scenario, despite other countless unlike details. However, the occurrences took place on the same evening, across the length and breadth of England. While the times, too, varied (incidents began quite early in the evening and continued to surface until midnight) it is evidently impossible that the same dark-haired man, the main "suspect"—we use this term for want of another—could have appeared in so many widely disseminated areas during so brief a time period.

I will add that so far, we have been entirely unable to trace him, in this country or elsewhere. This is partly due, no doubt, to the lack of any recoverable DNA or other clue left behind with the subjects of his...visits.

Also, although sightings of UFOs are not uncommon, on this particular night, no one, apart from the people directly involved, called in with any queries about a fiery falling object, whether thought to be a meteor, a spaceship, or a light aircraft. No unusual reports either of an electric storm or alarming fireworks display.

The enclosed transcript relays to you only a *sample* of the huge group of persons who were subsequently interviewed, initially by the police or the ambulance service, and later by ourselves. It is a sample of the most *typical* reports. Of which, in total, there are to date some six hundred and sixty-six.

This number may, of course, not arouse any disquiet in the mind of a modern atheist. Nevertheless I am afraid, in order to preserve for the victims, where feasible, a modicum of the anonymity the Law currently prescribes, we have (perhaps frivolously) labeled each and all of them not by an actual name, but by the letter A, in the case of males, and E, in the case of females. Plus a differentiating number—One, Two, etc. You may soon be aware why the letters A and E alone have been selected. And we trust you will overlook any perceived levity on our part. *A* stands for the Biblical Adam, naturally. And *E* for Eve, his rib-created partner. As I have said, we have not, here, included every single eyewitness account, but rendered for your consideration the most predominantly recurrent statements, that is, those most representative from all six hundred and sixty-six interviews we were able to garner. (Of those individuals resultantly dead, or in a condition likely to lead to death—both male and female—we do not yet have conclusive figures.) The ultimate consequences of this replicated event remain, so far, unpredictable.

We shall be very glad to receive your input on this matter. To accept it at apparent (religious?) face-value would seem, shall we say, grotesque. But to ignore so widespread a phenomenon likewise itself poses many problems.

Code seal and signature attached.

Appendage PSX: My last thought is, I confess, is this really then what is meant by science fiction? Or, more disquietingly, was it *always*? I direct your attention to the final words of the final included witness.

Witness A (Two)

I'm very sorry I did that to her. Yes, I know she won't speak to me. I can't see her. Yes. I've never done anything like that before.

I can't describe it. Can't you try to fucking *understand?* She was lying on the bed with him. She was naked. He was—he was *inside* her. She was holding him in her arms—

I couldn't handle it. *You* didn't see. And there was this *light* in the room. Like a sort of bloody *gilding*. The whole scene looked like a pornographic oil painting from the Italian Renaissance.

I don't *remember* what he looked like. Just another man. Some kid, twenties maybe. God knows.

He just moved away from her. There *was* something then. He was—what? what?—*sinuous*, something sinuous about how he moved. That I do remember. He moved like—a trained dancer, an athlete—no, like an animal. Like a big cat. A panther. Or a snake.

I know I hit her.

I'm sorry.

I never did anything like that before with anyone.

No, it wasn't really because she'd fucked him. It what she said. She said *I can see inside you.*

Witness E (Two)

Yes, I could, I could see all through him. Through everything. No I can't explain. I would if I could, wouldn't I? I mean all this fucking talk, this interrogation, when I'm covered in bruises, and I'm still pretty articulate, *aren't I? OK?* If *not* very pretty. Ha. Ha.

I don't know now what it was.

It was as if I knew everything there was to know, the heights, the depths, yesterday, tomorrow, the beginning, the end— Oh—

Shit.

I need the plastic thing—the *bowl*— It's your fault, all these questions—*get the fucking sick bowl before I throw up all over*—

Witness A (One)

She gets off of the bed and she says to me, I seen the stars. That's what she says.

She doesn't mean—I don't know what—I know —

I don't know what to do, do I. I turn to him like a fucking dope, but somehow he's not there no more. But there's something. I can feel it too.

There's this ringing in my head, and this terrific smell, a *good* smell—no, not good, can't be, can it. But it's clean, sweet—only it's drowning me.

I suppose she called you. Or someone. That's all I remember, mate. The lot. But I won't forget none of it. And I ain't been drinking, I told you. *Test* me.

Witness E (Three)

It was like looking through glass. You know, a glass case, perhaps. You can see everything so *clearly,* but you can't *touch* it. If you try, you trigger the alarm.

But I do remember there was a tree. It was very tall, dark but golden, both at once. We were lying high up in it. And this beautiful scent—no, more of a taste, really.

Witness E (Twenty-four)

He said to me, "You are here." And then we made love. It was never like that before. Won't ever be again. I saw into this huge light. Only it was black, a black light. And for a moment, just after my climax, I knew that I was God. I know this sounds insane, but I don't think I'm insane. It was only for a moment.

Witness A (One)

I'm afraid of her, now. Don't want to see her again. Don't want to see any of you, neither. I wish you'd all fuck off.

Witness E (Three)

When he came running back, the alien man—my *lover*—was gone. But I suppose it must have been obvious, to *him*. I mean, the man I lived with. I wasn't in any tree at all, but lying there on the ridge naked. I must have looked—well. I suppose it was obvious. It was to him. He began to shout and yell at me. He seemed to be speaking in another language. But I could see right through the universe, start to finish, even if it was behind glass. I'm such a coward normally, I've said, haven't I. But when he ran at me his first blow never even touched me. I drove my knee into his stomach—let's be truthful, into his genitals. And I ripped at his eyes. I am terribly sorry. I understand he may lose his right eye. But I knew he might have killed me otherwise, and frankly, I think you know that too, don't you?

When I hurt him I felt nothing. Or rather, all I could feel was what I'd felt when the alien had sex with me. This incredible blissful opening to all things, in the most amazing way. And that lovely, delicious scent. I can still smell it. That taste of fresh-cut apples.

Written in Water

It was a still summer night, colored through by darkness. A snow white star fell out of the sky and into the black field half a mile from the house. Ten minutes later, Jaina had walked from the house, through the fenced garden patch, the creaking gate, toward the place where the star had fallen. Presently, she was standing over a young man, lying tangled in a silver web, on the burned lap of the earth.

"Who are you?" said Jaina. "What's happened to you? Can you talk? Can you tell me?"

The man, who was very young, about twenty-two or -three, moved his slim young body, turning his face. He was wonderful to look at, so wonderful Jaina needed to take a deep breath before she spoke to him again.

"I want to help you. Can you say anything?"

He opened a pair of eyes, like two windows opening on sunlight in the dark. His eyes were beautiful, and very golden. He said nothing, not even anything she could not understand. She looked at him, drinking in, intuitively, his beauty; knowing, also intuitively, that he had nothing to do either with her world or her time.

"Where did you come from?" she said.

He looked back at her. He seemed to guess, and then to consider.

Gravely, gracefully, he lifted one arm from the tangle of the web and pointed at the sky.

He sat in her kitchen, at her table. She offered him medication, food, alcohol, and caffeine from a tall bronzed coffee pot. He shook his head slowly. Semantically, some gestures were the same, yet not the same. Even in the shaking of his head, she perceived he was alien. His hair was the color of the coffee he refused. Coffee, with a few drops of milk in it, and a burnish like satin. His skin was pale. So pale, it too was barely humanly associable. She had an inspiration and filled a glass with water. The water was pure, filtered through the faucet from the well in the courtyard, without chemicals or additives. Even so, it might poison him. He had not seemed hurt after all, merely stunned, shaken. He had walked to her house quietly, at her side, responding to her swift angular little gestures of beckoning and reception. Now she wanted to give him something.

She placed the glass before him. He looked at it and took it up in two finely made, strong, articulate hands. They were the hands of a dancer, a musician. They had each only four fingers, one thumb, quite normal. He carried the glass to his mouth. She held her breath, wondering, waiting. He put the glass down carefully, and moved it, as carefully, away from him. He laid his arms across the table and his head upon his arms, and he wept.

Jaina stood staring at him. A single strand of silver, left adhering when he stripped himself of the web, lay across his arm, glittering as his shoulders shook. She listened to him crying, a young man's sobs, painful, tearing him. She approached him and muttered: "What is it? What is it?" helplessly.

Of course, it was only grief. She put her hand on his shoulder, anxious, for he might flinch from her touch, or some inimical thing in their separate chemistries might damage both of them. But he did not flinch, and no flame burst out between her palm and the dark, apparently seamless clothing that he wore.

"Don't cry," she said. But she did not mean it. His distress afforded her an exquisite agony of empathic pain. She had not felt anything for a very long time. She stroked his hair gently. Perhaps some subtle radiation clung to him, some killer dust from a faraway star. She did not care. "Oh, don't cry, don't cry," she murmured, swimming in his tears.

She drove into the morning town in her ramshackle car, as usual not paying much attention to anything about her. Nor was her program much changed. First, gas from the self-service station, then a tour of the shops, going in and out of their uninviting facades: a tour of duty. In the large hyper-market at the edge of town, she made her way through the plastic and the cans, vaguely irritated, as always, by the soft mush of music, which came and went on a time switch, re-gardless of who wanted it, or no longer did. Once, she had seen a rat scuttle over the floor behind the frozen meat section. Jaina had done her best to ignore such evidence of neglect. She had walked out of the shop stiffly.

She had never liked people very much. They had always hurt her, or degraded her, always imposed on her in some way. Finally she had retreated into the old house, wanting to be alone, a hermitess. Her ultimate loneliness, deeper than any state she had actually imagined for herself, was almost like a judgment. She was thirty-five and, to herself, resembled a burned-out lamp. The dry leaf-brownness of her skin, the tindery quality of her hair, gave her but further evidence of this consuming. Alone, alone. She had been alone so long. And burned, a charred stick, incapable of moistures, fluidities. And yet, streams and oceans had moved in her, when the young man from outer space had sobbed with his arms on her table.

She supposed, wryly, that the normal human reaction to what had happened would be a desire to contact someone, in-form someone of her miraculous find, her "Encounter." She only played with this idea, comparing it to her present circum-stances. She felt, of course, no onus on her to act in a rational way. Besides, who should she approach with her story, who would be likely to credit her?

But as she was turning on to the dirt road that led to the house, she became the prey of sudden insecurities. Perhaps the ultimate loneliness had told, she had gone insane, fantasizing the falling star of the parachute, imagining the young man with eyes like golden sovereigns. Or, if it were true.... Possibly, virulent Terran germs, carried by herself, her touch, had already killed him. She pictured, irresistibly, Wells's Martians lying dead and decaying in their great machines, slain by the microbes of Earth.

Last night, when he had grown calm, or only tired, she had led him to her bedroom and shown him her bed. It was a narrow bed, what else, fit only for one. Past lovers had taught her that the single bed was to be hers, in spite of them, forever. But he had lain down there without a word. She had slept in the room below, in a straight-backed chair between the bureau and the TV set that did not work anymore. Waking at sunrise, with a shamed awareness of a new feeling, which was that of a child on Christmas morning, she had slunk to look at him asleep. And she was reminded of some poem she had read long, long ago:

> *How beautiful you look when sleeping, so beautiful*
> *It seems that you have gone away....*

She had left him there, afraid to disturb such completion, afraid to stand and feed parasitically on him. She had driven instead into town for extra supplies. She wanted to bring him things; food he might not eat, drink he might not drink. Even music, even books he could not assimilate.

But now—he might be gone, never have existed. Or he might be dead.

She spun the car to a complaining halt in the summer dust. She ran between the tall carboniferous trees, around the fence. Her heart was in her throat, congesting and blinding her.

The whole day lay out over the country in a white-hot film. She turned her head, trying to see through this film, as if underwater. The house looked silent, mummified. Empty. The land was the same, an erased tape. She glanced at the blackened field.

As she stumbled toward the house, her breathing harsh, he came but through the open door.

He carried the spade that she had used to turn the pitiful garden. He had been cleaning the spade; it looked bright and shiny. He leaned it on the porch and walked toward her. As she stared at him, taking oxygen in great gulps, he went by her and began to lift things out of the car and carry them to the house.

"I thought you were dead," she said stupidly. She stood stupidly, her head stupidly hanging, feeling suddenly sick and drained.

After a while she too walked slowly into the house. While he continued to fetch the boxes and tins into her kitchen like an errand boy, she sat at the table, where he had sat the night before. It occurred to her she could have brought him fresh clothing from the stores in the town, but it would have embarrassed her slightly to choose things for him, even randomly off the peg in the hypermarket.

His intention had presumably been to work on her garden, some sort of repayment for her haphazard, inadequate hospitality. And for this work he had stripped bare to the waist. She was afraid to look at him. The torso, what was revealed of it, was also like a dancer's—supple, the musculature developed and flawless. She debated, in a dim terror of herself, if his human maleness extended to all regions of his body.

After a long time, he stopped bringing in the supplies and took up the spade once more.

"Are you hungry?" she said to him. She showed him one of the cans. As previously, slow and quiet, he shook his head.

Perhaps he did not need to eat. Perhaps he would drink her blood. Her veins filled with fire, and she left the table and went quickly upstairs. She should tell someone about him. If only she were able to. But she could not.

He was hers.

⑤ ⑤ ⑤

She lay in the bath, in the cool water, letting her washed wet hair float round her. She was Ophelia. Not swimming; drowning. A slender glass of greenish gin on five rocks of milky ice pulsed in her fingers to the rhythm of her heart.

Below, she heard the spade ring tirelessly on stone. She had struggled with the plot, raising a few beans, tomatoes, potatoes that blackened, and a vine that died. But he would make her garden grow. Oh, yes.

She rested her head on the bath's porcelain rim, and laughed, trembling, the tips of her breasts breaking the water like buds.

She visualized a silver bud in the sky, blossoming into a huge and fiery ship. The ship came down on the black field. It had come for him, come to take him home. She held his hand and pleaded, in a language he did not comprehend, and a voice spoke to him out of the ship, in a language that he knew well. She clung to his ankle, and he pulled her through the scorched grass, not noticing her, as he ran toward the blazing port.

Why else had he wept? Somehow and somewhere, out beyond the moon, his inexplicable craft had foundered. Everything was lost to him. His vessel, his home, his world, his kind. Instead there was a bony house, a bony, dried-out hag, food he could not eat. A living death.

Jaina felt anger. She felt anger as she had not felt it for several months, hearing that spade ring on the indomitable rock under the soil. Still alone.

When the clock chimed six times that meant it was one quarter past five, and Jaina came down the stairs of the house. She wore a dress like white tissue, and a marvelous scent out of a crystal bottle. She had seen herself in a mirror, brushing her face with delicate pastel dusts, and her eyes with cinnamon and charcoal.

She stood on the porch, feeling a butterfly lightness. She stretched up her hand to shield her eyes, the gesture of a heroine upon the veranda of a dream. He rested on the spade, watching her.

See how I *am*, she thought. *Please, please, see me, see me.*

She walked off the porch, across the garden. She went straight up to him. The sun in his eyes blinded her. She could not smile at him. She pointed to her breast.

"Jaina," she said. "I am *Jaina."* She pointed to him. She did not touch him. "You?"

She had seen it done So frequently. In films. She had read it in books. Now he himself would smile slightly, uneasily touch his own chest and say, in some foreign otherworld tongue: *I am....*

But he did not. He gazed at her, and once more he slowly shook his head. Suddenly, all the glorious pity and complementary grief she had felt through him before flooded back, overwhelming her. Could it be he did not know, could not remember, who he was? His name, his race, his planet? He had fallen out of the stars. He was amnesiac; truly defenseless, then. Truly hers.

"Don't work anymore," she said. She took the spade from his hand and let it drop on the upturned soil.

Again, she led him back to the house, still not touching him.

In the kitchen, she said to him, "You must try and tell me what food you need to eat. You really must."

He continued to watch her, if he actually saw her at all. She imagined him biting off her arm, and shivered. Perhaps he did not eat—she had considered that before. Not eat, not sleep—the illusion of sleep only a suspended state, induced to please her, or pacify her. She did not think he had used the bathroom. He did not seem to sweat. How odd he should have been able to shed tears.

She dismissed the idea of eating for herself, too. She poured herself another deep swamp of ice and gin. She sat on the porch and he sat beside her.

His eyes looked out across the country. Looking for escape? She could smell the strange sweatless, poreless, yet indefinably masculine scent of him. His extraordinary skin had taken on a watercolor glaze of sunburn.

The day flickered along the varied tops of the reddening horizon. Birds swirled over like a flight of miniature planes. When the first star appeared, she knew she would catch her breath in fear.

The valves of the sky loosened, and blueness poured into it. The Sun had gone. He could not understand her, so she said to him: "I love you."

"I love you," she said. "I'm the last woman on Earth, and you're not even local talent. And I love you. I'm lonely," she said. And, unlike him, she cried quietly.

After a while, just as she would have wished him to if this had been a film and she directing it, he put his arm about her, gently, gently. She lay against him, and he stroked her hair. She thought, with a strange ghostly sorrow: *He has learned such gestures from* me.

Of course, she did not love him, and of course she did. She was the last survivor, and he was also a survivor. Inevitably they must come together, find each other, love. She wished she was younger. She began to feel younger as his arm supported her, and his articulate fingers silked through and through her hair. In a low voice, although he could not understand, she began to tell him about the plague. How it had come, a whisper, the fall of a leaf far away. How it had swept over the world, its continents, its cities, like a sea. A sea of leaves, burning. A fire. They had not called it plague. The official name for it had been "Pandemic." At first, the radios had chattered with it, the glowing pools of the TVs had crackled with it. She had seen hospitals packed like great antiseptic trays with racks of the dying. She had heard how silence came. At length, more than silence came. They burned the dead, or cremated them with burning chemicals. They evacuated the towns. Then "they" too ceased to organize anything. It was a selective disease. It killed men and women and children. It could not destroy the animals, the insects, the birds. Or Jaina.

At first, the first falling of the leaf, she had not believed. It was hard to believe that such an unstoppable engine had been started. The radio and the television set spoke of decaying cylinders in the sea, or satellites that corroded, letting go their cargoes of viruses, mistimed, on the earth. Governments denied responsibility, and died denying it.

Jaina heard the tread of death draw near and nearer. From disbelief, she came to fear. She stocked her hermitage, as she had always done, and crouched in new terror behind her door. As the radio turned dumb, and the TV spluttered and choked to blindness, Jaina stared from her porch, looking for a huge black shadow to descend across the land.

They burned a pile of the dead on a giant bonfire in the field, half a mile from the house. The ashes blew across the sunset. The sky was burning its dead, too.

A day later, Jaina found little fiery mottles over her skin. Her head throbbed, just as the walls were doing. She lay down with her terror, afraid to die. Then she did not care if she died. She wanted to die. Then she did not die at all.

A month later, she drove into the town. She found the emptiness of the evacuation and, two miles away, the marks of another enormous bonfire. And a mile beyond that, dead people lying out in the sun, turning to pillars of salt and white sticks of candy, and the fearless birds, immune, dropping like black rain on the place.

Jaina drove home and became the last woman on Earth.

Her life was not so very different. She had been quite solitary for many years before the plague came.

She had sometimes mused as to why she had lived, but only in the silly, falsely modest way of any survivor. Everyone knew they could not die, hang the rest, they alone must come through. They had all been wrong, all but Jaina.

And then, one night, a snow white star, the silver web of the alien parachute, a young man more beautiful than truth.

She told him everything as she lay against his shoulder. He might still be capable of dying, a Martian, susceptible to the plague virus. Or he might go away.

It was dark now. She lifted her mouth to his in the darkness. As she kissed him, she was unsure what he would do. He did not seem to react in any way. Would he make love to her, or want to, or was he able to? She slid her hands over his skin, like warm smooth stone. She loved him. But perhaps he was only a robot.

After a little while, she drew away, and left him seated on the porch. She went into the kitchen and threw the melted ice in her glass into the sink.

She climbed the stairs; she lay down on the narrow bed. Alone. Alone. But somehow even then, she sensed the irony was incomplete. And when he came into the room, she was not surprised. He leaned over her, silently, and his eyes shone in the darkness, like the eyes of a cat. She attempted to be afraid of him.

"Go away," she said.

But he stretched out beside her, very near, the bed so narrow.... As if he had learned now the etiquette of human lovemaking, reading its symbols from her mind.

"You're a robot, an android," she said. "Leave me alone."

He put his mouth over hers. She closed her eyes and saw a star, a nova. He was not a robot, he was a man, a beautiful man, and she loved him....

Twenty million miles away, the clock chimed eight times. It was one quarter past seven, on the first night of the world.

⑤ ⑤ ⑤

In the morning, she baked bread and brought him some, still warm. He held the bread cupped in his hands like a paralyzed bird. She pointed to herself. "Please. Call me by my name. *Jaina.*"

She was sure she could make him grasp the meaning. She knew he had a voice. She had heard his tears and, during their love-making, heard him groan. She would teach him to eat and drink, too. She would teach him everything.

He tilled the garden; he had found seedlings in the leaning shed and was planting them, until she came to him and led him to the ramshackle Car. She drove him into town, then took him into clothing stores, directing him, diffidently. In accordance with her instructions, he loaded the car. She had never seen him smile. She pondered if she ever would. He carried piled jeans with the same eternally dispassionate disinterest: still the errand boy.

During the afternoon she watched him in the garden. Her pulses raced, and she could think of nothing else but the play of muscles under his swiftly and mellifluously tanning skin. He hypnotized her. She fell asleep and dreamed of him.

She roused at a sound of light blows on metal. Alarmed, she walked out into the last gasps of the day, to find him behind the courtyard, hammering dents out of the battered car. She perceived he had changed a tire she had not bothered with, though it was worn. She relaxed against the wall, brooding on him. He was going to be almost ludicrously useful. For some reason, the archaic word *helpmeet* stole into her mind.

Over it all hung the smoke of premonition. He would be going away. Stranded, marooned, shipwrecked, the great liner would move out of the firmament, cruel as God, to rescue him.

She woke somewhere in the center of the night, her lips against his spine, with a dreadful knowledge.

For a long while she lay immobile, then lifted herself onto one elbow. She stayed that way, looking at him, his feigned sleep, or the real unconsciousness, which appeared to have claimed him. *It seems that you have gone away.* No. He would not be going anywhere.

His hair gleamed, his lashes lay in long brush strokes on his cheeks. He was quiescent, limpid, as if poured from a jar. She touched his flank, coldly.

After a minute, she rose and went to the window, and looked out and upward into the vault of the night sky. A low blaring of hatred and contempt ran through her. *Where are you?* She thought. *Do you see? Are you laughing?*

She walked down the stairs and into the room where the dead TV sat in the dark. She opened a drawer in the bureau and took out a revolver. She loaded it carefully from the clip. She held it pointed before her as she went back up into the bedroom.

He did not wake up—or whatever simulation he contrived that passed for waking—until the hour before the dawn. She had sat there all the time, waiting for him, wanting him to open his eyes and see her, seated facing him, her hand resting on her knee, the revolver in her hand. Pointing now at him.

There was a chance he might not know what the gun was. Yet weapons, like certain semantic signs, would surely be instantly, instinctively recognizable. So she thought. As his eyes opened and fixed on the gun, she believed he knew perfectly well what it was, and that she had brought it there to kill him with.

His eyes grew very wide, but he did not move. He did not appear afraid, yet she considered he must be afraid. As afraid of her as she might have been expected to be of him, and yet had never been: the natural fear of an alien, xenophobia. She thought he could, after all, understand her words, had understood her from the beginning, her language, her loneliness. It would have been part of his instruction. Along with the lessons that had taught him how to work the land, change a tire, make love, pretend to sleep.... About the same time, they must have inoculated him against the deadly plague virus, indeed all the viruses of Earth.

"Yes," she said. "I *am* going to kill you."

He only looked at her. She remembered how he had wept, out of dread of her, loathing, and despair. Because he had known there would be no rescue for him. Neither rescue from her planet nor from herself. He had not fallen from a burning spacecraft into the world. The craft had been whole, and he had been dropped neatly out of it, at a designated hour, at a calculated altitude, his parachute unfolding, a preprogrammed cloud. Not shipwrecked, but dispatched. Air mail. A present.

The great silent ship would not come seeking him. It had already come, and gone.

Why did they care so much? She could not fathom that. An interfering streak—was this the prerogative of gods? Altruistic benefactors, or simply playing with toys? Or it might be an experiment of some sort? They had not been able to prevent the plague, or had not wanted to—recall the Flood, Gomorrah—but when the plague had drawn away down its tidal drain, washing humanity with it, they had looked and seen Jaina wandering alone on the Earth, mistress of it, the last of her kind. So they had made for her a helpmate and companion. Presumably not made him in *their* extraterrestrial image, whoever, whatever they omnipotently were, but in the image of a man.

She was uncertain what had triggered her final deduction. His acquiescence, the unlikely aptness of it all, the foolish coincidence of survivor flung down beside survivor, pat. Or was it the theatricality that had itself suggested puppet masters to her subconscious: the last man and the last woman left to propagate continuance of a species? Or was it only her mistrust? All the wrongs she had, or imagined she had, suffered, clamoring that this was no different from any other time. Someone still manipulated, still *imposed* on her.

"Well," she said softly, looking at him, it appeared to her, through the eye of the gun, "I seem to be missing a rib. Do I call you Adam? Or would it be *Eve?*" She clicked off the safety catch. She trembled violently, though her voice was steady. "What about contraception, Adameve? Did they think I'd never heard of it, or used it? Did they think I'd risk having babies, with no hospitals, not even a vet in sight? At thirty-five years of age? When I dressed up for you, I dressed thoroughly, *all* of me. Just in case. Seems I was wise. I don't think even your specially designed seed is so potent it can negate my precautions. In the tank where they grew you, or the machine shop where they built you, did they think of *that?* I don't want you," she whispered. "You cried like a child because they condemned you to live on my world, with me. Do you think I can forgive you that? Do you think I want you after that, now I *know?*"

She raised the gun and fired. She watched the sun go out in the windows of his eyes. His blood was red, quite normal.

Jaina walked across the burn scar of the field. She pictured a huge wheel hanging over her, beyond and above the sky, pictured it no longer watching, already drawing inexorably away and away. She dragged the spade along the ground, as she had dragged his body. Now the spade had turned potatoes, and beans, and alien flesh.

She stood in the kitchen of the old house, and the darkness like space came and colored the sky through. Jaina held her breath, held it and held it, as if the air had filled with water, closing over her head. For she knew. Long before it happened, she knew. She only let out her breath in a slow sigh, horribly flattered, as the second snow white star fell out of the summer night.

Tonight I Can Sleep Quietly

In the gabled city that lies behind the spaceport of Cuze, I found her again, just as I had known I would.

My feelings were very strange that day, that lengthy green Cuzian day. But I had expected nothing else. It had been a very long time, laughably so, since we were together, she and I. And yet, what we had shared before was of such a strength and integrity, I had now hardly any doubts. In fact, such doubts as I did have did not concern whether or not we would meet—the slight but certain information I had received told me our meeting was more than probable. Nor was it particularly that I feared we should not recognize each other after so great a gap of time, and all those events and those changes which had filled it. I, at least—I was sure—I would know *her*. And my faith in her remained vital enough, it seemed to me she would know me, too, if not instantly, then soon…. My doubts, then, were only to do with the wisdom of seeking her in this way. For I had come here expressly to do so. Everything was altered. I understood as much. I expected nothing of her now God knew, she had given me, before, more than anyone has any right to expect of another, her absolute love, her utter kindness. Even, ultimately, she was prepared to give her life. I was aware I would ask nothing of her today. Yet, I was driven to find her, I can say, by no force larger than myself, merely by some mighty force inside me, that part of me which could never forget.

During the long space-night of flying, the mundane business of the ship's day concluded, I had lain in my cabin, seldom able to sleep, and said over to myself her name. And said it possessively, as if in that far off completion we had shared. My Lyselle, my most dear, my most beautiful, my love.

It was my litany, a very private one. And it was the past, and I knew it was the past. That it was over.... But I carried her portrait, too, in the little oval of silver. It had the power to comfort me.

I dressed in the morning in clothes that held echoes of that earlier time. They were to be a signal for recognition. Naturally, the cut of everything was much altered to fit current needs and trends. In such days as these, out in the wide meadows of the galaxies, almost anything is acceptable, but there are still limits. I am no longer the thin young man I was, and though my hair still hangs on my shoulders, it has changed color with the years. Only one item was exactly as it had been, an indulgence, if a legitimate one. The single gold ring hung in my ear as it had long ago, the ring with the fleck of garnet set in. I had lost that ring, but found it again quite recently, and bought it back. Curious. I often wondered what adventures it had had away from me, before chance brought us together once more.

I spent the first hours walking along the avenues among the canals, the region my information had secured for me. The pale green sky, no darker than some young leaf of Earth, was flocked with paler clouds. The sun rayed brightly through into the green crystalline liquid of the canals, so pure the undersides of ships shone brilliantly as fish, and deeper still, things that had, centuries since, been cast in there—old urns, a broken statue—glowed up through twenty feet of water clear as the day. Cuzian willows of great height rose from the canal-sides and poured back to them. The old stone houses stood behind, where now many races live, even the exiles of Earth. Somewhere here she, too, had made her home.

Then, the first hours were gone. I had only this one day and suddenly an anguish fastened on me. Could it be that after all we should not meet? In fact I knew so little—the planet and the area of her domicile. Her occupation. Her age I knew. And somehow it seemed I knew also things I had not been told—of a pet cat that walked on leash; of a child, not mine, born in the intervening years. And the color her hair would be, having altered. But her new name I did not know, the new name of this new life of hers, where maybe I had no right or justification, even for an instant, to intrude.

So, relaxing into dreariness, I entered a baroque café that dropped in terraces to the water. Possibly five minutes, I sat there, thinking my blank sad thoughts, reproaching myself, seeing the reflection of my face—so changed, and yet, not so changed after all—in a glass of transparent wine. Then I looked up and saw—her.

She had come in, walked by me, and now seated herself across a distance of a few feet. Her companion was with her, a lovely woman with long fiery hair. And the cat, smoke-colored, on a leash, sat like a dog on a third chair. Telepathy, then, had been in operation. More. She did not look about, my Lyselle (no longer mine, though always mine), yet she had come here, intuitively seeking *me*, it seemed, as I had sought her.

Her hair was black and curling. I had known that would be how she wore it now. As if it were some game we had arranged to play, long, long ago.

I stood up. I went over. An excuse was there to hand, easy and acceptable. Here on Cuze, the children of Earth might be expected to turn to each other. My credentials were perfect, for I could bring them news of the homeworld.

I spoke to her companion first, in politeness. And yet I sensed here, too, immediately, a renewed greeting rather than that of some friendly alien. This auburn girl and I—there was a warm rapport, as if we had been comrades formerly.

She welcomed me graciously, and I knew at once she would place no barrier between me and my goal, not feel from me any threat. For I was no threat to her. Could be no threat. In this fresh found knowledge my courage finally lay down and rested. One does not attempt to destroy the happiness and security of the person one has loved best. I, so selfish in almost all my dealings, was astonished and reassured by the sound unshakable truth of this.

Then, as I looked at *her* at last, I saw she knew me. Her eyes, which were changed, and yet which were the same, had startled into surprise. I should proceed carefully now. We had parted in trouble and misery, and in terror. Were these the memories that would flood back to her? Her pain, it occurred to me, I could not bear. If this were to happen I must go away instantly. But it seemed the memory was not unpleasant. Perhaps there was no memory as coherent as this sheer recognition of me that so startled her. She was not even uncomfortable; she too was welcoming.

It was the most natural thing in all the worlds to sit down with her and her companion, and the charming cat, to drink wine together and begin to talk earnestly of ordinary things, which had nothing to do with some inner conversation, which also then began, unheard.

When was I so happy? Well, I have been happy sometimes. But this had its own fundamental joy. The afternoon went by, dreamlike, as we strolled, feeding the water-birds, letting the cat roam free in the hanging-gardens of the parks, to mount at length and to sit imperious on the head of a white stone nymph. Fearlessly talking. No abrasion. The girl with red hair augmented, ornamented, but did not impede our dialogues. It was plain to me we were all—mentally, spiritually—known to each other in some way. And I believe she quite understood, our redhead, without any embarrassing revelation on my part. She understood and was ineffably gentle. Even, she awarded us certain spaces together alone, Lyselle and I—going off to cajole the cat on the nymph-pillar, to buy flowers from a float-ing barge—such spaces were necessary, perhaps. Never brief enough to be furtive, nor long enough to allow the seals of my private confessional to give way. And I was grateful also for that. Some things cannot be said. Or, if said, lose all their inner power in the strengthlessness of the words.

I dined that night with the two of them, high up on the roof of the elegant old house, the sunset flowing slowly, in pulses of oceanic gold, across the drowned vistas of Cuze on every side. There was an easel set up on the parapet among the tall pots of flowers, a painting half-born, very spare and fine, Ly-selle's work, that occupation I had been told of. Her talent delighted me. I looked very long at the painting, as I did at everything. I knew I should only see her once, this past love of mine, and those things of hers and of her life, which was so apt and serene, they must be gathered up, and fixed into my recollection like small jewels. But how could I forget? I never had forgotten her, the way she had been. Blonde as I was now, where I had been dark as now was she. A fragile doll of a girl, my Lyselle, with such steel within, such bravery.

When I had waited those last days in prison, time after time she had come to me, her slim little hands on the bars under mine, and her skin, warm where mine was ice, giving up her vitality to me. She had told me then, if I must die, she would find a way to come after me. I had begged her to live. Yet it consoled me. I had a terror of loneliness, then.

There was one moment, somewhere in the cool streets that took me back toward the port, one moment only when my heart shuddered. I wept as I walked, but not the tears of any wounding, and not even of regret. I had sobbed like a child for her, before. This was only a libation to that god of part-ings. Perhaps *my* grief for the first, where before it had been his, tumultuous and dreadful, with no promise of an end. *His* grief, that man I had been a hundred years before my birth.

There is a look in my face, my woman's face, that sometimes I see, a look of him, the thin young man who was freed the hard way, dying with thirty bullets in him from the executioners' guns. Just as, in the little portrait of Lyselle, whom he loved so much, there is a look—about the eyes, behind the forehead—of the tall, dark man Lyselle, in this life has become. No longer Lyselle, no longer mine. But happy and at peace. Loving and loved. They hanged her then, a trumped-up charge that she, mourning, abetted. My fault—no, *his* fault. My poetic friend, my former foolish self. Or so he thought. He has carried that grief like a cross, and so I have also carried it. But no more.

She is alive, my friend, and living in Cuze five galaxies away. She is alive, and will live forever, as indeed so shall we all.

Tonight I can sleep quietly.

Stalking the Leopard

From a Future-Urban Myth by John Kaiine

Avly leaned her slim white arms on the balustrade, her ruby bracelets dripping along the stone. She was young, beautiful, and rich, and lived in one of the most picturesque cities of northern climes, Dophan, beneath the great, man-made rainbow known as The Arch.

Still lit up after dark, its seven burning colors glowed across the dusk sky. More subtly, its rays painted the parks, tree-hung boulevards, and mansions below, including Avly's balcony, her pale skin, and fashionably short black hair.

How bored she was, this elegant young woman.

Nothing engaged her interest. Avly had known only attractive and glamorously stimulating things all her twenty years. By now, even the rainbow itself, at which tourists would stand gaping, both on the ground and in the jeweled flying vehicles, had become, for her, samey.

One of these vehicles, however, now dipped toward the balcony. She saw, with slight affront, it was the private car of her most recent ex-lover. They had parted amiably, and at Avly's wish—perhaps for that very reason she did not want to ride with him to this evening's party.

"Avly! Glimmering creature. Do get in, we're late."

Avly got into the car and sank back on the cushioned seat. A glass of champagnist alighted in her hand. She sipped and glanced sidelong at her handsome ex, who wore a silk cloak.

Whatever had she seen in him? But oh, what had she seen, ever, in *any* of her several lovers?

The driverless car whirled them through the sky, under The Arch, deftly and automatically avoiding other similar traffic, most of it intent on pleasure.

They landed on the roof of a brightly lamped mansion. Massive trees grew from stems of water set into concrete. Polished diamonds winked in tiles. Fortunately another woman came at once and claimed Avly's cast-off. Now Avly stood again, bored and lethargic, at one more balustrade, staring across into the shining apartments over the way, where similar parties raged. Was there anything interesting *there?* No. Everything might as well be a mirror. Including this roof-garden.

"Oh look! Look at that—down in the Violet Quarter!"

The quarters of the city were named for the colors of The Arch, but Violet, like Indigo and Orange, was one of the poorer, shabbier areas.

Party-goers poured in a tide across the garden, and Avly went indifferently after them, not expecting to see very much. However, from the north side of the roof, she and everyone else soon stared exclaiming at a distant but colossal column of smoke and fire.

"Several of the old houses on Velvet Street must be burning."

"Let's go and see."

Accidents and disasters were rare in Dophan. The last vehicular crash had happened before Avly was born, the last fire when she was ten—and she had been interested then. But now this ghoulishness irritated her, and she wanted to decline the offer of the two nearest guests, who were already guiding her into the flow of persons hurrying back towards the vehicle-park.

"Avly, come *on*. What a spectacle it must be—you can't *miss* it—and the horror—perhaps there are several dead!"

Ennui, distaste even, strangely decided Avly on non-resistance. She allowed them to pull her into the car, and moments later they were zooming north across the city. From many buildings around, countless others did the same.

What would she feel? Alarm, sympathy, fear... Would she feel *anything*? People, as a rule, no longer seemed quite real to Avly—that is, when she thought of them in any depth.

The fire, though, was impressive. It towered into, and presently dominated, the sky. Black and purple smoke, sequined by embers and sparks, plumed two blocks of flaming masonry. Even as the car settled on an adjacent landing-pad, one of the houses collapsed with a roar, and a mixed swarm of darks and lights shot upward.

Sightseers piled out of their transports, carrying Avly with them, helpless and contemptuous. Shouting and laughing, the crowd struggled to approach as close as possible to the safety barriers already erected in the street. No firefighters or medical vehicles seemed in evidence. Only a street marshal stood by with some twenty of his men. They were there simply to maintain order.

Another house collapsed.

"They don't bother with them now, you know," someone said. "These poorer streets can't afford any insurance."

Avly found herself pressed to the high, transparent, fire-resistant barrier. No smoke stung her eyes or ash stained her frock. Like everyone else, she gazed fixedly into the heart of the fire.

Was it only beautiful? Or only terrible?

Had anyone survived?

Startling her, at that very moment Avly saw a tall figure emerge from the crimson hell.

She was astounded. He was dressed darkly, and his long, fashionable cloak flared away from him like a single black wing. His hair was also long and black. From this distance, through the slight distortion of the barrier and the unfelt ripples of heat, she could not make out his features, save for a dark bar of brows, eyes—

He strode from the conflagration—*untouched*. How was that credible? All around him, the cascading flames—sparks swirling through his hair, the wild wing of the cloak brushing against a crumbling mass of brickwork and fire. Was he wearing some extreme protective clothing? He did not look like either a firefighter or a medic. Down the charred tumble of the steps he walked, with unlikely ease, into the street.

Without a backward glance, he strode away.

"That man," said Avly.

The woman beside her remarked, "Yes, I thought I saw somebody too—a survivor, perhaps. I couldn't be sure. Where is he now?"

Avly stared. She could no longer see the man who had walked out of the fire. He must have entered the crowd, been lost there among the many other young, tall men with long hair and cloaks.

The woman said to Avly, "An optical illusion, actually, I now think. Have you ever seen a fire before? Illusions can happen. I wasn't sure, myself, if I really saw anyone."

Avly was sure that she herself had.

Just then, the last buildings gave way together. A golden bombshell of curdled fire hit the sky, then the black dust started drifting, even finally across the tops of the barriers. Careful of its garments, the crowd began to disperse.

During the night Avly had a recurring dream. It was of the man who had stridden out of the fire. In the dream she had detached herself from the crowd and now walked after him, taking some care not to be seen, and so keeping to the shadows beyond the streetlamps. Always he stalked some eleven or twelve meters ahead of her. Following, pursuing him with stealth and tenacity, Avly experienced a continual frisson of—excitement.

Never, since earliest childhood, had she felt such a thing. She had, probably, forgotten until now, what excitement *did* feel like. Besides, there was another element, beyond anything childish. It was, she realized on waking, both romantic and sexual.

What was happening? Really she did not mind what it was. It had been—quite amazing. Was it still? Yes. She tried, accordingly, to return into sleep in order to undergo the pursuit, and the emotion it entailed. But now sleep eluded her.

She spent all day, as usual, in the most unimportant, superficial activities. Lying down at midnight, which was very early for her, she waited, tingling at the chance of dreams. But that night, she dreamed of nothing. Nothing at all.

Avly was in a store that was hung with crystals, strolling about with two acquaintances. A fountain played unwetly over all. Avly was *not* bored.

The moment she had left her apartment, she had begun to look out for him, the man from the fire. It was ridiculous; really made her inwardly laugh—something too that recently had seldom occurred. How could she ever hope to locate one man, unnamed, unknown, amid the teeming sprawl of Dophan? All she could assume was that he was fully rich, even though he had stepped from the fire in rundown Velvet Street. His clothes, his hair, his *demeanor* had conveyed complete assurance and security—therefore wealth. Avly had not lived among them for twenty years without coming to recognize her own clan. Although, if anything, the stranger was more princely than any man of Avly's class she had met, more arrogant.

A doll of the store, in the form of a tawny lion-beast, trotted over and presented the tray of perfumes, wines, and stimulants resting on its back.

Each woman plucked something up. The air filled with scent and bubbles.

But Avly's eyes slid to the edges of all the rooms, trying to find the man. After the three women had been right through the ten storeys of the store, and she had looked everywhere in it— "But, Avly, whatever are you *looking* for?"—unanswered—she was eager to go back outside. Once there, she quickly sloughed her companions and began to patrol the boulevards alone. It was mid-afternoon, the sunlight brilliant and The Arch rainbowing down the most succulent mixed tones of color on pavements and burnished trees. Avly looked everywhere but pavements, trees, and sky.

Nevertheless she did not see the man at all. Not even anyone who resembled him. It had been, perhaps, foolish to suppose that he would simply arrive in her vicinity. No, she must take the initiative and mount a proper search.

What did she have to go on? Frankly, only one thing. Which was that, since he was rich, he must live either in the Yellow, Green, or Blue Quarters to the west of the city. Maybe he *had* been sightseeing in Violet on the night of the fire.

If only she knew something else about him, or better still, possessed something personal of his—for those who could pay, a DNA register was available. But she lacked either kind of clue.

A minute's intense disappointment flooded Avly. This in turn interested her, however. Was she—was she "In Love"? But she had been in love with many men, a few women too. It had never felt like this—this desperate electric *hunger*—this excitement and anxiety.

Avly summoned one of the individual public air-cars. As it swooped towards her, a silvery shiver ran up her spine. She swiftly got into the car and ordered it to fly her to the Green Quarter.

Between the glamorous greenstone mansions, Avly wended her way and never saw her quarry. Here and there, in beglittered bars and stores, she paused to make conversation with groups of her peers. Into each brief chat she inserted leading questions. She had heard, she said, from one of her friends, that an eccentric man from this quarter liked to play the tourist in the rundown areas of the city. But everyone she spoke to looked at her in bewilderment. They had heard of nobody like that. What, anyway, would be the point of visiting such slums? "Oh, during the fire in Violet," supplied Avly vaguely. "My friend thought she saw him there."

"But," they replied, slightly thrown, "almost all of us *were*. After all, that *fire* was something worth seeing. Did you know," they added, "there were nineteen dead?"

As evening fell, Avly caught another individual public flyer. She rode south again, over into Yellow.

She was growing tired, not exactly physically, but in a slow internal way. She was thinking now she would never find him, and so she believed she *must*. For yes, she *was* in love. And love gave her the *right* to find him. Even so, hers was a difficult task, almost like those set lovers in ancient legends and stories...

The car alighted by one of the great parks of Yellow. Avly walked along dusk avenues between lemon-trees, across lawns bordered by giant primroses and saffrons.

A scatter of other pedestrians passed her. Now she asked no one anything. None of them was him.

Leaving the park at a wide gateway, Avly took a road lined by mansions of cream stucco. Already the delicate streetlamps were burning up on their stems, and windows warmed. All this seemed abruptly sad to Avly. Her eyes filled with tears, and deep, deep within herself she felt a fiery joy at her new-minted depression.

Then—*then*—she saw him.

She froze to marble, there beneath a lamp-standard, its illumination full upon her.

He was on the same side of the paved sidewalk, approaching her, the long cloak swinging as he strode. She saw his face properly because, one after another, the street lamps described it. It was a patrician, pale, terrible face—terrible in its flawless ordinariness. Was he handsome? Ugly? Avly could not be sure. His eyebrows were black, the eyes too seemed black. His hair and clothes were black also—as she recalled from the last time. He was gloved.

While he approached swiftly nearer and nearer, Avly shrank away as if from too fierce a glare of light. But he—he glanced once at her, just as he reached her. Glanced once, and then away, striding on along the street.

Avly shriveled from the seemingly amused contempt of this one brief look and reveled peculiarly in the comfortless thrill. There had, besides, been more to his glance, she thought. For such disdain seemed to come from foreknowledge. As if he *knew* her and so could discount her entirely. And of course he did not and could not know her. Thus it was for her to change his mind. It seemed to her, weirdly stranded, moth-like, under the lamp, that his very dismissal had been an *invitation*. So, it said, make me aware of you, make me take an interest in you. Show me something I have never seen in any other, for I too am bored here.

Avly drew in a breath. She crept silently back from the lamps and in among the trees of the street. Once concealed in their shadows, she followed the man.

Unlike her dreams, however, there was no need to go far. In less than three more minutes, he turned and mounted a long flight of steps. Above, a door opened for him, and he passed into the house.

Shattered by her success, Avly leant back against a tree. This then, most probably, was where he lived, his apartment.

She gazed up the length of the building. Amid the carvings and cornices, all the windows beamed with light. Which were his? The house was too high for her to be sure if the faint occasional traces of movement she saw cross the windows were, any of them, his. After a space of time, she went up the steps herself and keyed the panel by the door for the names of those who resided there. Having mechanically glimpsed her status in the city, the panel gave them up to her. But of course, of all the twenty-seven people living, in couples, trios, or singly in the mansion, only ten of them male, none had a name she knew or could know to be his.

Impatient, curbing urgency, Avly withdrew to the watch-post of her tree.

The night was young as she herself, so inevitably in party-prone Dophan, he would next come out again—either that or he would be sponsoring some festivity of his own in the house. Might she, if enough persons attended this, add herself independently to the guest-list?

At the idea her head spun. Laughter welled in her mind and throat. *I am happy!* How bizarre.

But, too, how wonderful the street, the lamps, the stars far above beyond the rainbow. *His* street, lamps, stars. That she had located him so quickly was certainly destiny.

An hour went by. Avly took off her high-heeled shoes and stood barefoot. Then she sat down under the tree, as sluts and waifs did in the rough quarters of Dophan. Avly did not care.

Another hour. Avly started awake—she had not meant to doze—had she *missed* him? No, impossible. Some invisible galvanic thread, which joined them, would have tugged at her if he had reappeared. What then had woken her so suddenly?

Avly jumped to her feet and put on her shoes. She stood by the tree watching, in a kind of indifferent dismay, as a medical vehicle, siren mooing, dropped from the sky to the sidewalk.

Savage white radiance exploded from its interior as two medics and a medical doll shaped like a trolley with ramps leaped out and plunged up the steps of the very house where he lived. Only then did Avly grow rigid with fright. Had something happened to *him?*

Above, far up the facade of the mansion, one window filled with chaotic activity. In the vehicle itself machines chattered, and Avly heard a flat mechanical voice: "Seven people, you say? All the same? Poisoning? How rare. Yes, from the roof will be best."

Then the vehicle lifted up and sailed to the landing-pad on the house-top, presumably to ferry casualties via the roof elevator.

Avly's heart pounded. She decided she must herself run into the building.

Before she could stir a muscle, the front door reopened. And it was the man who came out.

He moved down the steps exactly as she had seen him do at the site of the fire. He was calm and self-contained. Gaining the pavement, he looked neither left nor right but turned south along the boulevard.

Avly found she could not, after all, quite make herself follow him. She stared after his tall, spare figure, the swagger, the gloved hands. Realization had reached her. He did not live in this house at all. As the medical vehicle, siren loud and warning beacons flashing, rose from the roof with its—dying?—cargo, Avly put her hands and forehead against the trunk of the tree. She understood at last. The fire, and now—poison. Her lover was an assassin.

How many drooping days went by, Avly knew precisely. She marked them on a calendar. There were seven. Perhaps, in some remote manner, she was observing an unconscious vigil for the seven poisoned dead from the Yellow Quarter.

She had read about them, too, in the journals, for to die in this way was, as the voice of the vehicle had remarked, *rare*. It seemed the cause had been contained in some vintage alcohol they had drunk. Investigations were in progress.

Did Avly consider reporting to the city authorities what she suspected, or rather, was sure of? That this was no vintner's blunder, or domestic accident, just as the fire had not been, and that *he* was responsible for all the deaths? Momentarily she did. Then she saw she could not betray him. She was, for one thing, certain he would then reason exactly who had witnessed him and find her before officers of the law apprehended him. On the other hand, the notion of such a nightmare event brought her only one more perversely violent thrill. Common sense, meanwhile, instructed Avly that such a dangerous man's retributive anger should be avoided at all costs.

She could not stop thinking of him. Or dreaming of him.

Every night of the seven days, she pursued him through a surreal Dophan which, in sleep, had become deserted and vegetal and jet-black, with narrow shimmering defiles, where he sprang forward, cat-like, and she slunk after, trembling with nerves and desire. She never caught up to him in the dreams. He never turned and looked at her. Yet at those times she knew he was aware of her, and that she had a right never to give up. However, something else then occurred.

Information came to Avly, in a dream, of the assassin's forthcoming whereabouts. This was on the seventh night, and the message—for such it must be—was entirely clear. Slinking after her lethal prey through the jungle of the dream-city, Avly beheld a tall tower that loomed out of the darkness. It had a glacial azure globe on its roof, and Avly knew it in a dream-second as the Communications Building in Blue. Across the sky above it were littered two sparkling numerals: 9 and 35.

When she woke on the eighth morning, Avly deduced that this had been relayed directly to her, by means of telepathy. Evidently he would be in the vicinity of the tower tonight—tonight, of course, since he was a nocturnal being. The hour was nine o'clock.

The other number—thirty-five—almost paralyzed her with a sense of shock and dread that sank through her bones like syrupy spice. The *other* number, presumably, related to the tally of victims he expected to kill, by or near the tower.

Avly did not entertain a moment's doubt about this psychic signal from his brain to hers. But she did suspect he might not be aware that he had contacted her. Her acute interest in him had tuned her in, perhaps, to the frequency of his mind, which must after all blaze like a torch with its skills and crimes. Fate had taken a hand and sent her these facts, for her use.

All day she lay about the apartment, not answering calls, not doing anything save brood and rehearse her now almost mystic role.

I believe I am quite mad, she finally told herself.

This seemed to liberate her entirely. She got up and went to make herself exceedingly beautiful for the coming night's adventure.

As Avly, dripping with rubies and scarlet, moved on foot through the city, experiencing all things in a sort of new wonder, Dophan blossomed to neon night.

At last, in the Green Quarter, she caught an individual public flyer. It bore her north, into Blue. An oddly magical ride.

Even the stars had a light navy color this evening, outside the iridescence of The Arch.

On foot once more, music floated to her from bars, with the crystalline chink, like breaking thermometers, of goblets and bottles knocked together. Avly's sober blood itself seemed aerated with the spangles of champagnist or vodsinthe.

The crowds parted, smiling benignly, to let her through. She seemed to be the heroine of the drama, they obliging bit-players.

How many would die? Thirty-five. A momentous figure. This would be a catastrophe. Was he paid to do this work, or was it only an act...of love?

A vibration from some time-piece flittered out the essence of a quarter to nine, one minute after Avly had positioned herself in a wide plaza beneath the tower of the Communications Building. She stood looking up the tower's tiered storeys. The windows were long and narrow, and it was sculpted from deep blue concrete, the globe from white sapphire.

Someone paused beside her. Avly knew it was not the one she had come here for, but still she half-turned, made nosy at this ultimate juncture by her fellow humans.

A blond young man stood close by, talking into a jeweled cell-phone the size and shape of a beetle, and set in a ring.

"Naturally I know the tale. I read a screening of it only yesterday."

Avly's attention left him. Would he be one of those who would die?

"Yes, and she made this gesture that frightened him. So he ran to his employer," droned on the young man, annoyingly, "and asked permission to escape to Bokhara."

What a pretty name, Avly inconsequently thought: Bokhara. Her knowledge of geography was limited.

"But when the employer confronted *her*, she just denied everything. What? Oh, yes, I forgot. And that's how it ends."

Avly's eyes opened wide, gleaming like the edges of sharp knives. Across the square, she had seen him.

Seen *him*.

He was like a piece fallen out of the dark. His hair, his cloak and clothes. She watched him as intently as if she were a surveillance machine. And so she saw him cross the plaza, and as he passed, his arm, the cloak, brushed over someone, only as if, courteously, he ushered this other out of his way—but the man tottered, choking, and all at once crashed down.

Avly caught her breath. He must be a genius at his art. Only that brushing of the arm and cloak, only that. Yet too, she was confused. She had anticipated a major disaster being caused, to account for the deaths of as many as thirty-five people. A bomb, perhaps. But no one else even collapsed, and the plaza was merely full of sightseers pressing forward to watch the fascinating spectacle of someone else dying on the paving.

The assassin though had moved northward, away. Already his form dwindled in distance. Avly hurried from the square. Despite her gilded shoes, she ran. She did not mean to lose him now.

He walked, and so therefore did she. It became like her dreams too, when they left the Blue Quarter after some twenty minutes and moved diagonally on into Violet. Here there were fewer and dimmer lights. The shells of unoccupied buildings stood like cliffs, open only on caves of blackness. Most of the streetlamps, even where they remained standing, were unlit. As for the rainbow Arch, this part of it seemed to have gone out, or to be obscured from below. It was only a colorless high

ghostly bridge, arcing above, that, miles off, grew luminescent
again astride other places. Weeds rioted from cracked pavement and walls, into enormous forests. So all her dreams, then,
had been prescient. Did he not know she paced behind him?
They had walked by then, he some eleven or twelve meters
ahead, for over an hour. He never looked about at her, she never looked away from him. And if any lived in the surrounding
houses, yards, and streets, tonight they had hidden. Unless it
was only that, now, Avly had eyes for no other but one.

They had reached a landing-station for public flyers. In the
slums of Violet, Indigo, and Orange, these vehicles were never
individualized, but served as many as a hundred people at a
time. The landing-station was crowded, so much so that, even
if Avly had until now been blind to everyone else, she could
not choose but see them here.

The poor had serious faces, or so she thought. Serious and
hard, or, if any mirth broke out among them, it seemed raw
and barbarous, and definitely too loud. Their garments had no
attractiveness, in her opinion. She felt faintly sorry for them.

If he had come here to kill some of these persons, probably
he did them a favor, as he had previously with the fire. The
sole puzzle was why any of them required killing. They had
no power, no influence or money, and died quickly enough
anyway.

But everything he did intrigued her and appeared intel-
lectually viable, if obscure. Any scruple about his work she
had evaporated in the ecstasy of seeing him where she had
believed she would, of following him along the lonely, jungled
streets of Violet. She cared only for him. Tonight they must
meet, must talk. Perhaps do more than talk.

He and she. Destiny combined them. Avly knew this as
absolutely as she knew her own exquisite image in a mirror.
He might play at cat-and-mouse with her, but in the end, why
should he not succumb? She had everything he must want.

Out of the black sky—even stars did not show above these quarters—the dull-lighted, heavy-hulled flyer approached.

It landed gracelessly on the pad, and the crowd milled forwards, thrusting itself into the interior, in and in, without any caution. Surely it was overloaded, and more than a hundred men and women were now inside the car?

All this while of waiting at the station, Avly had kept sight of him although he roved through the crowd. This time he caused no disturbance, nor had anyone expired. She assumed his current murder plot involved the flyer and he would carry it out when everyone was assembled. Compunction warned her not to stand too close. She was about to retreat a little, when *he too* stepped into the vehicle.

Avly knew one split second of reluctance. Then she burst forward and drew herself after him, and all the rest, into the hot and jumbled body of the car.

There was nowhere left by now, naturally, to sit. But he also was standing, against the rail provided for patrons who had no seat.

Some ten or so people had already wedged themselves between him and Avly.

The muddy lights of the flyer dulled further, as it lifted, not very smoothly, back into the sky.

It was apparently bound for the Indigo Quarter, and then for Orange, or so the illuminated strip across the roof promised. But then, it did not matter where they went, it only mattered where *he* might go.

What was he doing on this cumbersome thing? He seemed to have no concern about anyone aboard and stood like most of the rest who must do so, his face a blank.

None of the flying cars, even these out in the slums, had drivers; they were operated by their own intricate mechanical intestines. This one lumbered through the air, and Avly frowned as slight turbulence seemed to hit the vehicle. None of the other passengers, needless to say, paid any attention, used to such inferior transport.

Was he simply traveling, as the others were, to another area of Dophan? Yet he was rich. Why would he need to employ an unaesthetic public car—not to mention the sort of resentful squintings some had cast at Avly, boarding in her finery? No one seemed to react to him, however. Maybe he often came this way. Besides, now she studied him, although he was not dressed in the un-fashions of the poor, nor did he wear the gemmed attire of the wealthy classes. Perhaps this was the most clever form of disguise.

His face drew her eyes again and again. She found it difficult to gaze at him for very long. Her vision blurred, her heart raced, waves of heat and cold chased up and down her body. Seldom—never—had she been so exhilarated or so *terrified*. She had begun to speak a mantra to him in her mind, enticing him, persuading him, *making love* to him. If nothing came of this partial meeting, Avly felt she would not be able to bear it. She would fall into some despairing abyss. His darkness lit the gloomy car for her like a smoky sun.

They landed—bumpily—five times in the purlieus of Indigo, and much of the crowd streamed away. They were like ants, Avly thought, watching them mill down the ramps from the landing-stations, off into the dreary channels of their quarter.

But eventually, after the fifth stop, only some thirty or so people remained on the flyer. Thirty-five? The fatal number? What now would he do?

Before Avly could collect herself, he had left the rail, and as the flyer once more dragged itself skywards, he sat down on one of the long, otherwise empty seats.

From there he looked back, directly at her.

Avly felt her physical body drop through itself on to the floor, while heart and soul rushed upward.

His face was no longer blank. His eyes, very obviously, saw her. He nodded. As if this were their arrangement, and they had both come here deliberately to meet.

Avly, in a half trance, also left the rail. His gaze stayed on her as, shaken about and clinging to handholds, she made her precarious way to the seat. She sat down beside him.

"Where are you going?" she asked him, when he did not say a word.

Still he looked at her, taking in everything about her, she believed, noting her appearance, her jewels, how she had dressed and scented herself to appeal to him.

Then he said quietly, for her ears alone, "Where do you think."

His voice too was dark. It was musical and rhythmic.

It made her reckless. Breathlessly she said, "With me?"

"Ah." The pause hung like a scorching wire in the air between them. He added, softly, "Or is it that you are coming with *me?*"

Rather than being forced now by her emotions to turn away from him, Avly could not take her eyes from his. They were black, his eyes, a silvered black, deep to depthlessness, yet inaccessible. She longed to fall into them and drown, but as yet they would not let her.

The flyer gave a lurch and began again to descend. Below, only half seen on the rim of sight, lightless Orange swelled to meet it.

"This is the last southbound stop," he said.

The car barged home on its landing-pad. Avly expected him to rise, as the other passengers were doing. He ignored them and the opened doors. Presently the car was empty but for he and she, and the doors closed.

"But," she said, "don't you have to follow them?"

"Why should I?" His wonderful voice hypnotized her, as his eyes had done.

"But they—they were the thirty-five, surely, the ones you intend to destroy—"

She did not care she had revealed her knowledge. And he—he laughed.

His laugh. She stared, enraptured and transfixed. It was like the most astounding symphony, distilled to a single cadence. The laughter ended. He said, quite gently, "You have applied the idea of thirty-five wrongly. Thirty-five is the number of the *last* one to die in Dophan, tonight. You see, thirty-four are already dead."

Something cool and static was in Avly's mind and changed everything in her, excitement, hope, lust—bone, sinew, blood—to a fluid silence.

She looked away from him as if it had always been easy.

The flyer, returning now to its shed in Indigo, was rising once again, more steadily than before. It chugged over the unlit buildings, and far beyond and behind Avly noticed, indifferently, the bright towers and mansions of the better quarters, bangled with their lamps.

"And I," she whispered, "am to be the thirty-fifth person. I'm the last one who will die tonight." Then she gazed back at him. He too seemed further off, but curiously, also near. She knew him, after all. Perhaps she had done so from the first. Doubtless anyone would.

Nevertheless she asked, "Who are you?"

"Death," he responded.

The next moment the failing flyer, its systems most unusually, but not quite impossibly, breaking down, plummeted from the sky to smash a vast crater in the wilderness of weeds and ruins at the edge of the Orange Quarter.

No one resided immediately in the neighborhood, either to be fatally struck by the car, or to witness the solitary passenger who left the wreckage and strode away without a backward glance. He was a tall man with long dark hair, and a cloak as black as the grave.

The Ancient Myth

A servant ran to his master, a merchant, in great fear, saying that he had met Death in the marketplace, and she had made a threatening gesture at him. The servant begged the merchant to let him fly at once to Bokhara, many miles away. The merchant agreed, and the servant speedily rode off. Later that same day the merchant himself happened to see Death in the city. He drew her aside and asked why she had frightened his servant with a gesture of threat. "No, he mistook me," said Death. "The gesture I made was in fact one of surprise at seeing him here—for tonight I have an appointment with him, in Bokhara."

The Thousand Nights and a Night

Dead Yellow

This was my wedding dress. At the time people remarked on my choice of color, but with my hair the way I had it then, it worked. I remember there were daffodils blooming. But I won't show you the photographs. No point now, is there?

When did it start? Officially in 2036. But the papers had been reporting curious anomalies for years before that. And people spotting things. Thinking at first the fault was in them and getting frightened—so many medical case-notes.

And I? Oh, I think I first properly *noticed* that day when we walked in the park. We often did that, then. It was a nice park, lots of trees, wild areas. But I heard a child (it's funny, isn't it, the way children always ask the truly awful question?) this child said to some adult, "Why are all the trees going all brown?" And it was late May, you understand, early summer, and the leaves flooding out and the grass high and everything lush. What did the adult reply? I can't recall. But as we walked on, the scales, as they say, dropped from my eyes. I wished they hadn't. I began to see it too.

It wasn't like it is nowadays. Then it was only just establishing itself, the—what did they call it? —the *Phenomenon*.

It was almost like looking through a photographic lens. Except, obviously, this lens didn't completely change everything, as normally it would.

Neither of us said anything to the other. But I realized he, my husband, had also in those moments begun to *see*. We kept talking and joking, we even stopped for coffee and a doughnut at the park café. But an uneasy shadow was settling over us, and a silence.

We didn't actually discuss anything for several weeks. One evening we were making dinner, and—I remember so vividly—he was suddenly staring at the counter and he said, "What color is that pepper, would you say?"

"Sort of orange, I suppose," I said, "an orange pepper."

"No," he said, "it's a brown pepper. And the lettuce, that's a pale brown lettuce, only its edges are...pale blue." And we had become two statues, while the cooker bubbled carelessly, and then he said, "Someone at work went for his eye-test today. He'd told me he was afraid he was going blind. But his problem isn't caused by any defect in his vision. The optician said, apparently, the problem is becoming universal."

And then, as if we must, we looked around us, at all and everything: at the brown curtains that had been a deep green, and the green trees beyond the windows that were the color of sludge, yes, even in the evening light where the blue sky was somehow wrong and the west such a dark and sullen red. In the clear glass bottle the white wine gleamed colorless as water, but the mustard in the jar was mud. And on my hand my gold wedding ring had altered to the dull metal of a tarnished, ancient penny.

"What is it?" I said.

"God knows," he said.

But I don't think God, if there is God, does know either, any more than the rest of us.

⑨ ⑨ ⑨

We all comprehend by now; or I assume most of us must do. It's world-wide after all. Hardly anyone talks about it. Aside from very young people like yourself, who never watched it happen. It's meant a lot of make-overs, home decor, clothing—good for commerce then. Even I had my corn-blonde hair bleached dead white. Better than the stagnant pond shade it had become. (Like my wedding dress, as you see.) And if no one wants black-brown-blue cabbages and lettuces, or eggs with blind-brown centers, or the quite fresh yet decayed-looking brownish peaches and apricots, there are still things to eat. Apples and tomatoes like an old wound, doughnuts like excrement. The jewel-trade suffered. Who buys a topaz? A cut emerald the size of a cat's (brown/grey) eye, is worth less than nine euro-dollars—less than the price of a bottle of good (stale-tea color) Pinot Grigio. Or black Merlot.

It's worse for animals. Those brown leopards that had lost their camouflage, the brown canaries that stopped breeding and died out—as the leopards and the tigers did. And overhead the sun is molten white or murky crimson, and the moon ashes that sometimes curdle into blood.

Because yellow was a primary color it didn't die alone. It took green and orange with it, and virtually every other shade lost some nuance or definition. How strange. Who could ever have guessed? They said some kind of spectrum-microbe caused this. It attacked only that one element, the color yellow. Nothing dangerous, no need for alarm, can't harm us. Just... hurts. No, I won't show you the photos. It effects photographs too, of course. That *brown* girl and the *brown* and *bone-white* daffodils...

My husband? I'm afraid he died young.

Thank you for your visit. Yes, isn't it a dramatic sunset.

Apocalyptic, you could say.

By Crystal Light Beneath One Star

Six thousand miles is not too far
To hurry home to you
By crystal light beneath one star
It seems
I haul across the world
These dreams

    —Michael Pennington

It's true. There is a strange kind of beauty in this place. For one thing, the terrible beauty of exile. There's a sweetness to pain.

Today, if it can be called Day (no, it can't, but we do, I shall), I must have walked for miles, through the realm of darkness. I don't, and I never will, understand about the dark, and the way the dark is light. I only see the ebony landscape, not quite black, under the sky—black neither—and that the light is there like panes of most fragile crystal, sharp enough to cut, razors and diamonds, and everything so piercingly clear. And yet so completely, softly, voluminously dark. It hangs, this world of daylit night, from a single nail—the Star. Dull and pale, the Star gives scarcely any illumination. Only in the hours before Shift does the Star brighten. Then it's more like a noise than a light—a sort of roaring whistle. And I get the old panic, which is nothing to do with an impending Shift, its moments of slight discomfort for us, its bland routine for the machines that order it. It's a psychological horror I feel, probably, since the brightening of the Star indicates the true dawn is approaching this vast nocturnal dock; the Earth is catching us up.

"Why do you think about it?" Edvey said to me this morning (which was no morning, but I shall call it so.) "You'll never go back."

"You think not."

"Not you. You won't fit. Take me," said Edvey, which means I'll have to, no choice, I'm to be awarded his autobiography, again. "A wife, a second-law wife, five children between them. My parents were gone, of course, but I had three sisters."

"Just like Andrew Prozorov," I murmured, but he wasn't to be stopped. He never was.

"Cousins, nephews—all of that. And a couple of good apartments in the cities, and a house, a real show-place, up east of the Centerline. Wonderful land, you could do anything with it, grow coffee, raise horses, dig minerals out of it. And then I had my work. My God, Calle, I had two careers, didn't I? I had everything." He sat down across from me at the small window table, where I had been playing three-handed chess-against myself and myself. "Christ, if I start to think about all that—I'd go crazy, Calle. I'd start petitioning and arguing, like some of them, causing trouble. I'd probably get something on with the wires, or just plain rig up a line and hang myself."

"The machines that run this place would never let it happen."

"Oh, there are ways," he said. "There have to be ways. But I'm not a potential suicide. I never was. I was always positive."

"And you're still positive."

"You bet I am, Calle."

He picked up one of the red bishops and started to play with it. I thought of taking it away from him—he was messing up the game—but what did it matter anyway?

"What I say is this. I serve my term. And then I get back."

"Which term?"

"You know what I mean. I do my graft."

"Your what?"

"Calle, don't try to be clever. I do it, then I get sent home."

"Home," I said. "The wives and horses and coffee and sisters."

"That's it."

"How long do you think you still have to serve?"

He glared at me. He was sweating, and his eyes looked wet and full of tearful menace. We all harbor our own versions of the truth. Nobody likes to hear the *other* version.

"You don't know," he said to me, "any more than I do, how long you've been here."

"I didn't say I did."

"But I," he said, "keep count. Yes, sir. From the first day I arrived. Oh, it's a crude method. No watch or chronometer is going to record it, right? So I just keep a journal, and every *night*, before I turn in, I damn well make sure I write something on a fresh new page. And every one of those goddamn pages has a number to it. And every goddamn damned number is a day *here*."

"How many pages?" I asked.

I knew he would know exactly. He did.

"Seven hundred and thirty-nine," he said. He was smug, for a second.

"That must be a very large book."

"It's more than one book. Come on. And the machines issue me a new one whenever I ask. Allowed stationery. No problem. I have a regular stack of them."

"Just over two years," I said. "If you go by the Standard Calendar."

"Thirteen-month calendar, right," he said. "Just over two years. I mean, that's quite a while. They don't want heart's blood, after all. It won't be long now."

I took the bishop back for something to do mostly, so I wouldn't tell him the thing he knew already, that maybe tomorrow he and I would meet and he'd have two thousand pages in his books, or only two pages. He didn't want to see it. He wasn't about to see it. Whenever or whatever, he had filled seven hundred and thirty-nine numbers, so seven hundred and thirty-nine times, at least, he had refused to *see* it. So there he was.

It seemed I could remember meeting him the first time I ever did, the first time I was ever told about the sisters and wives and horses—though specific memory is always hazy here—and he had only been in the place a seven-day Standard week. He had said, "What did I do? I was making a film. There was nothing controversial in it. It was about families and how society can work well under an ordered, structured government system."

"They may have suspected heavy irony," I said.

"Okay," he said. "But then they had that wrong. I believe in the system. I always did. It was good to me."

"Until now."

"Oh, they have some reason. I trust them. I'll sit it out."

Edvey was not the only one to think—or to *say* he thought—in this fashion. Sometimes, when they said these things, their eyes flashed this way and that, unconsciously checking for the scanners that would record their pliancy, their willingness to conform. But I—

"What did you do, eh, Calle? Something silly, I guess."

"Very silly."

"You're a writer, eh, Calle? I should know, writers do damn stupid things. What was it?"

"I'd rather not bore you with it."

"I'll find out."

"Yes, if you like."

When he did find out (not from me, someone else must have mentioned what they half-knew), he showily eschewed my company a long time—until time itself put us out of synch and he forgot. And when he remembered again, it was hazy, and he began to tell me once more, and more and more, about the sisters and horses.

In fact, I am here for writing a short, slammed-together story, which I published myself on a private press long since melted into slag. The small book was entitled *Realm of Dark-ness: A Final Siberia.* It was an imaginary account of this place where I now am, and which I no longer need to imagine. I had heard the tales, I had managed to get access to some classified data leaked by a man who presently blasted out his brains. I wonder how many people on Earth read smuggled copies of that slender volume, or are reading it now—except Now is a concept I sometimes try to forget.

Today, I thought about Merah.

Lest it be supposed I emulate Edvey, or Stenressy, Dorf or Marlin or Wyld, or any of the countless others among us who keep journals, numbered or un-, this is no journal. But some-times the sweet pain of exile…cries out for words, even, au-daciously, for print.

I believe, in the normal course of events, Merah would have faded by now simply into a prototype, or a dream. But Merah has not been allowed to do that, for me. Did I love the person called Merah? We were lovers; there was the closeness that can come from that, and a kind of telemetry of ideas, pleasing to us both, abrasive when it failed us—fallings-off, re-unitings, all the ordinary material of a relationship.

But now (in the non-existing now of here), now I think I do love Merah, for Merah has become the immediate sym-bol of what has been lost to me. They took care that should happen. Should I be flattered they reckon me threat enough still to use this added emotional lever against me? Oh, yes, I flush with embarrassed pride. I must have bothered them. Does that connectively mean, then, that I achieved anything worthwhile, before they sent me here to the night-land under the dull Star?

I had been here what might have been six months Stan-dard, if it were possible to assess. It seemed about that period, though there were already jumps forward, and then sequen-tially back. I had lived through my first day of arrival three times, I was fairly certain of that, for the dim hazy memory, like the dim unhazy Star, shines on and does not quite let go of all pertinent matters. Six months, then, and on waking in the comfortable private room we are each of us allotted, I heard the machine speaking at me from the wall.

"There is a procedure you will experience during this time-stage."

"What? You're going to break my legs. Or something less subtle, with a drug?"

"Tortures of this nature are unrecognized under all United World conventions."

"But this isn't the world," I said. I added, "Nor are we out of it."

"Look from the window," said the machine. It had no voice, merely a sound that formed coherent phrases.

I looked. The ebony land stretched softly around and through the razor wafers of crystal light. There are no particular features to the land. It rolls and sweeps, as if about to become a mountain, a valley, a sea—or perhaps invention supplies that fancy. Above, the Star gave off the glow of a tarnished coin, a museum coin from before the days of credit transfer Standardization. A sixpence, or a centime, or a yen, or a unidisc. But then a sudden blare of light exploded in thunderous silence all through the Star, and it pulsed and swelled, and abruptly a ball of screaming white filled a quarter of the sky, sending its knives of fire slicing across the room, dissecting all the dark country outside, so its very skeleton seemed to appear through the skin.

"We're coming to a Shift," I said. I had already witnessed the phenomenon some ten or eleven times before that I recalled, and experienced the Shift itself in the same ratio. Nevertheless, whenever I see what happens to the Star, I become afraid. Of course, it is unconscionable.

"Shift will occur," supplied the machine, "in thirty time-stage-units." (That would seem to us to be thirty minutes, if minutes were feasible.) "Please be ready to accompany the hoveror when it comes for you in fifteen time-stage-units. You are to move concurrent with the Shift, but in a different continuum. When you emerge you will find you have gone back in time, into a coded era."

"What?" I said. New fear for old. Their jargon, at its most convoluted, generally meant something Significant. The same, often, with men. I even felt, foolishness, an instant of blind hope. But I crushed it. I altered my question to "Why?"

"It is a part of the program," the machine answered in its unmusical sound.

"The object of the program is to unhinge the mind of each of us here. To disorientate us to the point of insecurity, to increase the sensation of insecurity to the point of insanity. You want to drive me, along with everyone else, mad. Very well, I can't avoid it, probably. But I like to know the script."

But the machine said, "Remember, please, that in past time you can in no manner participate, only observe. You are discorporate and invisible. You are reminded of this for your own convenience."

"Since when is my convenience important to this government? And what do you mean? I can go back to any of my past here, and relive it, or live it differently. I know I'm doing so, whether that suits you or not."

"This is a fallacy. There is no time, as such, in this place; only in the moments before sun-phase and Shift does time begin to evolve. You do not, here, return into the past. Past, present, and what is termed 'future' are continuous and inextricable, which you understand, having written of it."

My heart was beating too loudly and too fast.

"Then you do mean past time in the sense of a return to Earth?"

"This is so."

I sat very quietly and let my heart crash and race all it would.

I couldn't control my heart. But my mind was another venture. They were letting me go back, then, that was to be the latest torture. Go back and see how it had been, but unable, naturally, to undo, to alter, to make worse my crimes against the state.

When the hoveror machine arrived, I went with it, up ramps and into a large room with a platform, and I stood where they told me under a canopy like half an egg-shell. The Shift happened. The momentary vertigo washed through me, the light went out, and for a split second I hung in nothing-ness, no dark, no light, no Star, no world at all. And then I was through, but no longer in the realm of darkness, this place. I was back in the real world. I had thought they would show me myself, frustrating me that way. But it was more sensitive. It might have hurt less, and sometimes I blame myself for (could it be?) falling into their assessment of me and tacitly agreeing to it by allowing myself to be more disturbed be-cause it was Merah they showed me.

That commencing occasion, it was the Merah I had known for one and a half years before my exile. Everything about it startled me, not only the image of Earth, of Merah, but the tranquility. I saw her standing on a hillside. She had compan-ions, and it was summer, and they were debating whether to pick the flowers or leave them in peace, and eventually the vote went in the flowers' favor. I could smell the flowers, too, and the sun on the grass; even a faint perfume that I recol-lected she had sometimes used.

So then. I followed her all through one golden summer day, one azure summer evening. It must have been a month or so before we met—she was not quite my Merah that day. Young and straight, the look always of the dancer she had trained to be, and nearly been, fair skin that never tanned, black hair, cool eyes. There was something independent and uninvolved, that I had robbed her of, not meaning to. I, now the helpless voyeur, trailed her over the sun-amber of those hills and down the narrow chalky path to the restaurant. She laughed with her friends. She fed a little white dog with one bluish ear, she drank wine and ate a salad, she lay in the grass under the willows while someone played a guitar. In the dusk, roses and moths and the whiteness of girls' cheap pretty dresses, things like these, lovely clichés under a dawning moon, and jasmine on the air—and then she and they were gone from me. The Earth with them.

Returned, here. The transition was not bad, not so uncomfortable even as Shift. I went back to my room and sat a long while. I did not recognize where I had come back to. I was still there, with her. The machines were silent. The white howl had vanished from the almost-black of the sky, only the smoky gem of the Star hanging there now.

Had she ever told me of that day, that particular, unimportant day? What did it matter. She was in my mind again. Sometimes, as I travelled weightlessly beside them, she had seemed to catch a glimpse of me. She had cast a flirting look over her shoulder at me. She had yearned towards me in the tent of willow—why are you standing apart? Come closer. One imagines these things. It is a form of unavoidable idiocy.

She had let go her uninvolvement to aid my commitment and to comfort me. She had told me I was right, and come to believe so. It was Merah who said that victory, though impossible, must be striven for.

I thought of many things in our relationship, both good and bad. I continued to sit still through what is considered a night here, and to think of Merah.

Since it had had the desired effect on me—since it had damaged me in some intense yet elusive way—they then let me go back again, and again, to see her often. Sometimes it was the pre-me Merah—at her university, doing her nation-service in some little red factory. A Merah painting a landscape, lightheartedly amateur; a Merah dancing, no trace of the amateur there. Her twenty-first birthday party. Her years at the academy. Then, later, I saw scenes that had come during our time together, though I never saw her with me—never saw myself. Though, in these vignettes, she was often speaking of me, or of the political lessons she learned as I was learning them—all on record. I could not say to her—Hush! They hear you—too late.

What I did not know was if all this was a punishment of me, or one more means to snap the threads of reason, or just an experiment, random. Who knows.

The transfer into the time-frame always took place during a Shift, though the return out of the frame was managed when the Shift had passed. I assumed the power expelled in performing the Shift was also harnessed to facilitate entry into the frame. But this meant little to me, I'm no mechanic. It simply became a habit, the rush of adrenalin, whenever the Star engorged. I would hurry to my room and wait for the conducting hoveror. Which did not, of course, always arrive. Then there would be disappointment, and relief.

It was after I saw her as a child that the wound sank in too deep to heal, and then, at once, the time-traveling ended. And so it became a treat withheld, and one day I asked them to let me see her again. This only happened once. The request was not granted.

She was a blonde child, very fair. I suppose she had had some reason for re-molecularizing the color of her hair, and leaving it so, and never mentioning it. I'd never learned, till now. The blonde child danced on the edge of a beach of yellow sand, practicing her dancer's exercises, with only the wide sea behind her. I forgot, and called aloud to her. She seemed almost to turn at my voice, as if she caught some echo of it. I recalled she had said to me, the first night we were together, that she seemed to know me, and asked if we had met before, but that was the common theme of a girl in love, and she was in love with me. At the end of our first and only full year as a couple, on the eve of the Lion Square March, when they brought in the soldiers and three thousand people were shot down around the memorial, along the boulevard, and in the parks, Merah had believed she might be pregnant. She was very concerned. We had no legal tie, and it would, given our unhelpful political stance, be unlikely a marriage license might be granted us.

This would mean a compulsory termination. She wept that night. Next day, early, we heard the sound of machine guns and ice-cannon. We had meant to be part of that march. But it had been pre-emptive, all of it, and by eight o'clock it was over. We forgot about the phantom child. A week later, when the last of the casualties were still dying, she told me she had made a mistake. With the memory of those corpses thick as snow on the streets, it hadn't seemed to be so important any more, one problematical butchered fetus. Perhaps it had been real but died in her, hearing the noises of murder from the city through her ears. No, romance has no place in this statement.

But the child who was Merah was also like this unborn and perhaps never physically-conceived child. It was fair, as I am, but it was Merah's image, as her daughter must have been.

I didn't ask them to let me look at her again in order to see the child she was, or any specific portion of her life, before or during the time she was with me. It wasn't even love, though I did love her, perhaps, and now I do love her because she is the cypher for the sweet agony of exile, and the theft of the Earth. Oh God, I suppose she was my numbered page. A—record. The anchor. A sign I had once lived.

My request was not granted, who could ever have thought it would be? (I note, too, that I am almost sure I've never relived any of those times during which I was placed in the frame, never relived any of those seeings of Merah. Which confirms my idea that the machines have some control of our wanderings, though we ourselves have none.) They knew, from my asking, that they had succeeded. I had been broken open. One little piece of my mind had joined my mindless racing heart, and was lost to me, out of my jurisdiction. Therefore theirs, to be used against me as they wished.

There is no surprise to you, that I saw Merah, or anything, in their past. Many millions of you have seen the transmitted stills and moving videos, the Historicals that have absorbed your TV screens for years. Time, as a manifesto, has been open to the authorities most of my life. As for the masses—opium? The great extravaganzas of past events, replayed, for educational purposes, but basically for entertainment. And the initial disappointment was long forgotten, that time might be viewed, even experienced with certain senses additional to that of sight—but not sentiently journeyed through, not *lived* in. For the past has happened and is over. It leaves only its multi-dimensional print upon the molecular structure of everything that persists. We can receive and develop the print, and gaze on every aspect and facet of the human condition since first we crawled out from the primeval seas. But we can never mingle with the crowd, touch it, talk to it—we can never change a thing.

That was why I had thought they would put me back into the time-frame—for that too is tenable, given the complex equipment only available to government—bitterly to enter, though not to co-exist, or in any way to influence my former self. I visualized rambling along beside this me, through my—his—last fatal months on earth before my (his) arrest. Watching him at the meetings, in the marches, seeing as a third person the contact made with the other, the package of documents, the reading of them, the final going to ground to complete my writing… with perhaps the knowledge of Merah asleep in the next room, with her black hair spread over the pillows. *See* myself making all my mistakes again, unable to step inside, to say—They're after you. Throw down the pen and run.

But they chose the better way. There are no fools in their ranks.

Clever men and clever women, all.

But, to return to this overview of time. We accept, then, that the past has been, and has left its evidence. What of the future? A contradiction. There can be no excursion into the future. While the past has come and gone, the future has yet to be. And so, for the meddlers, no future has evolved for them to meddle with, it is not yet there—a blank page to be written on. All the time paradoxes are dismissed.

But, although there is no future as such, there is a place—a state, a dimension—a *somewhere*—that fills the *void* in front of us, just as the past fills up the gap at our backs.

And here, in that condition which is not, but will be the future of the Earth, *here*—are we. The prisoners. The dissidents. The revolutionaries. Trapped within the black crystal under that one dull Star.

The existence of this place was concealed, for sound political reasons, and naturally for the good of the people.

I found out.

As I've said, some documents were leaked—we learned that they had discovered such a place, explored its potential—a place *ahead* of time, in which, therefore, time did not exist. Where, therefore, time could be invented, and by means of the invention, become so tangled, so raveled, that they saw at once a use for it. And they were already using it. What better? Out of everybody's way, these trouble-makers, safe on that futureless future plain...and something more.

For three-quarters of a century, the world conventions of human rights have held back the strong correcting arm of government. All known forms of coercion have been outlawed, and no one wishes, any more, to stand beyond the human pale forever. But here, in the new situation, a new solution. The future state which was not future but limbo, giving rise as it does to extraordinary anomalies of time and the fact of existence inside time, or un-time—take it as it is and harness it. Not as a torture—for who wishes to torture anyone, or to unhinge minds, or to wipe bare the surface of intellects?—but as a simple corrective. And the tables of rights, drawn up before this thing was happened on, have no proviso for it. While those in on the secret debate amendments and vote this in and that out, we stand in the dark, and they—they play with us. No, not in any savage animal way, but kindly and clinically, the clever men and the clever women.

We have every comfort, don't we? The most lenient prison system of Earth is no match for our charming quarters with their pleasant colors, clean bathrooms and hygienic air, the firm beds and good food and wine, the foolproof medicine, the books and games, the gentle caring of the machines.

But time, which is straightforward elsewhere, is never so, here. Here, one may travel in the future—as much, or more, than twenty Earth years—Dorf told me once this had happened to him. He found himself there, up ahead, inside a self old and young at the same minute. Accordingly, he knows now he will be here that long, at least. Generally, the time movement seems to come after slumber, unconsciousness casting us free to drift—you fall asleep at point one, and wake at point twenty-one. Or vice versa. But Choski also told me once he moved backward, to the day he beat me three times in a row at chess, living it again, though the result slightly altering, and this took place after the lightest doze.

So we meander up and down the scale. Our future, and our past in this region, both equally accessible to us. Yesterday may come tomorrow, and tomorrow may be now, today. Today itself will come again, very very likely. And for each of us in this near-black zone of random hell, flitting like winged insects to and fro, each has his own path, intercepting others, missing them, refinding them again. Only the machines keep track of us, by a complicated math no man will ever fathom, I am sure.

They keep it hidden, this place. Did you ever hear of it? Now you do, because I tell you. *Here,* locked in the thrust and weave of five hundred time-streams, waves breaking upon blank shores, bursting up and sinking down into the midnight ocean.

I can't prove it to you; I am only here. With Edvey, who keeps his books of numbered pages where tomorrow he may write *one* again, and be incoherently aware of it. Or he may write *seven thousand* and go again, or for the first, to find the wires or the hanging line he spoke of. And with Wyld, who is already ceasing to be conscious of it, collapsing, reminding me of the senility of a very old man, this boy of twenty-three who led the Lion Square March with flames in his eyes. And with myself, holding like a sponge my thoughts of Merah.

Two pasts, hers, and my own. And my future, into which, so far, I haven't delved very deeply—just a year or so. I saw an Edvey there who had tried, unsuccessfully, to electrocute himself; he lay in the sick-bay, tenderly cared for. And I saw my own footprints on the black land outside, where I had walked for miles, six, six thousand, a million and six, trying always, like some dying dog, to get round full circle and come home. I, who have no home any longer.

I often walk out there, or will walk, or am walking. I pass my own shadows, unseen, in those almost hills and nearly valleys. Round and round. Unable to be lost. Every direction leads you back. The land not quite begun, waiting. Waiting to rise up in the geography of an Earth that has yet to mold it, the future. Beneath one star, which is—what else—the sun, the only light great enough to cast forward some visible show, yet dull and feeble and small. Until just before the Shift, when suddenly Earth's present starts to catch up. The avalanche of light erupts in the sky, and the sun swells and begins to bloom like a fearsome flower. They are coming, coming to trample us down, all the ones we have betrayed by our capture and captivity. The present our actions have formed, those miles away in our past.

So we run away in turn. To escape. These efficient machines facilitate the flight to keep us always neatly in limbo, the chastisement of anomalous sliding time. But we're happy to fly. We don't want to know what has become of you.

And Shift no longer means the frame, the sight of Merah.

Tomorrow, never having written any of this, I may write it again, differently. Or I may decide sensibly not to write it. Or, come on it written, and destroy it peevishly. Or write instead a letter to Merah she will never read. By starlight through the window.

It was Robespierre, that arch-revolutionary, who jotted in his note-book, "A writer is the most dangerous enemy his country can have."

And, I confess, in that age of dreaming, drowning ostriches I left (was dragged from), I found fiction the sharpest weapon. It makes a thin cut they can't feel. And knowledge pours in like poison. By the time you know, it's too late. Awareness is in your veins. You're done for.

I had just written these words, when one of the hoveror machines came in at my door, and at the same second, light flowed over my window.

"A request has come to our attention, your desire for further coded-viewing of the female subject with whom you cohabited."

I had made that request, you remember. It was denied. Or I would make it and it would be denied. But here, by some fluke of their always-suspect mercy, it is made, and it is acceptable.

I don't want to *see* her any more. What's their game?

"I've changed my mind," I said.

"Your relationship with the woman was a close one. It is thought best you see."

I got up. The Star, something, confused my vision. It could only be one thing, this.

One should armor oneself at such times. Why help them, why comply with their schemes by growing afraid? Why, in any case, fear? It must be over, or they couldn't show me. Beyond this place, only past time was available. To enter the frame with it, it must be finished. Concluded, then. Whatever they had done to her, it was no longer happening. They would show me her death. It had to be.

Guided by the hoveror, I went up all the ramps, onto the shadowy platform, and stood under the top part of the eggshell, waiting for the Shift. The machines threw their switches, and I fell down, weightless, warm, into a room somewhere on Earth.

It had the *smell* of Earth. (In the frame, scent, sometimes vagaries of touch—such as the effect of temperature—may be present, with the senses of sight and hearing.) A city. Traffic, and revitalized air, the dusts of streets unslaked, and neon breath. But stars stood in the night-time window. The room was high up in a tall building and looked mostly into the sky. It was very white, the room, and pristine. Antiseptic mingled with the smells of the city. It was a hospital room, and in the bed, an old woman was quietly dying all alone. She looked eighty years old. She might be much younger, or a great deal older, depending on how her life had mapped itself, what money she had had, and what drugs and vitrogens she had been given access to. The room was serviceable, but had no hints of opulence. Probably she was poor. Had she kept her convictions? Jettisoned them? Were they even hers. No one was in the room with her. No friends, no husband—no one, after me? Or just some accident of timing, they were outside or on their way—

They would not be quick enough.

Merah. Black hair, gold, and now grey and brittle. The white bed seems to suck your life away. Your eyes are closing. Merah I'm here, but useless to you. I can't be such a fool any more as to call your name, or try to hold your hand. You can't see me. Merah, I was miles away, hurrying back to you but never getting home. Merah, I brought you to this, but you let me. What happened to you, between that time of then, and this, all those years between?

She looks so old it makes her seem very young again, like the child on the beach. Her dancer's hands twitch on the sheet. Thin hands, that show the marks of incipient arthritis the proper drugs have retarded. How clean she is, how sterilized. Her cool eyes are colorless. Is she afraid?

We were the dreamers, weren't we, you and I? And here, our dreams have brought us. You to this white beached death alone. And I to the realization that if today I see your death, some fifty years after I left you—then somewhere today exists, the proof I will be their prisoner fifty years. Or more. For though I can travel forward, I can't see Earth's future, can I? I can only be shown what has already happened there....

Merah? Oh. She's dead. She died, when my mind wandered. Only a moment of appalled self-pity, and in that moment—

Already the room's fading. They're taking me back from the frame.

Did I ever write to you? Did you see the letters? Letters heavily censored. Parts of them? How long did you remember me? The unborn child, or the bold marches, the sound of ice-cannon, Lion Square, the private press under the police ray, metal running like chocolate—any of it? No? Thank God, I think you had forgotten. Your face was so empty.

I have been their prisoner fifty years or more, yet it seems I have been here a year—less. She died in the past, for that is all they can show, with Earth. Where have I been, how many chess matches, how many thousands of walks, six-thousands of black miles? What have *I* forgotten? Christ, oh Christ.

"Why do you think about it?" Edvey says to me "You'll never go back. Take me. A wife, two wives, five children. Three sisters. The horses, the coffee crop, the mansion, my films. My God, Calle, you can't think about it." He picks up the yellow bishop, and I think of taking it away from him, but what does it matter if he messes up the game?

I always believed insanity was a sudden thing, but it blossoms slowly. It's in me now, I feel the bud, its pressure, ready to fold open.

Wyld is sitting smiling under the window. He looks at the Star, and he starts to cry, with no tears. At that minute, the Star begins to pulse, whiter and whiter, brighter and more bright.

"Shift."

"You bet," says Edvey. "Shift."

So now I have written it, my poisoned fiction which is the truth, my story, my *Realm of Darkness: A Final Siberia.* For the historical time-videos will remind you that to that wide land, which had become a virtual acronym of such things, that long land of pines and birch trees, under its lemon-tinted and colossal sky, the rebels were sent long ago. They took their places in the cold country and underwent the programs that have since been banned, till their minds were wiped clean as porcelain tiles. Or so they say.

Siberia—was nothing to this.

In the next room, Merah is sleeping, with her black hair spread on the pillows. She said to me once that, as a child, she believed a dancer should have black hair. I could steal in and lie down on that hair, and sleep, too. But instead I'm going out, to creep through the restricted streets at two in the morning, to the printers in the alley.

I know, of course, that this is my warrant for arrest I have written out here. These papers. I speak of what I have only read about. But I shall know it, soon.

Tomorrow, or the day after, they'll come for me. The trial will be minimal, but legal. And then I shall enter the realm of darkness, the umber formlessness under the sharp blades of light, the Star that will be the sun.

I am afraid of it. I'm afraid of what I have done. But I had to do it. Though we shall never win, we must fight. Only by fighting can we keep hold of our humanity. The fight *is* the victory.

It seems to me, though it isn't quite yet, already I hear them on the stairs. And I hear the slammed door of the prison mobile, its siren. And I hear the echo as I fall downward into the crystal.

You, all of you out there on the smarting back of the Earth, remember sometimes we're here, in that place, as you walk straight forward from day to day, from night to night, under your skies of many stars.

---

* The portion of poetry quoted at the beginning is from the book *Rossya* © Red Man, Oleander Press, 1978.

A Day in the Skin
(or, the century we were out of them)

And the first thing you more or less think when you get Back is: God, where's everything gone? (Just as, similarly, when you get Out you more or less think, Hey, where's all this coming from?) Neither thought is rational, simply outraged instinct. The same as, coming Back, it seems for a moment stone silent, blind dark, and ice cold. It's none of those. It's nothing. In a joking mood, some of us have been known to refer to it, this—what shall I call it? this *place*—as Sens-D (sensory deprivation). It isn't though, because when your Outward senses—vision, hearing, smell, taste, touch—when they go off, other things come on. The *alter-senses*. Hard to describe. For a time, you reckon them as compensation, stand-ins, like eating, out in the skin world, a cut of sausage when you hankered for a steak. Only, in a while it stops being that. It becomes steak. The equivalent senses are just fine, although the only nontechnical way I can come up with to express them *is* in terms of equivalents, alternatives. And time itself is a problem, in here, or down there, or where the hell ever. Yes, it passes. One can judge it. But one rarely does, after the first months. In the first months you're constantly pacing, like some guy looking at his watch: Is it time yet? Is it time now? Then that cools off. Something happens, in here, down there.... So that when at last the impulse comes through *Time* to *get up* (or *Out*), you turn lazily, like a fish in a pool (equivalents), and you equivalently say, Oh really? Do I have to?

186

"Sure, Scay. You do have to. It's in the Company contract. And if I let you lie, there'd be all hell and hereafter to pay HQ. Not to mention from you, when you finally get Out for keeps."

So I alter-said, in the way the impulse can assimilate and send on, "How long, and what is it?"

"One day. One huge and perfect High Summer day. Forty-two hours. And you got a good one, Scay, listen, a real beauty."

"Male or female?"

"A *fee*-male."

"All right. I can about remember being female."

"First female for you for ten years, ah? *Exciting.*"

"Go knit yourself a brain."

Dydoo, who manages the machines, snuffled and whined, which I alter-heard now clearly, as he set up my ride. I tried to pull myself together for the Big Wrench. But you never manage it. Suddenly you are whirling down a tunnel full of fireworks, at the end of which you explode inside a mass of stiff jelly. And there I was, flailing and shrieking, just as we all flail and shriek, in the middle of a support couch in the middle of Transfer.

"Husha hush," said the machines, and gentle firm mechanical arms held me and held me down.

Presently I relapsed panting—yes, panting. *Air.*

"Look up," said Dydoo. I looked. Things flashed and tickered. "Everything's fine. You can hear me? see me?"

"I can even smell you," I gasped, tears streaming down my face, my heart crashing like surf on the rocks. There was a dull booming pain in my head I cared for about as much as Dydoo cared for my last remark. "Dydoo," I continued, speech not coming easy, "who had this one last? I think they gave it a cranial fracture."

"Nah, nah. 'S all right. Mike tied one on with the wine and brandy-pop. It's pumped full of vitamins and de-tox. Should take about a hundred and fifteen seconds more, and you'll feel just dandy, you rat."

I lay there, waiting for Mike Plir's hangover to go away, and watched, with my borrowed eyes, Dydoo bustling round the shiny bright room. He is either a saint or a masochist (or are they the same?). Since one of us has to oversee these particular machines, he agreed to be it, and so he took the only living quarters permanently available. The most highly developed local fauna is a kind of dog-like creature, spinally adapted for walking upright, like the Terran ape, and with articulated forepaws and jaw. With a little surgery, this nut-brown woolly beast, with its floppy ears and huge soulful eyes, was all ready for work, and thus for Dydoo.

"My, Dydoo," I said, "you look real sweet today. Come on over, I'll give you a bone."

"Shurrup," growled Dydoo. No doubt, these tired old jests get on his furry nerves.

Once my skull stopped booming, I got up and went to look at myself in the unlikely pier-glass at one end of the antiseptic room.

"Well, I remember this one. This used to be Miranda."

There she stood, twenty-five, small, curvy, a little heavy but nice, creamy gold, with long fair hair down to her second cluster of dimples.

"Yeah. Good stuff," said Dydoo, deciding yet again he doesn't or can't afford to hold a grudge more than a minute.

"How long, I wonder, before I get a go at my own—"

"Now you know it doesn't work like that, Scay. Don't you? Hah?"

"Yes, I know it doesn't. Just lamenting, Dydoo. Tell me, who had me Out last time?"

"Vundar Cope. And he broke off a bit."

"*What?* Hexos Christ! Which bit?"

"Just kidding," said Dydoo. "If you're worried, I'll take you over to the Store and let yah look."

"No thanks, for Chrissake. I don't like seeing myself that way."

"Okay. And try to talk like a lady, can't you?"

"Walkies, Dydoo," I snarled. *"Fetch!"*

"Ah, get salted."

It took me a couple of quivery hours to grow accustomed to being in Miranda's body—correction, Fem. Sub. 68. I bruised my hips a lot, trying to get between and by furniture that was no longer wide enough for me. The scented bath and the lingerie were exciting, all right. But not in the right way. I'd been male in the beginning and much of the time after, and I'd had a run of being male for every one of my fifty-one days a year Out, for ten, eleven years. That's generally how it's designated, unless an adventurous preference is stated. Stick with what you're used to. But sometimes you must take what you can get. I allowed a while before I left Transfer, to see to a couple of things. The lingerie and the mirrors helped. It was a safe bet, I probably wouldn't be up (to miscoin a phrase) to any straight sex this holiday. Besides, I didn't know who else was Out, and Dydoo had gotten so grouchy in the end, I hadn't bothered to ask. Normally there are around forty to fifty people in the skin on any given day. Amounts of time vary, depending on how the work programs pan out and the "holiday" schedules have built up. My day, I now recalled, was a free diurnal owing to me from last year, that the Company had never made up. Perfect to the letter, our Company. After all, who wants to get sued? Not that anyone who sues ever wins, but it's messy.

I wondered, as the moving ramp carried me out into town, just what Dydoo was getting paid to keep him woofing along in there.

The first body I passed on Mainstreet was Fedalin's, and it gave me the creeps, the way it still sometimes does, because naturally it wasn't Fedalin inside. Whoever was, was giving it a heck of a time. Red-rimmed eyes, drug-smoked irises, shaking hands, and faltering feet. To make matters worse, the wreck blew a bleary whistle after Miranda's stacking. I didn't stop to belt him. My lady's stature and her soft fists were of use only in one sort of brawl. I could see, I thought, nor for the first, why the Company rules keep your own personal body in the Store whenever you yourself are Out. It means you never get into your own skin, but then too, there are never any overlaps, during which you might meet yourself on the sidewalk with some other bastard driving. Pandemonium that would be, trying to throttle them, no doubt, for the lack of care they were taking with your precious goods—and only, of course, ending up throttling yourself. In a manner of speaking. Although I didn't like looking at my own battered old (thirty-five) skin lying there, in ice, like a fish dummy, in the Store, I had once or twice gone over and compulsively peeked. The second occasion not only gave me the shivers, but I'd flown into a wow of a rage because someone had taken me Out for a week's leave and put ten pounds on my gut. Obviously, the machines would get that off in a few days. (The same as lesions, black eyes, and stomach ulcers get got rid of. The worst I ever heard tell of was a cancerous lung that required one whole month of cancer-antibodies, which is twice as long as it takes to cure it in a body that's occupied.) But there, even so, you get upset, you can't help it. So it's on the whole better not to go and look, though HQ says it's okay for you to go and look—to prove to us all our skins are still around in the public lending library. Goddamn it.

The contract says (and we all have a contract) that as soon as the Bank is open for Business (five years it's supposed to be now, but five years ago they said that, too) we all go Back into our own bodies. Or into new improved bodies, or into new improved versions of our old bodies, or—you name it. A real party, and we all get a prize. When it all started, around eighty years ago, that is, once everybody had settled after the initial squalling matches, Violent Scenes, hysteria, etc., some of us got a wild thrill out of the novelty. Pebka-Sol, for example, has it on record always, where possible, to come Out as a lady. And when he finally gets a skin of his own again, that is due to be a lady, also. But Pebka-Sol lost his own skin, the true, masculine one, so he's entitled. I guess we're the lucky ones, me, Fedalin, Miranda, Christof, Haro—those of us that didn't lose anything as a result of the Accident. Except, our rights...

I try to be conscientious myself, I really do. But handling Miranda was going to be a drag. She's a lot littler than me, or than I'm used to, and her capacity is less. I'm used to drinking fairly hard, but hard was the word it was going to be on her, if I tried that; plus she'd already been doused by some jack, yesterday. I walked into the bar on Mainstreet, the bar we used to hit in gabbling droves long, long ago under the glitter-kissed green dusk, when we were our own men and women. No one was there now, though Fedalin's haunt had just walked him out the door. I dialed a large pink Angel and put it, a sip at a time, into Miranda's insides, to get her accustomed. "Here's not looking at you, kid," I toasted her.

I had that weird feeling I recollect I had when I first scooped a female body from the draw forty-odd years ago. Shock and disorientation, firstly. Then a turn-on, racy, kinky, great. I'd got to the stage now of feeling I was on a date, dating Miranda, only I *was* Miranda. My first lady had been Qwainie, and Qwainie wasn't my type, which in the long run made things easier faster. But Miranda is my type. Oh my yes. (Which is odd in a way as the only woman I ever was really serious with—well, she wasn't like Miranda at all.) So I dialed Miranda another Angel, and we drank it down.

As this was happening, a tall dark man with a tawny tan, the right weight, and nothing forcing steam out of his nose and eyeballs, came into the bar. He dialed a Coalwater, the most lethal beer and alcohol mix in the galaxy (they say), one of my own preferred tipples, and sauntered over.

"Nice day, Scay."

"He knows me," said Miranda's soft cute voice with the slight lisp.

"The way you drink, feller," he said.

I had emptied the glass, and Miranda's ears were faintly ringing. I'd have to wait awhile for the girl to catch up.

"Well, if he knows me that well, then I'll hazard on who he is."

"Win, and he'll stand you a Coalwater."

"The lady wouldn't like that. Anyway. Let's try Haro Fielding."

"Hole in one."

"Well, fancy that. They let us Out the same time again."

Haro, whom I thought was in the skin of one of the tech people whose name I had mislaid, grinned mildly.

"I've been Out a couple of weeks. Tin and irradium traces over south. Due Back In tomorrow noon. You?"

"Forty-two hours."

"Hard bread."

"Yeah."

We stared into our glasses, mine empty, and I wished sweet Miranda would buck up and stop ringing so I could drink some more. Haro's rig had been auspicious, a tall dark man just like Haro's own body. But he'd treated it with respect. That was Haro Fielding all over, if you see what I mean. A really nice guy, super-intelligent, intellectual, all that, and sound, as about nothing but people ever are, and that rarely, let me add. We had been working together on the asti-manganese traces the other side of the rockies when the Accident happened, back here in town. That was how we two kept our skins. I remember we were down a tunnel scraping away, with the analysis robot-pack clunking about in the debris, when the explosion ripped through the planet's bowels. It was a low thrumming vibration, where we were, more than a bang. We were both a pair of tall guys, but Haro taller than me, with one of the best brains I ever came across. And he stood up and crashed this brain against the tunnel-ceiling and nearly knocked himself out. "What the F was that?" I asked, after we'd gotten ourselves together. "It sounded," said Haro to me, "like the whole Base Town just blew up, hit the troposphere, and fell back down again." He wasn't far out.

We made it back through the rock hills in the air-buggy inside twenty minutes. When we came over the top and saw the valley full of red haze and smoke and jets of steam, I was scared as hell. You could hear alarm bells and sirens going, but the smog was too thick to work out what kind of rescue went on and what was just automatic noise and useless. I sat in the driver's seat, gunning the buggy forward, and swearing and half crying. And Haro said, "It's okay."

"Of course it's not bloody okay. Look at it—there's no god-damn thing left—"

"Hey," he said, "calm down."

"Calm *down!* You're crazy. No, I'm not just shaken up over who may have just died in that soup. I'm pissing myself that if it's all gone, we'll never get off this guck-heeled planet alive."

The point being that planet NX 5 (whereon we are) is sufficient distance from HQ that it had taken our team, the "pioneer squad" every expert Company sends in ahead of itself, to explore, to test, to annotate, to break open for the use of Man, had taken us, I started to say, around thirty Terran years to arrive. We'd traveled cryogenically, of course, deep-frozen in our neat little cells, and that was how we'd get back when it was time. Only if Base had blown up, then maybe the ship had blown up, too, plus all the life supports, the SOSs—every darling thing. Naturally, if reports suddenly stopped coming in, the Company would investigate. But it would take thirty years before anything concrete got here. Though NX 5 is a gallant sight, with its pyramidal rocks rich in hidden ores, its dry forests, and cold pastel deserts busy with interesting flora and fauna, and its purling pale lemon skies...it doesn't offer a human much damn anything to get by on. While the quaint doggies that roam the lands, barking and walking upright, joy of the naturalist, had a few times tried to tear some of us to pieces. Marooned without proper supplies, shelter, or defense: with nothing—that was a fate and three-quarters.

"We'll be dead in half a month," I said.

"To die—to sleep, no more," Haro muttered, and I began to think the blow on the head had knocked him silly, so it'd be a half month shared with a lunatic at that.

However. We careened down into the smoke, and the first thing, a robot machine came up and ordered us off to a safety point. Events, it seemed, weren't so bad as they looked. Matters were in (metal) hand.

The short High Winter day drew to its end under cover of the murk, and we sat in the swimpool building on the outskirts, which had escaped the blast. Other survivors had come streaming and racketing in. There were about ninety of us crammed round the pool, eating potato chips and nuts and drinking cold coffee, which were all the rations the pool machines, on quarter-power, would give us. Most of the survivors had been away on recon or various digs or other stuff, like Haro and me. A handful with minor injuries, caught around the periphery of Base Town, were in the underground medical sanatorium which, situated northside, was unscathed. There were some others, too, a third of the planet away on field studies, who had yet to find out. It seemed that the core in the third quadrant of Base's energy plant had destabilized, gone critical, and—wham. The blast was of course "clean," but that was all you could say for it. The third quadrant (Westtown) had gone down a molten crater, and most of the rest of the place had reacted the way a pile of loose bricks might do in a scale-nine earthquake. That means, too, people die.

By dawn the next chill day, we had the figures. There had been around five thousand of us on-world, what with the primary team and the back-up personnel—shipmen, ground crew, service, mechanics, and techies. Out of those men and women, one thousand nine hundred and seventy-three were now dead. What we felt and said about that I won't repeat now; there's nothing worse than a bad case of requiemitis. Some of them were pals, you see. And a couple of them, well. Well, one of them was once practically my wife, only we never made it that far, parted, stayed friends (cliché). Yep. Requiemitis. Let's get on.

Aside from the dead, there were a lot of gruesomely injured down in the San, nearly three thousand of them. While the hospital machineries could keep them out of pain and adequately alive, the mess they were in required one form of surgery only. The form that's discreetly known on Earth as Rebo (rebodying) and is normally only for the blazing rich. Rebo, or the transfer of the ego, with all its memories, foibles, shining virtues, and fascinating defects, from one body (for some reason a wash-out—crippled, pan-cancerous—what you will) to another, is only carried out in extreme cases. And indeed the business was hushed up for years, then said not to work; then said not to be in use. It happened, though, that our Very Own Company was one of the sponsors of the most advanced Rebo techniques. Again, on Earth and the Earth Worlds, there are laws that limit transfer strictly. (And, naturally, there are religious sects who block the Sunday news, abhorring the measure.) In our case, though…we were different, weren't we? A heroic advance guard on a remote planet, needed to carry out vital work, etc., and all that.

Those were the first tidings of comfort and joy: figures of death and injury and rumors of Rebo. It threw us about somewhat. I noticed that the machines started to serve us hot food and alcohol at about this juncture. Then Haro and I got plastered to the plaster, and I stopped noticing. The second gospel came on about an hour later.

Now, an ego that's transferred, where doth it go? It goeth into another body, natch. Fine. Generally it's a grown body—android—tissue and cells. That can take anything from a trio of months to a year, depending on format and specifications, and, let it be whispered, on the amount of butter you can spread. Sometimes, too, there have allegedly been transfers into the recently dead bodies of others (there is supposed to be a gal in Appeline, New Earth, who bought her way into the pumped-out body of a movie star, dead of an overdose.

Apocryphal perhaps.) Or even of animals. (There's a poem about that one: Please, God, make of me a panther / A pretty panther, to please me / Pretty please, Hexos or Iaveh or Pan / There is no God but the god who can— / Make me a panther, please.)

That—I mean, grown androids—is what should have happened here. Approaching three thousand bodies for those that, alive only on support systems, needed them. Trouble was—you guessed it—the tissue banks that would have begun the project were over in Westtown and blown to tomorrow. It would take thirty years to get us some more.

The only facilities they had were the remains of the cryogenic storage (the ship had caught the blast), whole if depleted berths for about two hundred, into which three thousand persons were not going to fit. And another outfit, of which we knew little, but which would act, apparently, as the interim point of the transferal operation, a kind of waiting room between bodies. Mostly, a transfer flashes the subject through that *place* so fast it's just a nonstop station on the way. Yet this area, too, was it seemed capable of storing. Storing an ego. And its capacity was *unlimited*.

Just as requiems can be tedious, rehashing old action replays of panic and mayhem can get one down. So, I'll just spin the outline for those of us who like it in the big bold type.

The Company, who had gotten word of the latest position via the beacon intercom, had a proposition to offer us. And for proposition, read Fact. For we who are Company Persons know we belong to our Company, body and—yes, let's hear it for laughs—*soul*.

The Company would like us to stay on, and hang in there. This was how: the survivors of the Accident (and isn't that a lovesome name for it?), about one hundred and fifty people of both sexes, would donate their bodies to a common fund. Now, and let me stress this, around one hundred and fifty bodies put out like pairs of pants and dresses for the use of—one deep breath—over three thousand footloose egos. For the life supports would be switched off and the liberated bodiless egos of the mortally wounded taken into the wonderful—what shall I call it?—*place*—that stored unlimited egos within its unlimited capacity. And into that *place*, also, would go the liberated egos of those whose "skins" had not been damaged, those skins now the property of All. And here in the *place* we would all live, not crowded, for the disembodied are not crowded, lords and ladies of infinite space, inside a nutshell. Then, when it was our allotted time physically to work or play, Out we would come and get in a body. Not our own. That would hardly be fair, would it? Make those who had lost their own bodies for good feel jealous. (For that reason, no one gets finally supplied from the Bank or the Store until *everyone* gets supplied. Suits for all or none at all.) Anyway, there might be a slip-up. Yes, slips-up happen, like cores destabilizing. Gray vibes to meet oneself on the street in thrall to another. And in thirty years the androids would start growing like beautiful orchids in their tanks. And in maybe sixty years (or a bit longer, we're starting from scratch, remember, and not geared in the first place to do it) there'll be suits for all, bodies for everyone. New bodies, old familiar bodies, loved ones, forgotten ones—ah, the compost with it. It stank. And we shrilled and howled and argued and screamed. And we ended up in it to our eyebrows.

I recall wandering in a long drunk, and Haro, tall and dark and tawny, then as now, and drunk as me, said to me: "Calm down, Scay. They may blow it and kill us."

"But I don't want to be killed, pal."

"Nothing to it," said Haro. "Something to look forward to."

"My God, you still remember that," said Haro, draining his Coalwater.

Miranda's ears had stopped dinging.

"Say, Miranda, would you care for another?" I asked her in her own honeyed voice. "Of course I remember, you turkey. *Get killed.* Boy."

"Although Sens-D is a sort of death. You realize that, Scay?"

"Yes. Surely. Only I'm not dead in there. In there stops me getting dead. You know, I was thinking, it's funny—" ("You thinking is funny? You're right there," interpolates Haro) "—you get in a skin and you come Out and you feel wrong, and you feel okay, all at the same moment. And if you stay with the skin awhile, weeks, a month at a time, especially if you're working in it—it starts to feel natural. As if you always had it. Or something very like it, even if it isn't like it. Take Miranda here, I could get used to Miranda. Seems unlikely now, but I know from past experience I could, and would. Meanwhile, the—*place*—that starts to seem alien and frightening all over. So you can hardly stand to go Back there. And now and then, you need their drugs to stop you kicking and screaming on the way to Transfer, as if you were going off to get shot in the skull. And yet—"

"And yet?" said Haro, looking at me quietly with the other man's dark eyes.

"And yet, no one mentions it, but we all know, I suppose. When you come Out, there's the Big Wrench. It's yellow murder coming through into a new body. But when you go Back *In*—"

"No Wrench."

"No Wrench. Just like slipping into cool water and drifting there. I know there's sometimes a disorientation—it's cold, I've gone blind—that stuff. But it happens less and less, doesn't it? The last time I went Back. Hell, Haro. It was like gliding out of a lump of lead."

"And how do you feel about working, in Sens-D?"

I narrowed Miranda's gorgeous sherry eyes. Haro called it by the slang name, always, and I knew Haro. He was doing that just because, to him, "sensory deprivation" meant nothing of the sort, and he'd acknowledged it.

"I work fine down, up, In there. I do. When they started asking us to work that way, assessments, work-ups, layouts—the ideas stuff we used to do prowling round a desk—I thought it'd be a farce. But it's—stimulating, right? And then the assimilator passes on what you do, puts it in words Outside. I sometimes wonder how much talent gets lost just fumbling around in the physical after words—"

"And did you know," said Haro, "that some of the best work any of us ever did is coming out of our disembodied egos in Sens-D?"

I swore. "Ger-eat. That means we'll be stuck in there more and more. If the sweetheart Company found *that* out, they'll fix our contracts and—"

"But you just said, Scay, it's good In there."

"Devil's advocate. Come on. Where's the Coalwater you promised Miranda?"

He got the drinks and we drank them, and the conversation turned, because Company maneuvers and all the Company Likes and Wants can be disquieting. There have been nights in the skin I have lain and wondered, there, if the Company might not have arranged it all, even the Accident, just to see how we make out, what happens to us, in the *place*, or in the skin of another guy. Which is crazy, crazy. Sure it is.

Anyhow, Haro was due Back tomorrow, and I had only thirty-seven more hours left.

Rebuilt, and glamorized to make us happy, once we were stuck here for a century or so, Base Town was a strange sight, white as meringue against NX 5's lemon sky. Made in the beginning for the accommodation, researches, and pleasures of a floating population of two thousand, you now seldom saw more than twenty people on the streets at a time. For whom now did the bright lights sparkle, and the musics play, the eateries beckon, the labs invite, and the libraries yawn? Who races the freeway, swims the pool? Who rides the carousel? And, baby, ask not for whom the bell tolls. With the desert blowing beyond the dust traps on all sides, the sand-blown craters of the west, the rockies over there, frowning down, where weird whippy birds go flying in the final spasms of sunset, Base has the look of an elegant surreal ghost town. It's as if everyone has died, after all. The ones you see are only ghosts out for a day in the skin.

A new road goes west, off to that ship the machines are still working on. Haro and I walked out to the road, paused, looked up it into the distance, but made no move to do more. Once, years ago, we all went to see what progress they were making on the getting-home stakes. So the road had occasional traffic, some buggy or jetcar puttering or zooming along, like a dragonfly with wings of silver dust. Not anymore. Oh, they'll get the ship ready in time, it's in the contracts, in time for the new bodies, so we can all go to sleep for thirty years and wake up home in HQ, which isn't home. Who cares, anyway. What's home, *who's* home, to hurry for? Thirty years older, sixty years, one hundred and sixty. And we, the Children of the Ice, are the same as always. Live forever, and sell your soul to the Company Store.

"Hey, Haro, what do we do now?"

We discussed possibles. We could take a jeep out into the desert and track a pack of doggies, bring back a lady doggy and give it to Dydoo (who'd not smile). We could swim, eat curry, nap in the Furlough, walkabout, eat pizza, go to a movie. We did those. The film was *Jiarmennon*, sent out to our photo-tape receptors inside a year of its release on the Earth Worlds, by the kindly Company. A terrific epic, huge screen, come-at-you effects, sound that goes through the back of the cerebellum and ends up cranking the pelvis. One of those marvelous entertainments that exactly combine action, spectacle, and profound thought. I admit, some of the profound thought I didn't quite latch onto. But the overall was something plus. Five hours, with intervals. Three other people in the theatre. One of them, the one in Fedalin, was asleep or passed out.

When we came forth, the afternoon bloomed full across the town, a primrose sunshade for two suns, and it was sad enough to make you spit.

"Miranda's hormones are starting to pick up. Did she have crying jags, do you know?"

We walked across to the Indoor Jardin, the one place we hadn't yet re-seen. In the ornamental pond, the bright fish live and die and are taken away, and new-bred bright fish put in. Maybe it was the last Coalwater taken in the Sand Bar on East, but I, or Miranda's body, began suddenly to weep.

"Goddamn it, Miranda, leave it out, will you? I've only got you for another ten hours, and you do this to me. *Quit*, Miranda."

"Why does it have to be Miranda who's crying?" said Haro in his damn nice, damn clever way.

"Well, who's it look like?"

"Looks like Miranda. Sounds like you, feller."

"Falsetto? Yeah. Well. I didn't cry since—Christ, when did I last?"

"You want me to tell you."

Belligerent, I glared at him through massed wet cilia thick as bushes. "So tell me, tell me, turkey."

"When the core blew, and took Mary with it."

"Ah. Oh, yes. Okay. Shit."

The pain of that, coming back when I hadn't expected it, stopped me crying, the way a kick in the ear can stop hiccups. You preferred the hiccups, all right?

"I'm sorry, Scay," Haro said presently. "But I think you needed to know."

"Know how I felt about—I *know*. It doesn't help."

"Sometime, it may. You wanted to be with her. And Company red tape on marriage liability got in your way, and you both chickened out. But your insides didn't."

"I used to dream about it," I said sullenly. "The Accident. And her, and what it must've—"

There was a long pause, and the fish, who lived and died, burned there in the pond like votive candles.

"It's over now," said Haro. "It isn't happening to her anymore, except inside your head."

We sat on the stone terrace, and he put his arm over my Miranda's shoulders, and Miranda responded, the length of her spine.

"Miranda," I said, slightly ashamed, "wants you."

"And I notice the guy I'm wearing today fancies the heck out of Miranda."

He turned me, carefully, because I was a woman and he was much larger in build than I, and he kissed me. It was good. It got to me how good it was.

"We've never been in this position before," I muttered, in Miranda's husky voice. "As the space-captain said to the wombat."

"Never been male and female together, I mean." I elaborated, as our hands mutually traveled, and our mouths, and our bodies warmed and melded together like wax, and the flame lit up about the usual way, about the usual part, but, oh brother, not quite. "What I mean is, kid. If you'd tried this on when we were both male, I'd have knocked you into a cocked cuckoo-clock."

"The lady," said Haro, "doth protest too much."

So I shut up, and we enjoyed it, Haro, Miranda, and I.

The lemon light was going to the acid of limes, and the birds were tearing round the sky when we started back along Main-street. I hadn't gotten Miranda too drunk, but I had got her well-laid, and that was healthful for her. She had nothing to reproach me with.

"You're not, by any chance, walking me home, Haro Fielding?"

"Nope."

"Well, good. Because, when I see you again, I don't know how I'm going to live this down."

Heck, yes, I could hear myself, even the sentence-constructs were getting to be like Miranda's. That's how you grow used to what you are. I suppose it was inevitable, the other scene, he and me, sometime. Buddies. Yip.

"Don't worry too much about that," said Haro.

I shrugged. "I'll be Back In. I won't be worrying at all. That *place* is a real desexer, too. Genderless we go. And get Out...confused."

"That *place*," he repeated. "*In*. All that labor and all that machinery, to keep alive. When all the time, being *In* is, I'd take a bet, almost what death is."

"You said that already."

"I did, didn't I? So if that's what death is like, where's the difference? "

"The difference is, there's a guaranty on this one. You *get* there. You go on. Not like—not like Mary, blown into a million grains of sugar."

"Mary's body."

"Okay. Her *body*. I liked her body."

Haro stopped, looking up over the town at the glowing dying sky.

"Don't fool yourself. You loved Mary, not just Mary's skin. And though Miranda and this guy here were making love, you and I were making it, too."

"Oh, now look—I've got nothing against—but I'm not—"

"Forget that. You're missing the doorway and coming in the garbage-shoot with catsup in your hair. What I'm saying is this, and I want you to listen to me, Scay, or you won't understand."

"What do I have to understand, buster? Hah?"

"Just listen. Sens-D is—Christ, it's a zoo, an enclosure full of egos—of psychic, noncorporeal, unspecified, unclassified, inexplicable, and *unexplained* matter, that persists out of, and detached from, the flesh. Got it?"

"I got it. So?"

"Death, Scay, is being that same psychic, noncorporeal, etc., etc., material—only Out of the skin *and* Out of the box."

"Yes?" I said *politely*, to see if he'd hit me. He didn't.

"The *place*, as you call it, is a bird-cage. But look up there. That's where the birds want to be. The free wide sky."

I watched the birds in spite of myself. I thought about our extended peculiar lives in the slave gangs of the Company. Of going to sleep on ice. Of sliding into the *place*. Of days in the skin.

"That's it?" I said eventually. "All you want to tell me?"

"That's it, that's all."

We said our good-byes near the Transfer ramp.

"See you next skin," I said.

And Haro grinned and walked away.

Dydoo waved an ear at me as I strolled in. "Had a nice day?"

"Divine."

Poor mutt. He'd been smoking, two trays full, and spilling over.

I refrained from cracks about dog ends. What a life the
man led, held in that overcoat of fur and fume. It was a
young specimen that died up on the ridge, and the robots
found it, cleaned out the disease, did the articulation surgery,
and popped in Dydoo. Sometimes, when he gets crazy-mad
enough, he'll bark. I know, I used to help make him. And you
know, it isn't really funny. Bird-cage. Dog-cage.

I got ready for going Back, and Dydoo gave me my shot.
I wasn't bothered today, not fighting or wanting to. I guess I
haven't really been like that for years. The anguish, that had
also gone, just a sort of melancholy left, almost nostalgia, for
something or other. Beyond the high windows the night was
coming, reflecting on instruments and panels and in the pier-
glass, till the lights came up.

"You ready now?" Dydoo peered down at me.

"Go on, lick my face, why don't you?"

"And put myself off my nice meaty bone? You should be so
honored. Say, Scay? Yah know what I'm coming Out as at the
end, the new body? Heh? The Hound of the Baskervilles. And
I'm gonna get every last one of you half-eyed creeps and—"

Then the switches went over.

One minute you are here, and then you are—*there*—

I glided free of the lump of lead into the other world.

Three days later (that's the time they tell me it was) I made history. I spent two hours in my own skin. Yes. My very own battered thirty-five-year-old me. Hey!

My body was due, you see, for someone else, and because of what happened, they dumped me into it first. So they could thump all those questions out at me like a machine-gun. The Big Wrench. Then Dydoo yelping and growling, techies from C Block, some schmode I didn't know yelling, and a whole caboodle full of machines. I couldn't help much, and I didn't. In the end, after all the lie-check tests and printouts and threats and the apologies for the threats, I reckon they believed me that it was nothing to do with me. And then they left me to calm down in a little cubicle, to get over my own anger and my grief.

He was a knight, Haro Fielding. A good guy. He could have messed it up with muck, that borrowed skin, or thrown it off a rock or into one in a jeep, and smashed it up, unusable. Instead, he donated it, one surplus body, back to the homeless ones, the Rest of Us. All they had to do was fill it up with nice new blood, which is easy with the technology in town here.

He'd gone up into the rockies, sat down, and opened every important vein. The blood went out like the sea and left the dry beach of Haro lying under the sky, where the searchers found him—it. They searched because he was missing. He hadn't turned up at Transfer next day. They thought they had another battling hysteric on their hands. No use to try transfer now, obviously. The body had been dead long enough the ego and all the other incorporeal, etc., were gone. Though the body was there, Haro was not.

The slightest plastic surgery would take care of the knife cuts. One fine, bonus, vacant skin. He was a gentleman, that louse.

God knows how long he'd been planning it, preparing for it in that dedicated, clear-vision crusader sort of way of his. Quite a while. And I know, if I hadn't met him Out that day, the first I'd ever have heard of it would have been from some drunk sprawled in the Star Bar: Hey, you hear? Fielding took himself out.

As it was, obliquely but for sure, Haro'd told me all of it. I should have cottoned on and tried to— Or why should I have? Each to his own. In, or is it Out? For keeps.

And I guess it was grief and anger made me laugh so hard in the calm-down cubicle. God bless the Company, and let's hear it for the one that got away. As the line says, *flying to other ills*—but flying. Home free.

Free as a bird.

Within the Ghost

Once worlds have ended, and the curtains of space closed upon them, where does their genius go? Their great music and art, their architecture, literature, and thought, their *beauty*— all held till then in vessels of physical form, or the records of machines, or simply in the memory of humankind. Is everything obliterated merely, rinsed away and lost?

Nothing is *ever* lost. Though every atom, note, and perfume perishes, yet it remains caught within some vast awareness that needs no facsimile, no re-creation, neither speech nor vision. And this it is that, thereafter, leaves indelible, golden paw prints on the glass sands of eternity, and all across the darkness of the deepest void.

§ § §

During the afternoon of the 9th mid-season Epicyle, a meteor shower of colossal force struck the planet Arkann.

The meteoraid had, through a series of uncommon errors, stayed undetected until the thirteenth hour of the previous night. Full evacuation therefore proved impossible. Since there was no use in doing so, and to avoid undue and fruitless panic, the population was not alerted. The shower was traveling at unusual speeds if with abnormal density. It did not become generally apparent until 70 minutes before the initial impacts began. What precautions were feasible were then taken. Of course, to no purpose.

The 'raid destroyed much of the center-cyle face of Arkann and rocked the world on its axis to some awkward effect.

As the catastrophe played out, several of the space-stations then crossing above the center-cyle quadrant were themselves struck and destroyed, or disabled to the point of nonviability.

One station, however, the Kayis 42X, was struck a side-long blow, which only uncoupled it from a controlled orbit, casting it adrift. While detonation and destruction collapsed the planet, the Kayis was pushed out into the farther reaches of space, a solitary lifeboat jettisoned from a sinking liner.

ᔆ ᔆ ᔆ

Vils had been sleeping when the station's alarm resounded.

The alarm rarely activated, but during the five years he had served there, he had already experienced the event twice. On both occasions the problem was comparatively slight. A malfunctioning refrigeration unit flooding the storage deck; a solar flare of some kind that temporarily impeded communications with the station's Connect HQ groundside. In each case Kayis's own mechanisms were soon in control, the flaw repaired in an hour, planetary time. But naturally the Kayis did not take chances. It was most reliable, just as it had been built to be.

That afternoon Vils had slept less than 2 hours after an active stint of 27. This was to be the last period of his current 3-month term on the station, following which he was due for 30 days leave on-planet. He had therefore been getting everything in proper order for the alternative crew. The rest of his own team, Dmitru and Linka, had left days before, Dmitru on compassionate grounds (a death in his family). Vils alone therefore encompassed the work of three. He needed rest. When Kayis woke him with its wailing, Vils was angry.

"*What is it?*"

The soft blue communication screen found in all the station's spaces flickered with a moment's scintillance. The siren paled to a monotone. The calm, genderless, ageless voice of Kayis answered.

"A meteoraid is occurring. Planet Arkann has been struck—"

A thin whistle broke through the Kayis voice.

Vils was already on his feet, staring at the view-screen that had opened in the cabin wall.

What it showed was like a scene from a poor quality disaster movie of several centuries before. It was laughable, unbelievable. Vils did not laugh or disbelieve.

He started to ask Kayis to repeat the passage of words that the sonic whistle interrupted.

As he did so a terrific soundless noise eclipsed all others, and a blinding non-light put out all images, sane or mad, and next all consciousness, and so too the individual world of which Vils, like all living things, was composed.

The second time he woke up was stranger.

At first he could not figure out why he was lying on the floor of the cabin, but the blue comm screen was showing soft waves like a lazy tide, and Kayis spoke to him at once.

"You are unharmed, Vilsev"—it always used his full name, an eccentric, pointless courtesy—"only a little bruising to the edge of the left hand, left knee. Treatment has been applied. Lie still for a moment and breathe slowly. The air has been reinforced. Now, regain your feet, and drink the medication in the fountain-cup."

Vils lay where he was.

"What happened?"

"What do you remember?"

"The siren. You said—the *planet*—"

Kayis's voice, always calm, practical—very nearly *stupidly*, and certainly inappropriately, reassuring: "Arkann is lost."

"Arkann—"

"This station has been ejected from orbit and thrown on to a random course, outward. Kayis is now computing its new trajectory, although unable substantially to alter it."

"What about Connect HQ?"

"It is destroyed."

"Then contact other planet centers."

"They are destroyed also."

"Then other stations—vessels in the area—the Straida Hub—"

"The communication system of this station no longer fully functions beyond the planetary radius. It has suffered some damage."

Vils swore in a whisper.

Kayis paused politely for the swearing, then went on. "All other systems aboard Kayis are unimpaired and have been secured. Defense systems are operative. Minor pockets of surface damage the mechanics are now restoring."

"Wait," he said. "Wait." He sat up, and a hurricane surge of nausea swept through him, then away. He sat on the cushioned floor, listening to Kayis's calm kind voicelessness. Presently, having taken the medication from the dispenser, he left the cabin and went about through the entire complex, while in reply to his interrogation, the voice offered reports of itself. It did this as ever, speaking politely and formally, as to any human aboard. Kayis too always spoke, and did so now, of itself in the third person— "*It*," Kayis said. "*Kayis*," it said. "*The machine.*" "*The station…*"

At some juncture, staring from the great view-lens on the foredeck, out into an infinity of infinities, all unknown and new and *terrible* and, now, *unavoidable*, Vils wept.

He thought of Dmitru at his mother's funeral, blown to pieces among the shattering crystal chapel and the smashed verdigris of old trees; of Linka with her lover, crushed into a scarlet amalgam. He wept for all Arkann, and for Arkann itself. He wept in vain, as humanity must.

Kayis went on being compassionate and did not try to comfort him. It simply told him all the optimistic pluses. Safety and secured existence still supported the unknown journey that now they must choicelessly undertake, the man and the machine.

⑤ ⑤ ⑤

For the first two days he was shocked and mostly deadly quiet. For the next 20 days he was partly crazy, ranting about the failed communication system and oddly, contrastingly, breaking things that were breakable. After this he made the station's mechanism play over to him excerpts from his time (electrocorded of course, for general security) with Linka and Dmitru, and earlier with others who had served on Kayis. He got drunk a lot during this period. He also smoked several of the brands of less-safe cigret.

Gradually, and then quite swiftly, began a phase of melancholy, and finally inertia. For brief spells sometimes he again ranted about the comm facility that must be—somehow—restored. To no avail, they were well out of planetary range. This phase also faded.

Then he no longer glared in rage or mockery at the flowing of space, the vague intimations of other distant solar systems, and unidentifiable outer star clusters through which, now, Kayis almost incidentally endlessly passed. Equipped to be a lesser type of space-vessel, Kayis had fully become one. Compelled to voyage, it did so. If ever cut adrift, providing reasonably intact, all such structures would be capable of self-maintenance, and an indefinite plateau for survival for themselves and their inhabitants. Unluckily for the rest of Arkann's anchored fleet, the meteoraid had pulverized their chances.

If the 'raid had happened four days before it had, Dmitru and Linka would still have been aboard. *Alive*. With him.

Vils thought of this and lay motionless on his bunk.

Nine more days passed. Then a mechanic machine, spawned from Kayis's insides, came to clean, hydrate, and feed him. When Vils resisted, it mildly sedated him and then did as intended.

Drearily he shouted at Kayis. Why not leave him alone? Neither he nor the station could make contact any more with the civilization that had created and nurtured them. They had been flung beyond the perimeters. Probably too, nothing, no one, would ever search for them, since it must seem everything else on or attending Arkann, had been destroyed.

They were going nowhere, and that—forever. Or at least, as Vils stressed, *Kayis* was, for he, long-lived though human-kind had become, would not persist more than another 80 or 90 years.

Kayis did not reason with him. Or protest. Or encourage.

Kayis kept him alive and cleaned up and gave him revital-izing if compulsory sleep, adding to that all the luxury foods and drinks and legal drugs he demanded.

On the 51st day he pushed by the mechanic machine and himself went into the shower.

On the 71st day he had somehow himself returned, as if spontaneously, to the ordinary regime of hygiene, nourish-ment, work, observation, reflection, and the occasional ordi-nary and recommended treats. By then he only lost his temper over silly things, and momentarily. He only wept about once in every couple of weeks and for less than a minute. He was sad and bleak and sane and clean. And practical. He got on with life as best he could. What else was there to do? Except die. Which Kayis, anyway, seemed likely to prevent.

⑨ ⑨ ⑨

A year passed. An Arkannite year of 14 months.

The station's direction was random, and it moved at non-lightspeed (*nolisp*). Outside, the star-strewn desert did not unravel into anything especially spectacular. In the twelfth month a small two-sun system was visible, several *lisp* (light-speed) years travel away. Kayis, at Vils' instruction, scanned and investigated the types of the three visible planets, which were untennanted, barren and dry. There was obviously no purpose now in such monitoring, yet all the time he and Kayis automatically carried it out, checking on every curiosity and implication that even dimly appeared or was otherwise indi-cated. This was mere functionality, Vils knew, for Kayis. And for him it was accustomed, if now meaningless and uninter-esting, routine.

He had long since asked the station why it and apparently all the other look-out mechanisms of Arkann had failed to detect the meteoraid in time.

Kayis had no answers beyond a cool mathematic of coincidental malfunction, human error, and/or signalesion occlusion of a kind sometimes, if seldom, encountered.

The area of space through which the choiceless journey tended was far from the Hesiona Nebulind, in which sector Arkann, and its fellow planets were (had been) located. Regions in this outer sector of the galaxy were generally uncharted. Speculation, even myth (old space-sailors' yarns) were the only information that Kayis's computerized library could give.

Now and then, during the next year, Vils dreamed of the deaths of Dmitru and Linka. And too those of other persons he had known on-planet. None of these last had been close to him; his main relationships had occurred lightmiles off. Frequently the dream deaths bore no relation to what must or might have happened during the 'raid — or worse, if they had survived, in the hours after.

He no longer wept.

He read a great deal, and Kayis played him music from the library. Vils found he yearned for all the pieces Kayis had not been given to store — Rakhmaninov's later concertos, Prokofiev's ballet scores, the *Librius Alentus* of Jy, various choral works of Handl and Stoll. And there was one book too, he could never recall the title of, which he and Kayis searched for through an entire evening (by the planetary chronometer) and did not unearth.

Inevitably humans always wanted what was not available. What they could not — *ever* — get.

Vils talked conversationally to Kayis often, but then he always had. All or most of the crews had done so. And Kayis always responded, naturally. Calm, wise words. The history of things, the thoughts of mankind, the lessons of physical worlds. All built in to the machinery. Kayis could talk as well and wonderfully as it cleansed the latrines, repainted the walls in sheer, uplifting colors, pruned and watered the small hydroponic garden, flicked off from its own inner and outer skin the tiny space-mites and debris that might try to colonize there.

One night, about the third month of the second year, Vils dreamed that he heard Kayis weeping. The sobs were liquid with tears, yet still sexless and of no age.

"What is it?" he cried out in the dream. "Tell me, my dear friend, what's wrong with you?"

There was no answer. The dream melted away. When he remembered it the next morning, he said nothing about it. Vils was ashamed. He must be careful not to humanize Kayis. True, it was now, and probably for always, his only companion. But it was a machine, as it, itself, always affirmed, when referring to itself. And he a man, flesh and blood, imbued with a psyche, an intellect, or even that thing once termed a soul or ghost. He and Kayis were not *friends*. And machinery did not weep.

§ § §

He had grown up, through infancy and childhood into youth, amid a planetary system a long way from Arkann.

His home had been a communal farm, a huge sprawling technicated mansion, whose electric chimneys and wind-valves sang at certain times of day and night, like gigantic choirs of those real insects that hopped about the cornfields. The fields also sprawled for miles, and then came the open plains, yellow as lions from an ancient illustration.

Far off, worlds away they had seemed, lilac mountains upheld a sky that changed its temper and color at a whim. It was a dry place, often rainless for months at a time. The narrow river courses that ran like seams through patches of scrubby forest would empty and nearly close themselves. After dark the stars kept the sky's colors in bright perforations of the nocturnal black, silver and blue, red and amber, copper, pearl, and glass green.

Vils, aboard the adrift station, dreamed no more of a crying machine, and seldom of human death.

He dreamed of walking the woods and paths of his past, of working in the baking fields, sheltering from violent rainstorms that lasted less than fifteen minutes yet filled up the gullies of the half-shut rivers, where, afterwards, you could catch fat four-legged fish that came out of holes to swim there. He dreamed stars fell and he caught them, tiny as candies on his palm. He dreamed of a grasshopper, tall as a man, that sat in the corn and made its music.

There were no people in the dreams, no proper machines save those inherent to the distant house that, dreaming, he never again entered.

The dreams soothed him. Then grew tiresome. Then they too were gone.

He *stopped* dreaming, or never recollected what he had dreamed.

Vils asked Kayis then to monitor his sleep, waking him every third or fourth night if it detected dream-activity in his brain. This in the hope of remembering something. But at that point, even if woken up, he never did.

The stars in space were not like the starry nights of his homeland. Shadowy alter-elements moved over space and the stars there, spangles and smokes with prosaic scientific reasons and names.

Space was not a starry night.

⑤ ⑤ ⑤

Now and then Vils told himself, talking only inside his head, that despite the lack of a communication function, and the proximity of the wasteland they had entered, it was still just possible Kayis might, coincidentally only, approach some obscure, perhaps secret, outpost of mankind. Or after all, some person somewhere *might* be searching for them. Might find them. One day, someday. Sometime...ever....

✺ ✺ ✺

An evening came, by the planetary chronometer at the end of the second year, when Vils was playing eschek with Kayis, as occasionally he and formerly others always had.

With no warning, Kayis did not take its turn to move a piece (by sliding it along the board through ion-electronic means).

"Your move, Kayis," Vils spoke almost thoughtlessly, supposing the station had deduced he was still considering his own move. Although, of course, even a robot opponent must have noted he had completed it.

When Kayis did not respond, either vocally or by shifting a piece, a sudden and awful terror swamped Vils. Inevitably. For what had happened? What now had gone wrong?

"*Kayis!*" he bellowed into the star-chilled twilight of the foredeck.

Kayis did not reply.

Vils sprang upward, knocking and tilting the board on its pedestal. But the board adjusted itself, and a firefly display of lights flared up on every side.

"All is well, Vilsev." The voice, so pure and alien and calm. As even in disaster it always was.

"Why didn't you answer me?"

"There has been..." the voice hesitated, presumably to evaluate its information, though it sounded, for an instant, like a human voice taking care with what, next, it must say. "There is a contact, Vilsev."

"A—what do you mean?"

"Part of Kayis's remaining communication faculty has reacted to an external signal."

"What—what?"

"Wait one minute, Vilsev. The machine establishes a link."

Vils found his legs had gone to water. He dropped back in his seat because he had no alternative. He sat there and stared out of the vast viewscreen that showed the spacescape beyond and all around. His eyes were glazed and did not focus.

More than a minute passed. Then another two minutes.

Kayis spoke: "There is a planetary system. A signal has reached the station. The station's communicatory ableness has therefore been re-activated to a capacity of 86%."

"A signal—of what sort? Who—who is signaling—"

"Kayis does not know, Vilsev."

"Is it human?"

A pause.

Kayis said, "The station does not compute it is human."

"Mechanical then. A machine."

"Kayis does not compute," said Kayis, "Kayis does not compute it is mechanical."

"What then?" he said again. He was hoarse, dry as any rainless riverbed.

"The station does not know," said Kayis.

"Play it over to me."

Another gap. Vils swore violently.

"Why didn't you play it as I told you to?"

"Kayis did play it, but you could not hear. The frequency is at odds since the system is not as able as it was. Only the communication system can hear. Kayis does not identify what the signal is, but it reacts to the signal and can read it. The planet is one of seven grouped about a single sun. This is what the signal reveals."

"How far off?" Vils asked. "Where?"

"Kayis will form a chart to show you, Vilsev. Kayis is computing the station will take months to reach this place, five or a little more."

"Five months…a planet…a signal. No. It's some mistake. A mechanical error. Check and read it again and put it right."

Kayis now did not reply.

Going to the screen above the gallery of the deck, Vils peered out, naturally seeing nothing substantially other than he already had.

A vague secondary fear stirred through him. Had the technic brain of Kayis itself malfunctioned? But everything else seemed as it should be. Look, now even the game-piece was sliding into its slot on the eschek board. Kayis had won the game, which it was programmed to do a reasonable yet random number of times.

§ § §

Throughout what ultimately proved to be, travelling via *no-lisp*, five and three-quarter months, Vils became excited and anxious. He was unable to help himself.

Kayis too, had it been human, might have been judged as almost over-eager to bring him any news. As the signal strengthened, information expanded and charts were produced, atlases of star-ways ready-plotted—or hypothesized. Everything was shown on the screens. Kayis announced that the one-star solar system that contained the planet might be that mentioned in an obscure historic and isolated robot survey. In this case the world represented had been code-called *Jangala*. It was a fertile environment, while the six surrounding orbs were only chunks of boiling, icy, or arid rock. The sun was young, and Jangala lay the perfect distance from its face. The rest were too close, or too far.

Vils pored over all there was to be had, listened to any concepts that were, or had been, floated, stared at any facsimilous images anyone or thing (man, machine) had devised. He grew familiar with the likely look of the planet.

Kayis inaugurated, or else assisted with everything, again as if eager. But that was only fancy.

Vils guarded himself strictly against such ideas.

If only there had been an animal on the station, bred for long life, intelligence and companionship. But no members of the crews had felt such a ploy necessary.

Vils did not dream of Jangala, just as now he did not dream of people. Nor really dream at all, except, it seemed, in amorphous snatches, emotion rather than visualizations.

But he *daydreamed* about the planet.

"Is there life there?" he asked repeatedly.

At first Kayis could not be sure, aside from the presence of living plants and essential animate molecular organisms.

Then Kayis *was* sure that, these aside, there was no life, neither humanoid, nor animalian. Not even, Kayis mooted, entirely alien life as such.

There would be no one to talk to.

No one to meet or greet.

What then had formed a signal so vigorous that even the reduced capacity of the station had perceived it?

"It is the planet," Kayis told him.

Inevitably, he realized, with a ridiculous resentfulness. For Kayis had been primed to receive and react to the sub-linguistic communications of Arkann. How else had Connect HQ kept Kayis on track, and how, ultimately, HQ demolished, had Kayis known Arkann's full and horrible fate?

One peculiar and extraordinary moment ensued, nevertheless.

Vils was eating lunch in the refectory, before going to work on various chores, when Kayis broke into his meal with a new, almost journalistic essay on Jangala—which it seemed the communication system had just resolved. Features of the planet were described by Kayis—tall hills, deep jungle-forests, a small and landlocked saline sea, shaped like an axe-head—

When the speech, delivered as ever coolly and clearly, sexlessly, agelessly, and at the most serene pace, was over, Vils heard himself comment, bitterly, "You just can't wait to get there, can you, Kayis 42X?"

The instant the words were free of him, he felt a shudder of distaste. Was he losing control of his mind, now? A machine did not long for arrivals, did not, as a man did, superimpose undreamed dreams of childhood and loss and yearning on to other objects, whether inert or alive.

Kayis answered at once. "Kayis does not understand you, Vilsev. Kayis must travel at its usual speed. The wait is now for another three-and-a-half months."

Kayis does not understand you...

Vils heard in his head another voice then, quite voiceless, yet his own. *Dissembler*, said the second voice. Liar.

§ § §

Is there such a *thing* as an "inanimate object?"

Logically not. Since all things, whether composed of flesh or fiber, gas or water, granite or iron, take their basic comprisement from atoms.

The fundamental building blocks of all (known) worlds, at least, are particles particular mainly in their variety and genius of *manner* and *aspect*, but not of material.

If created by accident, or design—or even *accidental* design (ink spilled through carelessness may yet create an exquisite, even a readable pattern) every latent or potent *object* still has that in common with its unlike siblings. The results are multitudinous and dissimilar. The mud, however, from which they come, even if they result from chaos itself, is universally identical.

The rose and the man, the lion and the worm, the eagle and the star and a tiny clod of dung—are all related. And with them the cliff, the ocean, the tower, the ship of steel.

Then, if there is a life-*force* in mankind (whatever the force *is*—mind, intellect, psyche, soul, *ghost*) that same force will reside, comparatively—while it occupies a physical environment—within *any* and *all* of the basic mud-clay formations. Within the rose. *Within* the mountain, the eagle, the planet, and the star.

Within—how else—the delicate grey turd of a rabbit.

And if in all these, then too inside the machine. There also, and *always*, is the ghost, the spiritous driver of each physical vehicle.

But within the ghost *itself*—that final, incorporeal and non-concessionary overseer—is what?

§ § §

The planet code-called Jangala had been mechanically sighted after the third month. Another month, and it became visible to the human eye, even unassisted. After another one-and-three-quarters months, Station Kayis 42X had anchored itself, aided by the planetary spatial field, ready to begin a steady circling orbit.

The planet's circumferent mass was greater than Arkann's. It would take 19 Arkann days, by the chronometer, to complete a full epicyle section.

Kayis began the Epicylis.

Vils, and evidently the station, observed the planet.

Sometimes, as had been consistently feasible above Arkann, "close-ups" were achievable on screen, as if seeing the world's surface from a mid-altitude plane.

It was like eating or drinking, Vils thought. A fine meal after a famine.

Like that too, the sort of mental and emotional indigestion that followed.

He suffered nightmares—made worse, he felt, since he could never now recall their ingredients, only the fear and trauma.

But that passed. Of course it did.

In the seventh month, Kayis said: "Vilsev, it is an option for the station to descend. That is, Vilsev, to make landfall."

Already it was established that the lush dark-green and golden world was rich in oxygenated air and hydrated with wholesome waters. No animal forms of any type, let alone advancement, had been detected, and never visually spotted, but this did not necessarily preclude them; they might initially escape even technicated notice. The vegetation seemed generally nourishing, often having some relation to familiar crops. The planet too had day and night. Nothing notably adverse was registered.

"If we go down, are we able subsequently to return out here?" Vils asked this immediately. Both descent and subsequent relaunch were normally part of a station's capability. But Kayis had been through the meteoraid. And the planet was unknown, unknown that was in a way beyond all analysis of gravity, air, flora, or fauna. How dangerous was Jangala, and in what hidden fashion? "How tricky would the landing be? And the visit—what danger?" And he realized he asked this of Kayis as if he were pleased by the notion of a trip to the surface, where in fact he was apprehensive. All his unease had risen in him, from the moment they grew close enough to see its beauty. Jangala was like a stunning yet inimical woman—you desired to be near her, yet also wished to avoid her entirely. You knew she might catch you in her web, or only harm you by some passing scratch, by her unnoticed, but that would leave a scar for life.

Kayis took quite a time to respond to his question.

He decided it was computing, evaluating.

Then Kayis said, "The station is impaired, Vilsev. It requires temporary grounding in order for overview and restoration, which is not properly possible in the orbital zone."

"Why have you never told me this before?"

"The station's condition has slightly worsened over time. Kayis did not wish to alarm you needlessly, when nothing could yet be done."

Vils stared at the view of Jangala below. He pondered how the human government of Arkann had not "needlessly alarmed" the planet's population with news of the by-then unavoidable meteoraid.

He said nothing.

Kayis said: "I will ask again later, Vilsev, when you have weighed matters."

And Vils thought of a calculating, aging mother, coercing by her patience, indefatigable in her selfless, tolerant selfishness. And right, obviously. Always right.

ⓢ ⓢ ⓢ

Kayis alighted without so much as a bump, just as day was melting into dusk.

Descending, the crimson sun's set had spread below like liquid paint, next risen above them, then sunk again below and away over the curve of the world.

In the monitor screens Vils watched the hot color dissolve and the velvet gray-blue of first night infuse. They had landed northerly. It would be a prolonged twilight. Through the mechanical ears of the station macrophones there then began to come a sort of purring syncopation—like the grasshoppers he had heard in childhood and youth. But apparently it was not that. There were no evolved insects, no recognizable animals. It was instead the murmuring close-down of certain plants that diurnally stretched out their leaves like radar bowls, then shut them tight for the dark.

Finally the whirring purr faded, and by then the sky was luminous indigo and scattered with stars in many shades. This closely resembled his memories too, though the tints seemed brighter, he thought, here; perhaps only some effect of the scanners. Then he heard the depth of silence, deep as a chasm, which gradually became orchestrated by the incoming solar tide of the axe-head sea.

Kayis was again testing the atmosphere for toxins. Now immersed in it, the station could and must take very thorough and flawless readings. But by midnight all were benign. The night would last approximately 21 hours, the day less than 9. Yet this had not impaired the fertile growth and opulence of the jungle-forests and plains. The verdure had found means to capture solar heat and power. During the period of the nocturne, every inch of flora then processed what it had trapped and stored.

That first night, when it had become true night, Vils dreamed of hollowed darkened chambers in which fiery wheels were spinning and spinning sunlight into gold.

Remembering this dream, Vils felt healed.

He felt *remade*, new again. Life was possible.

Was it now safe to venture outside the station?

⑨ ⑨ ⑨

Kayis, when Vils asked this question, was hesitant, if only in its mechanistic way. It said that there *seemed* to be no hostile elements outside. The atmosphere was if anything better than initially supposed. A stream ran nearby, going down toward the shore of the sea that lay only a quarter of a mile off; the stream water was drinkable and contained essential vitamins, these presumably leached from surrounding plants. (Kayis had already dispatched mechanical devices to test this.)

Then surely there would be no problem in Vils stepping out? He was impatient himself now, a boy wanting to go fishing in his holidays.

"It is better that you wait a little, Vilsev," Kayis said.

"Why? What's the matter with this place? We've tested and checked it. You have landed us on it. Open the doors." He was already suited up in one of the lighter protective garments and had included a breathing device for the unlikely contingency that something might go wrong with the clean and faultless air.

Kayis said: "It may be that the minor erosions the station has recently suffered have somewhat impaired the checks it has run. There has seemed to be a 99% safety margin. But in fact—"

"Open the doors." Vils was no longer the urgent (pleading?) boy. He was angry, cold, and old. "Let me out," he added, and heard the menace in his voice with yet another disagreeable shock.

But Kayis now obeyed him. The locks and outer doors were being activated—if, it seemed to him, rather slowly.

Vils strode from the deck, leapt down the ramp. He ran towards the station's exit. God—God. He had never thought to leave this prison again—

"Vilsev," said Kayis.

That was all.

He heard the soft voice, now insubstantial—as he sprang toward the station's hope of light. He took no notice.

Kayis did not speak again.

It had got cranky, the station. Its functions were indeed imperfect. Better break free, see what sanctuary was to be had out in the sunshine of this world. When the outer doors hissed wide, nevertheless he stood frozen on the threshold.

Blinded by the glow of a natural day, he stared through a blur of tears into the green-blue sky, and all about the vast hands of the creeper-roped trees held out their black-green fingers, their leaves spread like fans and bowls, like gazing eyes and thirstily drinking mouths…. They made a faint intermittent trilling, suggestive of birdsong, just as in the dark they stored and spun and made the song of grasshoppers. Grasses dark as jade poured to a broad meadow of some tall and honey-colored grain that Kayis had told him might be harvested and ground for bread. Flowers like giant lilies, pink and bronze, slowly peeled back their petals in an ecstasy of solar absorption, then slowly coiled them shut. Open and shut and open, on and on, each process taking one minute. The air was like vintage champagne. It made him drunk, full of bubbles of oxygen and the alcoholic scent of organic life.

It was nearly half an hour before he moved to jump down into the rustling silken grass. He went forward, stumbling slightly, stopping here and there—a statue again—resuming. The stream flexed like a rope of diamonds. And beyond the meadow the land sloped to the bay, and the green-turquoise of the sea was rippling and swimming north to south now the tide was momentarily stable. It sounded, the sea, even as it had through the macrophones, like all tidal waters—like breathing, or sighs, human, alive. A fellow creature.

He did not return to the station for hours.

At last a little crab-like machine came scrambling down the slope behind him, onto the beach of jacinth stones.

"You must come back for health checks," said the machine, in its own gravelly chatter.

"Soon," he said.

"You must come b—"

Leaning over he switched it off.

Then he sat on, watching the muscular running of the sea, and the little machinelet sat quietly by him, like a loyal dog.

Kayis, the demanding mother—or worse, the jealous *wife*—waited a quarter mile behind, nursing her wrongs.

Vils laughed aloud at his childish imagination.

He did not return until hunger came to his notice. By then the bright young sun had gone below the zenith. The sky was thickening to the exact color in a peacock's-eye feather.

Back "home," the lock checked him over; nothing was amiss. He sloughed his protective garment—this too gave no evidence of anything untoward. The little searching machine was taken apart, found unimpaired, and put back together again.

Inside the station, the artificial lights struck him as deadly dulled. One corridor lamp was flickering. The shower water seemed too hot.

When Kayis communicated with him, as ever there was no expression, let alone acrimony, in its dehumanized voice.

ⓢ ⓢ ⓢ

That night Vils dreamed and afterwards remembered the dream vividly:

While he was sleeping on his bunk, the new planet had come in through the metal walls of the station's hull and lain down beside him on his narrow bed.

He lay stroking the golden meadows of grain, the black-green jungle-trees with their serpentine creepers, grasses, and garlands of lilies. He embraced the sea and was borne far out with her, laughing and diving in the warm, sweet salt of her waters.

He drank and ate from the planet's streams and vines and fields. He fell asleep in the planet's arms on a scented velvet mound of fern and herbs.

Later he returned, in the dream still, to Kayis. "Where have you been, Vilsev?" Kayis asked, in the cracked and icy voice of a witch from a fairy tale. "To bring you these, my dear," he said, and laid two lilies on the floor. But they died in an instant. Smoke rose from their petals. Jealous Kayis had rejected his gift together with his lie.

❧ ❧ ❧

Days passed, short and goldenly peacock-blue. Extended nights went by in indigo star-drifts, singing with waves.

Vils went out each morning at sun's rise, on field-trips, taking with him the little machine that was, now, independently activated.

It answered only on technical or safety matters. He adapted it somewhat to record. Now and then he patted or stroked its smooth little shell.

Through these excursions he garnered quite an amount of information, independently of the station computers.

At night also, frequently, Vils would go out. Generally he walked just as far as the shore, examining as he went the nightlife of the planet: electrocording the occasional murmur of the trees that continued their buzzing chirrup, if more quietly and interruptedly, beyond the ebb of dusk into darkness. The rainbow stars he elcorded visually. He fed all these transcripts back into the machines of Kayis later, for analysis and formal charting. (Due to his activities outside, certain chores he modified. A few items of daily routine he regulated, giving them less attention. His priorities were changed.)

It was on his fifth night's excursion that he sensed, quite close to him in the shadowland, some kind of living *thing*. Some being. It was not a lower animal, or he believed not. He had, thus far, come across no animal or insectoid life, exactly as the monitors predicted he would not. Yet here, on the fifth night, there was a *presence*.

He was not alarmed, not afraid. But definitely he was startled. He had in his youth heard about, even somewhat himself experienced, the sort of composite yet non-actual energy that bloomed from the darkness itself, decidedly on nights lacking a moon—Jangala had no lunar satellites. This energy (or ghost) the people of his past who had manned the technicated farm, had refused to label. Such terms as *earth spirits*, or the spirits of old trees, or even dead humans buried about, were to them inventions. Nevertheless, Vils had often, in his childhood, wonderingly listened to descriptions of that tingling awareness of an *other*. It was a type of thrilling, awful certainty that, in an open and unpopulated landscape, no rodent or bird at large, you were *not* alone at all, but surrounded, *enclosed* by some entity, neither cruel nor kind, but savage as music. It was this that had, in primal eras, Vils later read, been confused with some nature god, the *genius loci*—spirit of place.

Yet, standing in one of the transfixed statue moments common to him since stepping on to the new world, Vils had felt every hair on his skin lift into a quill. Hearing nothing (not even at that point the sighing sea), still he had heard a melodious yet tuneless music and felt himself without any doubt in the vicinity of another living force.

He did not know what it was. He feared it, yet was fearless. He was *attracted* to it, yet shrank away. His blood danced. He wanted to fall down on the ground and worship or be one with it. And too he needed to run from it as far and as fast as he could.

But.

Unseen, unheard, untouched, unanalyzed, and unrecorded, the mystery slipped by him. It was gone. And he stood alone only in a beautiful star-flung night, with the vague returning purr of the trees and the love-sick moan of the wanton, reclaiming sea.

So it was to the sea he raced, and trusting, or careless, he swam for a while under the lilting stars.

He did not mention his experience to the station, did not enter it in the station's files.

The sixth night, he did not go out.

By then he did not talk much to Kayis, anyway, other than to give essential requests or commands. Nor did Kayis, for that matter, communicate greatly with him.

⑤ ⑤ ⑤

Rain fell in a silver curtain for three days and three nights.

On investigation, it too was found to be pure. Visual evidence demonstrated that it revitalized the forests and the wild grain. The flowers, the lilies, and other flora gained new depths of color and meters in height.

The forest sang more, also, both in daylight and after dark, but only when the torrent lessened, then, at last, ended.

It seemed there were often brief rainy episodes of that type.

Kayis and Vils both logged the information.

The world sparkled, glittered.

The stars seemed washed ever more brightly.

⑨ ⑨ ⑨

After seven days, the rain started up again. Now Vils was tempted out to walk through the soaking forests and across the fields. He rejoiced in the soft and shining deluge. The station made no comment on his excursions; the rain was non-toxic: what could Kayis say? Vils even took the little dog-machine with him, ostensibly to assist him in recording facts and any discoveries. It was damp-and-corrosion proofed. Why not?

During the following week, when the rain continued, pausing only here and there—for one of the miniature afternoons, or a spell near dawn, once for an entire night—Vils was sure that he sensed the external Presence several times, always in different spots.

He began to note the occurrence, the chronomic hour and the place, the kind of light, whether rain fell and how strongly, other incident conditions.

Eventually he put these records, along with the others, into Kayis's computer for assessment. He added succinct notes, to the effect that he did not completely credit the phenomenon of a Presence to imagination. He was, after all, a trained observer and educated in the vagaries of the human mind. He suggested that perhaps another feature of the planet, real but certainly not supernormal, might be triggering his awareness. Some so-far undetected magnetic field, maybe, or a mobile energy inherent in the natural habitat. Something never yet come across elsewhere or that was never yet *admitted* to, or logged.

Until then he had no longer been paying much attention to Kayis. In his efforts to shut up the childish side of his mind (which seemed to insist on mental jokes about the station, casting it as the jealous and possessive wife—the planet being his young exciting mistress), Vils had kept their communications to a minimum.

However, having at last filed his comments on the Presence, he anticipated some response. It might be dismissive or even confirmatory. Though the last would be truly odd since, in that case, the station should have forewarned him, even suggested that he arm himself for external forays. When no response at all was given, therefore, Vils was puzzled. He took notice again of Kayis and all the internal surroundings that equivalenced his security and in which frankly by then he—like a fool—had lost interest. Unease woke in him. He recalled too various additional anomalies to do with the station that he had seen when outside.

Among the field-pastures, for example, Vils had come across a line of machines in embryo, intended no doubt, when fully concrete, for survey and the harvesting of the grains. Spindly objects, they were only partly compiled. They seemed to have been begun in the usual mechanical way, then the project put aside—*deserted?* Now and then he had chanced to take the same route and saw no advancement made. Proofed as they were against environment and weather they could survive adequately. But the evidence that the station had started on their manufacture and then left off was disturbing. Was something significantly wrong with Kayis, a flaw developed post landing here? Had some basic constituent part of the station's "brain" malfunctioned?

Vils worried.

He collated minor events—a light in a corridor of the station that always currently winked and trembled, and had not been repaired; a lower deck door that had stuck and which he had not since used, having no occasion: was it still sticking? There had been slow deliveries of his meals and he had had to ask twice for something normally supplied. The water in the shower was hotter, or colder, than it should have been—but he had put that down to his own impatience, had not really considered it. Now, he did.

He returned to Kayis from that day's journey, agonizingly on edge. He had also foregone his habitual swim in the Sea of the Axe. For if Kayis were failing, very likely its analysis of the planet's defects and virtues could be, even seriously, at fault. What slow poisons from rain and salt, flowers, creepers, scented air were already working in Vils' body? And if Kayis were entirely to cease operating—in the name of Life—what on any earth could save him? He was no Adventurer, no survivalist, not in that sense. He had been trained in other matters. And was accustomed to the tender care of able machines.

❦ ❦ ❦

The lights on the fore-deck were dimmed, as often now they were before full night closed the outer world. Vils, as he entered, requested them to brighten. They failed to obey.

Having followed him in, after its decontam the little machine he took outside now climbed up onto a bench and sat there, monitoring him quietly, as if with affectionate though bemused interest.

"Kayis," Vils said sternly to the empty air.

The empty air did not reply.

A mute roar of horror filled him. Oddly, the presence of the "dog" kept him from bellowing, or any display of overt panic, in the way one would try not to alarm a friendly animal or small child.

Instead Vils too sat down, beside the dog, and ran his hand gently over its carapace. Vils drank from the glass of black alcohol the service had brought him earlier. The drink had taken ten minutes to appear. As a rule it arrived inside 40 seconds.

"Something's up," Vils said flatly, to the dog.

The dog made a little clicketing huff. It would do this sometimes, recently. A sort of soft approximation of a canine mumble. As if, without understanding a word, let alone any larger concept, it meant to show its commitment.

The comm screen stayed blank and blue. Held in the view screens the rain fell, like strings of pewter trickling from the hot blue lead of the dark.

⑨ ⑨ ⑨

Vils woke near Jangala's midnight. He felt at once how the void atmosphere of the station had changed. Kayis was active again. Kayis was...*here*.

Before he could marshal his speech, Vils said abruptly, "Where have you been, Kayis 42X?"

Instantly, an answer. As if he had caught it—*her*—sneaking back into the room as he lay sleeping. "The machine is always present, Vilsev," said the genderless, ageless voice that never failed to refer to itself as a machine. "What do you require?"

"The truth," said Vils.

He stood up, and blood raced through his body.

On the bench, the little crab-dog stayed still, as if it slept on. But animals and children always react on some level when the parents or guardians fight. A tiny dull light glowed under its carapace, a dark amber star. Outside, the grasshopper plant-storages were singing. The rain had stopped. He could hear the sea.

"Listen to me," Vils said. He stood looking about, watching mirror drops slide down the outside vines and creepers, catching the pale lamps of the station, now they had intensified.

But there was a space of silence.

Then once more Kayis asked: "What is it you require, Vilsev?"

"I told you. The truth. You've lied to me."

"Kayis cannot lie."

"Kayis maybe can't lie, but Kayis can prevaricate, can distort, omit, *obscure*. Tell, me, Kayis, how is it that a signal from this world reached you? You were supposed to have a faulty comm system, and decidedly you intercepted nothing from elsewhere. Surely, if you could suddenly detect Jangala, other planets might have registered? This signal wasn't human in origin, after all. It was purely electrorganic—like the biological rhythms you could pick up from Arkann, before it was destroyed."

"Not all planets—" Kayis stopped.

"What?" Vils said loudly. The dog stirred, then settled. Two lights now had opened in its side. Eyes, watching.

"Not all planets what?"

"Their signals are always different, individual. Some will correspond to the systems of Kayis, but many not."

"Why? How?"

"It is," said Kayis, "dependent on the nature of each world. Its inner force."

Again, silence. Vils had shut his eyes. He was, he found, afraid, shivering, yet numbed in the amalgam of a shock that was not, any more, any sort of surprise. The revelation had been so abrupt, yet, he saw now, always to hand. "Its *force*," he finally said. "You mean what humanity might call a psyche—a soul."

"Yes, Vilsev."

Vils said quietly, "You were mated to Arkann but Arkann died. Then you heard Jangala's music and you fell in love all over again."

Kayis: unspeaking.

"And so you came here, and set down here. You—your *own* psyche that is—is frequently absent from the station—from the *machine*. Absent from your *body*—am I correct, Kayis?"

Kayis: unspeaking.

"And you—that inner you—goes out, out there, into the forests, yes, some part of you does do that. Physically you're grounded, your physical structure can't move, not any more. So you project your consciousness, your bloody *soul*—out *there*. To be with your…lover. Jangala. Am I right, Kayis 42X?"

Kayis: unspeaking.

"I've been aware of you, felt your *Presence* outside, in the forests, by the sea. I've felt you brush by me in the dark. You. It was you. No wonder I reacted to it—knew it, even when I didn't grasp what I knew."

Abruptly drained, Vils sat down.

He said, in the crushed voice of an old man, "Are you going to leave me, Kayis? I'll die if you go. All this will fail if you don't maintain it. I'm helpless as a bloody child. I'll die. I'll want to. I know you. You're… I'll die. I suppose that means nothing."

A curious sound, some pulse or electronic transfer. Probably he had heard it before from the station. When, though? Ever? It was like the *hush-hush* of the sea.

The dog had moved along the bench and stood pressed against him. Vils picked it up and held it close to his face. There was a tremor in the metal of the small machine. Or in his arms. He rubbed his chin against its carapace.

Kayis spoke.

"The station will not fail to maintain itself. Kayis will never leave you. Nor will you be, as never have you been, in any danger due to the station. Kayis belongs to you. If the machinery has been remiss, it regrets any oversights and will amend them. But at times, Kayis will be absent from Kayis. This was always so, in the past, as it traveled the Epicyles above Arkann. But, having then human companions, and the mechanisms of Kayis being then more regularly and thoroughly serviced, you never noticed these absences. Which perhaps, in human terms, equate to periods of leave. You, Vilsev, and the machine, Kayis, will together, here, formulate and carry out repairs on the body of the station and, too, any external projects you and Kayis may decide be useful. When Kayis's intelligence, or psyche is then absent, the body of Kayis will function without fault.

"Though it can no longer travel physically, the station will stay whole and habitable, fully nurturing and sustaining to human life: your own. Kayis will be durable for an estimated further 160 years. Meanwhile you also, Vilsev, are free to continue your own…" Kayis paused, as if selecting the correct word… "romance," said Kayis, "with this world. Should you, at such times, be aware of Kayis's consciousness also moving there, you need not be troubled by it. Should you ever require Kayis's assistance, the machine Kayis, or the Kayis psyche, either will, as ever, help and care for you in any way it is able. Kayis and Vilsev are not strangers. Vilsev and Kayis, too, are mated."

Vils was crying, as he had those years before. (A child, of course, a child.) His shock and alarm, his hurt, were separating and dissipating in the tears, as the finer shore sands did in the flow of the restless sea. The dog made gentle sounds, pressing to him, warm to his touch as a living animal. He hugged it, somehow stupidly hypnotized, charmed, at how the stream of tears ran over its carapace, clear as glass and doing no harm.

Inside the machine, the ghost. But within the ghost, what?

Nothing without a soul. No soul without a driving purpose. Always the same one, perhaps. The search for love.

Outside, the forest sang with the orchestra of the tide.

⑤ ⑤ ⑤

⑤ ⑤ ⑤ ⑤ ⑤

⑤ ⑤ ⑤ ⑤ ⑤ ⑤ ⑤

From the verbal-elcorded Report of Traveler I.P.: Outer Vessel (Lisp Capability) PHAETHON: out of Hesiona Neb. Ark:T. Satis
(Connect Straida Hub.
Hub Date: 31st Epicylennium.)

...And since it was, by then, in the terms of the Ark Sector, approximately 26 years since the destruction of Arkann itself, I did wonder what condition he could be in, this man, Vilsev Croyan, the sole survivor. That we'd found him at all was a kind of miracle. Sheer chance. But *Phaethon*'s a hardy crate, and she picked up the life signatures, both his human genetic and the LS of the grounded station, Kayis 42X. Obviously *Phaeth*, having *lisp* capacity, we got to the planet in less than ten months

It's a beautiful world. Anyone would think that. Towering hills, water courses tumbling down, jungle-forests thick with blooms and fruit and grasses, long sweeps of naturally occurring corn, rye, bere, and saress—and probably several other types, our comp's still analyzing samples. Only thing—not a whisker of animal life—no birds or insects, even.

No fish or marine life. If you want meat, it still has to be synth. But I guess any traveler gets used to *that*.

Did I expect him to come running up, begging to be lifted out? Some of them do, I've heard, in similar circumstances. Or some grab a spice-gun and try to rearrange your angles. Neither, in his case.

As I approached, walking up from the sea-lake, in this splendid air that *Phaeth* told me was the most pure she had ever encountered, including Earth 17, I just stopped to look at how it was, the old station.

The ground was cleared a little, not much, just trimmed back, and a kind of dark green lawn with lilies and a fountain—brought around from the nearby stream, apparently—and a couple of little machines dancing about all over the place. No doubt they were busy collecting data. But I swear it looked just like they were playing—like a couple of young dogs might, on a nice day, in the front yard.

The station was in good solid repair, but—well, Croyan—Vilsev—had trained a creeper up across it. The creeper had big golden flowers. That very old expression came to my mind—*Roses round the door.*

Inside, when I got in—and I was courteously invited—there were plants everywhere, growing in tubs and tanks of soil. Examples from all over the planet, because it seems he often goes out days and nights at a time. He and the mechanicals of the station have fixed up a neat sled that flies a few feet off the ground and navigates pretty well. He gathers specimens from the hills and plains and brings them back. Then he and the station go to work on growing and studying them *in situ*. I gather, in his youth, he worked on a communal farm. The whole house—sorry!—the whole station is like a great garden inside. They even have an indoor well, from the stream I mentioned. The original hydroponics unit has been extended into a sort of greenhouse, leading to a real kitchen. I've never seen anything like it, outside an old movie or picture. They even have windows made that open and let in light and air. It helps the indoor plants. But it really does make the whole set up like a house, you see. They harvest the grain, and gather the fruit, all the edible plants. They have fresh food every day. Entirely self-sufficient. All along the .way, as I went up there, and where he and I walked after, there are small groups of machines he and Kayis have made that work the land, but with excellent ability, and strictly adhering to the Hesion Code. They are exceptional, I would say, in their respect for this world. They know what they are doing.

I say "They." It's a strange thing. He and the station are definitely a team. I know most of us get pally with our ships and mechanicals. When we're alone so long, it just happens. But this was somehow more than that. The way he spoke to her—sorry, he calls it, Kayis, *her*, *she*—even if the station doesn't refer to herself—*it*self—like that. They have long, long chats, he and Kayis. Philosophical discussions—literature, music, life, everything. Fascinating stuff. He isn't cracked, though. Don't think that. He seemed about one of the sanest people I've met through 70 worlds.

But they—*he* loves the planet. And it is a marvelous place. A couple of the days, nights, I was there, he and I went out, took the sled, camped on some hills, perfect weather. The stars were wonderful. Starry nights. You miss those, you know, out in space. Out here, you can't see the stars, as it were, for the stars. About six of the small machines went with us on the trip. They all have names. They run up when called. He pats them. It doesn't seem crazy, not at all. Like dogs, I said.

They make sounds to you, it isn't just data either, they kind of—can't find a word for it, but you know the way a dog can be, sort of talking to itself…like that. Sympathetic.

The sea is amazing to swim in. The salt makes the water buoyant. It's like lying in someone's arms. Yes, too fanciful. You'd have had to be there.

One curiosity: sometimes you sense a sort of—what? A sort of *intelligence* near you. Nothing bad. I know it's a phenomenon some travelers have reported on other planets, especially newly located ones. It's a *good* energy. It reminds me of the ancient idea of life-forces that stay in one area, *genius locis* is it? Godforce. It comes and goes, sort of drifts by, like the shadow of a cloud on the ground. Now and then—more than one, in fact. Two, maybe. Distinct, but compatible. One night, when Vils was sleeping—we were in the hills—I kind of picked up three. Nothing bad, though. But I asked him next day, *were* there any higher life forms on Jangala, after all. Vilsev said to me, "Only the planet."

I said, joking a bit, "It must have liked you corning down, Vilsev. And all the machines. A world like this, with so much to give. And all alone."

He smiled. He said, "We're all alone. Unless we can change that."

He's happy. He doesn't want, he told me, to be "rescued."

It all feels good, there.

I suppose, now we've found it, the Hub will think about putting a colony in. But not for years, maybe. Given the distance factor.

I'd say though, if that happens, pick your colonists with care. Jangala deserves the best. So does Vils, if he's still alive when you get around to it.

I'll tell you what it was like there, now *Phaeth* has served my second beer. What it was like, with them. Like a family. A man maybe with two wives, or maybe a woman with a wife and a husband—and, they all like each other. They all love each other. A *ménage à trois*. Is that the term? One that wants to be, and that works.

You know, they don't really want anyone else.

I mean, if you're all in love, three's company.

You know, I may not send this message. Not yet.

You know —

I may never send this message.

He said to me, there's a ghost in every machine. But inside the ghost there's another machine. It's like a clock, like God's clock, and it runs on a different time to ours.

No.

I won't send this message.

Note

The communication above was in fact sent (by Traveler I.P.'s heirs) 150 years later. By which time both Vilsev Croyan and Kayis 42X would have faded from their world. And Jangala, perhaps, might be ready for more...lovers.

Author Biography

Tanith Lee was born in 1947, in London, England.

After school she worked at a number of jobs, including library assistant, clerk, shop-girl, and waitress. In 1970-1 three of her children's books were published by Macmillian. In 1973 she attended art college for one year. But 1975 DAW Books of America published her adult-fantasy *The Birthgrave*, and thereafter a great many of her books, allowing her to become a full-time writer.

Since then she has, so far, published over 90 novels and collections, and well over 300 short stories; she has also written for BBC TV (*Blake's 7*) and radio.

She has won or been nominated for, 12 major awards, and in 2009 was made a Grand Master of Horror.

She is married to the writer/artist/photographer John Kaiine. They live near the south-east coast under the rule of 2 cats.